LETTER LATE THAN NEVER
GREEN VALLEY HEROES BOOK #3

LAUREN CONNOLLY

www.smartypantsromance.com

Copyright

To every postal worker. You kept this country running during the pandemic. (And I'm sorry I keep ordering cat litter through the mail.)

Content Warning: This book contains scenes depicting anxiety, panic attacks, and excessive drinking. It also includes scenes discussing suicide and drug overdose.

Chapter One

GWEN

Never take your eyes off your food if squirrels, seagulls, or Sebastian Kirkwood are around.

— POSTCARD FROM RYAN, FLORIDA

When I daydreamed about coming face-to-face with Sebastian Kirkwood again, I never envisioned myself covered in blood.

But the guy works as a paramedic, so maybe that indicates a lack of imagination on my part.

"Oh goodness. He's too handsome. Gwen, tell them to send me someone who isn't good-looking. Don't they know the state I'm in?" Agnes stares up at me expectantly as I apply pressure to the cut on her forehead.

"I'm sorry. I don't think they have a menu for us to order first responders from." There's true regret in my voice because, honestly, I'd rather not deal with him right now either.

When I arrived at my favorite stop on my mail route, I discovered sweet Mrs. Agnes Keen lying in her garden, bleeding. She tried to explain what happened. Something to do with slipping on a rock while holding garden shears.

All I saw was the blood, and my body went into freak-out adrenaline mode.

I

"What will he think?" She tries to pat her messy gray curls, but even that small movement has her wincing.

My initial plan was to toss out all of the packages and crates of letters that crowded my Ford Bronco, load Agnes into the passenger seat, and drive her to the hospital in Merryville myself. But the second I tried to help her stand, she let out a pained gasp.

So, that was a no-go. Last thing I wanted was to make her injuries worse.

Who knew my 911 call would result in sexiness in a paramedic's uniform?

"Sebastian is nice." At least he was back in high school. "And you look gorgeous. Are you wearing the mascara I gave you?"

She nods and offers a brave smile that breaks my heart. Not that I let her see.

"Told you it was good, didn't I? No clumps." My voice only shakes a little on the last word. I can't help the fear that grips me.

What if she doesn't make it?

"You're going to be okay," I say, equal parts for her sake and mine.

Then, Sebastian Kirkwood kneels at my side, and I start believing the words.

"Oh Lord. You're even better-looking up close," Agnes mutters.

I wonder if she knows we both can hear her.

"Hello there, Mrs. Keen. I heard you ran into some trouble, and I'm here to help." Then, Sebastian goes and does something terribly unfair.

He grins.

If my friend was hurting a moment ago, I'm betting she doesn't need any painkillers now. That set of perfect white teeth, paired with his trademark puppy-dog eyes and neatly trimmed beard, is enough to numb any hurt.

Well, almost any.

No matter how hard I try, I've never been able to escape the persistent ache that accompanies my long-lasting, bothersome crush.

Long-lasting because I've mooned over Sebastian's strong jaw and easy laugh since grade school.

Bothersome because the man is off-limits. Totally and completely not for me.

Never gonna happen, Gwen. Get over him already!

But as I watch Sebastian work, speaking kind words to Agnes as he checks her for injuries, I know I'll need even more time to demolish my silly crush. Hiding from him hasn't exterminated the unwanted, awkwardly flapping flamingos in my stomach that perform a lusty dance whenever he's nearby.

"Gwen?"

At the sound of my name in his friendly voice, I jerk my thoughts away from queasiness-inducing lust birds. "Yeah?"

"Anything to add?"

"To what?" My attention flits from Agnes to Sebastian, where his hazel eyes hold mine.

"To what happened to Mrs. Keen." He speaks slowly, as if worried I might not understand him.

Great. Now, he thinks I need medical attention too.

"Oh. No. Not really. I got here after she fell, and when she couldn't get up, I called 911."

He nods, then turns his head to speak to his partner, which only drives home how thoroughly distracted I was because I didn't even notice there was another EMT.

Damn it, Gwen. Focus.

As Sebastian's partner—who I now see is Grizz Grady—approaches with a stretcher, I focus back on my friend. Agnes just turned seventy last month, and she looks so small, lying on the ground. I want to gather her into my arms and pour my strength into her body. But I settle for keeping a paper towel pressed to the still-bleeding cut on her forehead.

"Okay, Gwen, why don't you let me take over?" Sebastian speaks to me gently as he reaches a hand forward to take the place of mine. The purple latex glove does nothing to hide the strength in his fingers.

Oh my God, what is wrong with me? We're in an emergency situation, and I'm fixating on his hand!

I blame the fact that I never expected to see *him* here. Last I heard, Sebastian was living in Merryville. No need for them to send ambulances all the way to Green Valley when we have a fire department of our own.

Trying to keep my thoughts to myself, I let Sebastian take my place and move out of the way, so he and Grizz can take care of Agnes. They put a neck brace on her before lifting her onto the stretcher. Agnes makes the same pained noise she did when I tried to shift her, but I comfort myself with the knowledge that they're trained professionals and she'll soon be in a fully medically equipped vehicle.

As the two men work, a flash of color at Sebastian's throat catches my attention. A tease of magenta. He must be wearing the bright shade under his uniform. The sight sparks a memory of a younger Sebastian. The lanky teenager who made a point to wear something pink every day. A pair of socks, a baseball hat, a T-shirt, even his shoelaces sometimes got swapped out for the softer color.

Sebastian never draped himself in pink, only added a splash to whatever he was already wearing. And as far as I know, no one ever teased him about the subtle fashion statement. It's hard to make fun of a guy who laughs along with you.

The quirk charmed sixteen-year-old me, and every day, my eyes would drag over the length of his body, searching for the bright spot.

That he hasn't given up the habit, even all these years later, tempts me to smile.

Then, I see Agnes's face pinched in pain, and I sideline those happy recollections. I want to reach out to her, but the group heads down the front drive. Plus, blood coats my hands.

Without thinking, I wipe them on my shirt. The second after I finish the motion, I mutter a curse. Now, my USPS polo sports two bloody handprints, and somehow, I also got spatters on my pants.

Wonder if there's any in my hair.

At least it wouldn't show up against the dark brown. Now, if it's on my face …

"Not important," I remind myself, jogging after the EMTs.

They're already rolling the stretcher into place in the back of their vehicle. The outside of the ambulance has a more rugged appearance than ones I've seen in

4

TV medical dramas. This looks like someone chopped off the bed of a truck, then stuck a box on the back. Rural roads require tough vehicles.

The residents of Green Valley, Tennessee, don't all live in neatly paved suburbs. A lot of homes creep up the sides of mountains while others sit, surrounded by farmlands and dirt roads. I can't imagine having to use a boxy city mail truck on my route. The low undercarriage would get lodged on a dirt mound or fallen branch on the first day. Luckily, the post office allows rural carriers to use their own vehicles, and Cletus Winston—local mechanic and master of all car knowledge—recommended I get myself a Bronco.

Thing drives like a dream, no matter the terrain.

Hopefully, the ambulance has a similarly smooth ride.

"You're going to be okay!" I call to Agnes while hovering just out of the way of Grizz as he circles around to the driver's side.

The sound of her voice drifts to me, but I can't catch her words.

"What did she say?" I look to Sebastian.

"She asked you to call her daughter." He clicks one door shut and reaches for the other.

"I will!" Hopefully, my promise is loud enough for her to hear. "You'll be okay!" I already said that, but I don't want her to worry. "I'll come to the hospital and check on you!"

"Gwen." Sebastian's deep voice captures my attention again, and I realize I'm shouting in his face as he tries to close the final door. "You did good. I've got her." Then, he gifts me one of those better-than-medicine smiles before shutting the ambulance up.

As they drive off, I stand in a daze. My body sways as I get hit with a wave of light-headedness. Adrenaline must be wearing off, and I press my fingers to my forehead, as if that might help steady me.

Wrong move.

In my distraction, I once again forgot about the gore coating my hands. Now, I've definitely got some crimson streaks on my face.

Crime-scene blood splatter is *not* the makeup look I planned for the day.

"Fuck a duck," I mutter, looking between my blood-covered person and my SUV, full of undelivered mail. "What am I going to do?"

Since my shirt is already stained red, I give up on the thing and scrub my right hand on the fabric, getting my fingers as clean as possible before sliding my phone from my back pocket and bringing up a familiar name.

"Hello?" The greeting comes in a deep, almost bear-like grumble.

"Hey, Arthur. I'm sorry. I know it's your day off, but can you finish my route for me? Morgan's already working yours or else I'd call her, and if I don't get back on the road soon, I'm going to miss the dispatch truck, but I'm covered in blood, and I don't want to get it on the mail. That's just not sanitary." My pulse pounds hard, causing my brain to rattle off the babble of words.

A pause on the other end of the line, then, "Is this a time-of-the-month thing?"

"God, no!" I choke on a laugh-scoff combo. "You think I got my period, and now, I suddenly can't do my job?" I love my coworker like a brother, but sometimes, it is almost too obvious that Arthur grew up with zero women in his house.

"Did someone hurt you?" His voice drops lower, like he's ready to dole out some violence on my behalf.

I try not to sigh at the protectiveness. Arthur should know I can take care of myself, seeing as how I regularly deliver mail to members of the Iron Wraiths, and the guys in that motorcycle club are none too friendly.

"No. The blood's not mine. Can you just come, please? I'm at 354 Oakwood Drive."

"The Keen house? Who's bleeding?"

Every second he spends interrogating me is more time with me looking like I'm cosplaying a Stephen King character.

"That is not how this works! You don't get gossip for free. Get your ass over here and help me if you want to hear about how I'm moonlighting as a superhero."

Arthur snorts, but I hear what sounds like the slam of a car door. "Be there in ten."

Relief washes through me, and I thank the universe I work with reliable, caring people. "Thank you."

As I wait for him to arrive, I pace around Agnes's front yard. Anything to dispel the jittery energy that flooded my body the second I saw her collapsed in her garden.

What if I had been running late? What if I hadn't gotten out of my car to say hello?

The what-if game is a horrible one to play, and there are never any winners.

"I did get here. She's going to be okay." I brace for my body to crumple. To dissolve into sobs.

Instead, laughter spills out.

Triumphant, glorious laughter.

Agnes Keen is going to be okay because I was here when she needed me.

Holy hell, does that feel good.

My comment to Arthur about being a superhero was a joke, but the realization that little old me—nothing-special small-town postal worker—showed up when it mattered and saved a woman's life has my body filling with euphoria.

"She's going to be okay!" I grin at the sky.

But the brief jubilation curdles like milk in the sun when I remember the words I called out before Sebastian shut the door. The spur-of-the-moment promise I made to an injured woman.

That I have to visit the last place I ever want to step foot in again.

Chapter Two

SEBASTIAN

Life is more vibrant when you're near.

— LETTER TO MARIA

"And how was your day, rescuing the human race?" My sister doesn't bother glancing at me while she asks, too focused on counting out pills.

"Oh, you know, uneventful." I brace my shoulder on the wall next to the pharmacy counter and give her a grin that charms most people. "Cruised around town. Turned on the lights to have a parking-lot rave. Handed out free condoms. The usual."

Kennedy smirks, the sassy expression taking away all the professional points she gets for wearing that white lab coat. "So, that's why you went to Mrs. Keen's place? To give her some condoms?"

Word travels through this hospital faster than gossip in a small town.

"Never too old for safe sex."

This bantering with my sibling is a surprisingly pleasant way to end an emergency call. Since Kennedy got an internship at the hospital, I didn't mind Grizz's request for us to linger a few minutes after this last drop-off. He's got a *will they, won't they* flirting game going with one of the doctors. Plus, this is our second run to Merryville of the day. We'd just gotten back to Green Valley town limits when a call came in for a middle-aged man who had a nasty run-in with his hedge clippers.

Beautiful days at the end of spring mean everyone is out in their yard, injuring themselves with gardening tools.

Seems condoms aren't the only form of protective equipment the public needs.

"Please say that in front of Daddy at dinner tomorrow." Kennedy bats her eyes at me, as if I could ever mistake her for innocent or sweet.

"God, no. I only want to pull out the defibrillator on work hours." I shove my hands in my pockets. "And what's this about dinner?"

Kennedy places her carefully sorted pills on the desk of her supervisor before hitting me with a glare. "I swear, you spend so much brain power on your job that you forget about your life. *Dinner*. I'm coming over to eat with you all. I texted you, and you *promised* to stay awake. Do not let me show up to find you passed out, dead to the world."

Guilt settles in my stomach as I think about the last time I promised to meet her for dinner. I was still living in Merryville, working hours no human could maintain. Kennedy called me five times before the buzzing of my phone woke me up. I'd fallen asleep on the couch after covering a last-minute shift for one of the guys at my old company.

"Of course. Dinner. I'll be propped up at the kitchen table with a smile taped on my face and eyeballs drawn on my lids."

"Sebastian," my sister growls like an angry badger.

"All right. With my eyes open. I swear." Hands held up in surrender, I back away from the pharmacy window, making my escape before she crawls over the counter and puts me in a headlock for the fun of it.

Kennedy might be a foot shorter than me, but she makes up for the height difference with cheap shots and willingness to pull hair to earn submission. I finger-comb my brown strands, reassuring my scalp it's safe from my vicious little sister.

At least for now.

I'm not worried about staying awake, no matter what I said. Already, I've noticed the different pace of working in Green Valley as opposed to Merryville. A lot less stress, what with the calls tending toward infrequent small-town shenanigans instead of life-ending catastrophes. Taking this new job and moving home seem to have solved most of my problems.

There's one though that lingers.

To avoid thinking about that dark cloud casting a shadow over the new chapter of my life, I seek out fresh air, navigating through the busy hospital halls until I find the closest exit. Outside the doors sits a set of benches with a view of where the ambulance is parked. I figure I'll spy Grizz making his way back to the rig, or he'll hail me on my portable radio when he's ready to leave.

I stop mid-step when I realize the bench is already occupied by one Miss Gwen Elsmere.

Two sightings in one day of the Green Valley postwoman, and I can't help thinking this is some kind of fate.

The good kind.

Thinking back, I can't recall a clear time I've run into Gwen since we graduated high school. Yeah, I moved to Merryville soon after, but I'm in my hometown plenty, visiting my family.

How have I rarely stumbled across Gwen in this tiny corner of Tennessee?

Has it really been a decade since we last spoke?

"Come on." Her muttered plea reaches me. "Just go in. Count of five."

Careful not to make a sound, I step closer.

"One ... two ... three ... four ... maybe count of ten." Gwen stares up at the sky, her teeth digging into a plump bottom lip, painted a dark purple. The color of her mouth against her pale skin, combined with dark eye makeup, gives her an almost-vampiric appearance.

Gorgeous and also odd when paired with her loose Genie's Bar T-shirt and ripped jeans.

The postwoman doesn't resume counting.

I hesitate, finding myself familiarly fascinated by the profile of her face. How many times in Biology class did I end up staring at Gwen just like this? Following the swoop of her nose and the rounded apple of her cheek. Eyeing the stretch of pale neck—more visible now that her hair is pixie short.

I stop myself before going lower. Reaching her legs would be a problem. I already know they're too long for me to keep thinking straight even if she does have them covered in a pair of worn jeans.

Yes, I had a crush on my lab partner. But it was hard not to fall for Gwen Elsmere with her ready smile, easy laugh, and hilarious pencil figure drawings. She made Biology my favorite subject, just by sitting next to me every class and being her adorable self. She charmed me without trying.

But that's how Gwen was with everyone. Friendly, kind, and her own version of awkwardly funny. I'd bet she still is from the jokes she was trading with Mrs. Keen when I approached them earlier.

"Fuck a duck," she groans before dropping her face into her hands.

And just like that, I can't hesitate anymore. I *have* to talk to her.

"You don't want to do that."

Gwen jerks her head up, wide eyes taking me in as I settle on the seat beside her.

"Sebastian!" She squeaks my name so high that I bet dogs'll come running any second. Recognizing this, she clears her throat. "Sebastian." This time, her voice is comically low.

Grinning at her is as easy as breathing. "Hey there, Gwen."

"Hey. Hi." She rubs her collarbone, like her skin irritates her, and I realize she must have taken a shower since I last saw her. No more blood speckled on her skin and clothes. "What don't I want to be doing?"

"Fucking ducks." I try for a serious face. "By all accounts, guy ducks have oddly shaped packages and are selfish lovers. No notions of consent. Best you can do is avoid them."

"Oh, really?" Her neatly shaped eyebrows rise a couple notches. "Well, in that case, I'd better cancel the date I set with a mallard tonight. He was a real sweet talker. Couldn't tell him no."

"Glad I could steer you straight."

As I let my grin slip back into place, she offers a matching one that has me stuck on her.

Why has it been so long since I chatted with Gwen? Why did we ever stop talking in the first place?

Every memory I have of her is a good one. Goofy and childish maybe, but still good.

But I guess, at some point, we meandered away from each other in life.

Until today's 911 call. Normally, I prefer my day without bloody emergencies. But—and I don't mean this to sound as if I were glad lovely, little Mrs. Keen was hurt—I think I might be a little grateful this bad turn led me back to Gwen.

"What's got you sitting out here, muttering to yourself?" I ask as I ponder the idea of becoming friends with my Biology buddy again.

"Oh." Her cheeks pink, and her teeth get back to gnawing her purple lip.

I wonder why the lipstick doesn't come off on her pearly whites.

Would the lipstick smear if she kissed someone?

I redirect my errant mind as she sucks in a deep, bracing breath.

"I promised Mrs. Keen I'd come see her. Remember? Course you do, seeing as how I shouted it in your face. Anyway, even though I called her daughter to come, I still don't want to break my promise, but I haven't been in a hospital since my gran died." The confession comes in one long, fast breath that immediately punches my gut with a guilty fist.

Here I am, teasing her, and she's going through some real mental turmoil.

"I'm sorry. I didn't mean to make you feel silly."

Her smile, when it returns, glows with such unfiltered happiness that I bask in the rays of her easy joy. "Don't apologize. I love being silly with you, Sebastian Kirkwood. That's the only way I dealt with Mr. Parish droning on about plant cell structures for weeks straight."

The memory of our old Biology teacher has me groaning. "That man loved the sound of his voice more than his own wife, I swear."

She chuckles, and I savor the playful sound. Better than a strong cup of coffee to keep me going. Recalling her confession, I try to act like a grown man rather than the irresponsible teenager I used to be.

"I'm sorry about your gran. I remember hearing about her passing a few years back."

She nods, her gaze leaving mine to focus on the glass doors over my shoulder. "Thank you. Normally, I'm not so messed up about it." Gwen grimaces, as if the words taste bitter on her tongue. "Here though … this is where she … well, you can imagine. So, I guess my mind is telling me if I walk through those doors, something bad will happen." Her eyes flick to mine and away. "I should move on, I know."

Every part of me aches to take away her pain. But there's no Band-Aid in the world big enough to cover the kind of wound she has.

"I get it." When she offers a half-hearted shrug and not-really smile, I try again. "You had a bad experience here, and it's stamped on you. No reason to feel shame over that. If you want, I could find Mrs. Keen for you. Let her know you dropped by but couldn't stay."

Gwen watches me, her expression revealing nothing but curiosity.

Am I interesting to her? The idea fills me with more energy until I wonder if I might start buzzing.

"You're kind. Thanks for offering, but I want to face this."

She rises from the bench, towering over me in a way not many people can do. I enjoy lingering under her presence and stay seated to prolong the sensation.

"Maybe …" Gwen begins, then trails off as she taps a nervous rhythm on her jean-clad thigh.

"Maybe?" I prompt.

"Maybe you could keep me company?"

Chapter Three

GWEN

Always clearly mark your pee bottle. And screw the lid on tight. Just trust me.

— POSTCARD FROM RYAN, KANSAS

K*eep me company?*

So much blood rushes to my face that I'm worried the heat will melt my makeup off. I shouldn't have asked. But for the first time since I parked in the visitors lot of the hospital, I'm able to breathe in a full breath.

All thanks to Sebastian.

Without him, I'm worried I'll pass out halfway to Mrs. Keen's room, and then *I'll* be admitted. The thought of lying in one of those beds has me wanting to run in the opposite direction until the hospital is only a distant, unpleasant memory.

"Sure." Sebastian fiddles with a knob on the radio clipped to his belt, pulls his phone from his pocket, gives it a quick glance, and tucks it away. "I've got some time."

"Oh." Relief crashes through me. "Good. Thank you."

Sebastian rises from the bench, the move seeming to take an extra moment as he achieves his over-six-foot height.

As shallow as it sounds, I think the first reason I had a crush on him was because of how tall he was. But when you're a girl who shoots up to five-nine in the ninth grade, things like whether you're looking up or down at a guy matter. At least, they seem to matter to the guy. All the tall boys thought my height was fine. All the ones below five-nine counted me out as a romantic prospect. Because—gasp—my genetics granted me with a longer set of bones than theirs!

How dare I!

That meant I gravitated toward the boys who were too tall to care. And Sebastian was at the top of that list.

In junior year, I gained one more dreaded inch, then finally stopped. Sebastian looks down at me now, and I realize it's nice to have someone at eye-level, but that's not the reason my crush hung around for so long.

"M'lady." He offers his arm with a half-bow.

That's why. Because he's kind and silly, and he *cares*.

I hook my arm through his and find, just like my breathing, entering the building is easier with him at my side.

Then, I catch a whiff of the overly clean hospital smell.

Oh, wait, it's not that easy.

"Shoot. Just a second." I shove away from the hot paramedic and sprint to a nearby trash can, where I proceed to hurl up my lunch of peanut butter crackers, an apple, and three Daisy's doughnuts.

Yeah, I said three. Don't judge me. I was stressed.

A soothing hand settles between my shoulder blades as I heave, making it impossible for me to ignore the fact that I'm upchucking in front of the handsomest man I've ever known. If I had hair long enough to fall into my face, I get the sense he'd hold it back for me.

Sebastian is so great, and I'm so gross, and could a mad scientist please spill radioactive waste on me right now, so I could immediately develop an invisibility superpower? Only, knowing my luck, I'd turn into Vomit Woman instead, the grossest superhero of all time.

When I'm done after what felt like hours but was probably only a few seconds, a long-fingered hand comes into view, holding a tissue.

"Thank you," I murmur, doing my best to wipe my mouth clean. "Okay. I'm ready." I keep my eyes on the concrete below my feet rather than meet his or look at the automatic doors.

"You still want to go in? No, Gwen, come on."

"I promised." It's the only argument I have, but it's a good one. "And my stomach is empty now, so I'm all set."

"Just the idea of going in made you sick."

"Weird, right, since hospitals are supposed to make you feel better?" I chuckle at my bad joke and step around Sebastian's imposing body, determined to do this. "You don't have to come. I'm fine now." Lies. But I want to give him an out. I also don't want him to associate me with any more unpleasant bodily fluids today.

Watch, the moment I step through this door, a nurse will spill a tray of urine samples on me.

"When did you turn stubborn?" Sebastian grumbles in his deep voice as he appears at my side.

His words have me pondering.

"Huh. I don't know." I tend to be a laid-back, go-with-the-flow kind of gal. "This morning maybe?"

The huff of his chuckle has me glancing his way, and for a moment, I'm distracted by the teasing curve of his mouth. Sebastian has a nice mouth. He has a nice everything.

And I'm so distracted that it takes me at least a count of five to realize we're inside the hospital. My anxiety ratchets up again. I need the gorgeous paramedic to take my mind off my surroundings.

"How have you been?" I ask. "I can't remember the last time I talked to you." That's not true. I remember exactly the last time we talked.

It was about a year ago. I was walking into Daisy's Nut House, the best donut making diner in the world, the same time he was leaving.

Sebastian held the door wide for me, barely got out, "Hey, Gwen," before I power-walked by, straight back to the restroom.

He probably thought I had an emergency requiring a toilet.

But I was doing what I normally did whenever I saw Sebastian Kirkwood.

Hiding.

The reaction became almost instinctual over the years. Now, I never went so far as to crawl into a cabinet to get away from the paramedic, but I am now a master at ducking into alleys, around building corners, behind displays at the Piggly Wiggly, and even using the closest large body as a human shield.

Unfortunately, the body must be particularly tall to obscure me. Luckily, Drew Runous was at the Friday night Jam Session a couple of months back. That mammoth of a man was the perfect obstruction when Sebastian wandered into the same room of the community center where I was enjoying watching some of my fellow postal workers perform with other folk musicians. One step to the left, and the game warden unknowingly aided my escape.

Yes, hiding from a man because his smile melts my insides is immature. But I have no other option. No other plan for obliterating this yearslong crush other than to minimize contact and hope that it withers to nothing more than a shell of a memory.

And as of today, I can safely say my plan has officially failed.

Which is why I'm contemplating a new one.

"How've I been? Now, there's a question." Sebastian guides me around a man in a wheelchair and then waves at a nurse. "Well, I just started a new job at the Green Valley Fire Department."

"You're working in Green Valley?" The question comes out as a yelp.

I wondered why he was the one on the scene when I called 911. But I figured everyone else was busy and they'd called an ambulance down from Merryville or something.

Sebastian nods as he pulls me up to a desk. The nurse working the computer doesn't hesitate to give him Mrs. Keen's room number, and I think we both swoon when he thanks her and offers one of those better-than-medicine smiles.

As the hospital's sterile scent creeps into my nose and down my throat to tickle my gag reflex again, I shove the back of my hand against my nostrils and ask him another distracting question. "How's Kennedy? I saw your mom a few months back at the pharmacy. She said your sister's following in her footsteps."

This earns me a happy glimmer in his hazel eyes, and I enjoy the way his face somehow gets handsomer when he describes how his baby sister kicked ass in college and is apprenticing at this very hospital. A minute later, I'm choking on giggles as he tells me how she went on a date with a guy who insisted she sneak him free Viagra. I'm so busy laughing that I stumble in surprise when he stops at an open door.

Sebastian steadies me with a warm hand on my waist, the hold dropping away as fast as it arrived.

"Here we are."

He waves me in ahead of him, and the nausea creeps back, curdling my stomach. For a moment, while listening to him talk, I forgot I was in a hospital. Briefly, I convinced myself I was just having a conversation with a cute guy.

My muscles tense as I shuffle into the room. The bed closest to the door sits empty, and a tan curtain hides the rest of the room. On the other side of that flesh-colored barrier, I'm convinced misery awaits me.

Don't look. Go home and hide under your covers and never come back to this horrible place.

But I promised.

When I step past the drapery, I find Agnes wearing an arm cast, eating apple-sauce and watching a daytime soap opera on a blockish TV mounted in the corner.

"Gwen!" Her gaze lights up.

Seeing her as perky as ever drains my anxiety—if not all my nausea—away.

"You're okay," I sigh, approaching the bed and taking her uninjured hand.

"You bet your bottom. A few stitches, a broken wrist, and they said I'mma have a collection of bruises. But otherwise, I'm right as rain. Even better, Sherry got ahold of the hospital after you called her." Agnes smiles wide when she says her daughter's name. "They held the phone for me. She's coming home! Promised to stay as long as I need her. It's been ages since we had a long visit. Shoulda slipped in my garden years ago."

"If it's all the same, I'd rather you stay steady on your feet."

I will never forget the image of my friend lying on the ground, covered in blood. I'm going to be even more vigilant on my mail route now, especially at the homes of the older Green Valley residents. Some of them live far from town. Anything could happen, and I'm the only one guaranteed to show up most days. I have an itch to go up to every door and knock, just to check.

"Oh no." Agnes drops her spoon in her snack, eyes widening in horror.

"What is it? Are you hurting?" My hands flutter a frantic, useless dance around her frail form. "Should I call a nurse?"

"You brought *him* with you?"

She waves over my shoulder, and I glance back to find Sebastian followed me around the curtain. His hands are shoved into his pockets while a rueful grin creases his close-cropped beard.

"How many times in one day must a man handsome as sin see me in this state?" Agnes pats her flattened curls and her pale cheeks.

"Afternoon, ma'am." Sebastian dips his chin. "Glad to see you're doing better."

"Sorry." And I really am. I know what it's like to step out of the house with or without a full face of makeup. Whichever I'm doing that day, I want it to be my choice. "But I brought something that might help."

From my back pocket, I slide out a tube of lipstick and a container of blush.

"Oh, you perfect girl!" Agnes claps her hands.

"I was going to give them to you today, but you had to go and be dramatic," I tease, cracking the seal on the new items of makeup.

Sometimes, I see a color that I love but know won't work well for my complexion. But if I can think of someone to give it to, that's just as fun. Agnes is one of my regular makeup-chat friends.

"Can you put it on? I'm afraid my hands are none too steady at the moment."

She sits up straighter on the bed, and I settle beside her. After years of practice, I find applying the makeup meditative. This is something I can control.

Something I can make beautiful.

"Gorgeous," I declare when I finish, no need to be humble when I'm talking about someone else.

"As always." Agnes primps. "I think I've watched your smoky-eye video a hundred times now. I've almost got it right." She grimaces at her cast-covered arm. "Seems I'll be out of practice for a time."

"You let me know when you want it done, and I'll pop over."

Anything to make her feel better. Last week, Agnes mentioned how her joints were paining her. Now, this accident? She must feel like she's falling apart.

"That's so sweet of you, but I think Sherry can help. She watches your videos too. Said she can finally do one of those cat eyes after your tips. I'll just make her watch the smoky-eye one till she can get it right."

"Ah, so it's the Keens getting me all the views." I give her uninjured arm a gentle squeeze of thanks. "You're making me feel like a real internet star."

A loud throat clearing from over my shoulder has me realizing what I just admitted in front of my longtime, bothersome crush.

"Did I hear what I think I did?"

At Sebastian's question, I turn to spy the paramedic wearing an alarmingly delighted grin.

"You publish makeup videos? Online?"

I've never been particularly secretive about my hobby. But I also don't advertise. Ever since my grandmother showed me the basics, I've been fascinated by makeup and all the beautiful things it can do to an ordinary face like mine.

"You heard right." I narrow my eyes, daring him to mock me. "But it's just for fun. I turn the comments off, so I don't get any trolls harassing me."

Please don't be a living, breathing troll, I silently beg.

High school Sebastian would never have made fun of me. Not in any hurtful way at least. But the man could have changed.

It's disconcerting to realize I don't truly know Sebastian Kirkwood anymore. We're not friends. Haven't been in years.

Which is entirely my fault.

A box full of frogs shares the blame, but let's not get into that right now.

"And it's how-to kinda stuff?" he asks.

As far as I can tell, there's no mockery in his voice.

"Yes—"

"It's more than that." Mrs. Keen talks over me, wiggling to sit higher in her bed. "Sometimes, she does these wild, lovely designs. Why, I remember one time, Gwen colored clouds on her cheeks and rainbows across her eyelids. I've never seen something so clever in my life!"

"Let me introduce you to my biggest fan." I give Sebastian a sheepish smile as I gesture to Agnes.

"Can I watch them?" he asks.

For a moment, all possible answers escape me. *Why would he want to sit for a half hour, watching me apply cosmetics to my face? Maybe he's just curious? And he probably doesn't realize how long the videos are.*

"Okay. Sure. I mean, anyone can."

The paramedic is already pulling out his phone, swiping across the screen, and finally handing it to me. "Can you pull it up? I'll bookmark it and watch later."

With him standing close to my side, watching over my shoulder as I navigate to my video channel, I try to remember if I styled the back of my hair after my shower. The short strands sometimes stick up in a weird cowlick if I don't tame them into submission before leaving the house.

When I reach the website, I hesitate for a moment, deciding which video to bring up for him. Then, inspiration strikes, and I bite down on my lower lip to keep from chuckling. A couple of months ago, I did a bubblegum-inspired look. All shades of pink.

Perfect.

The second after I click the link, an incoming call notification blurs half the screen. The name of the caller douses my happy buzz in dirty mop water, and I get the sudden urge to find the closest hiding space.

"Here." I pass his phone back, doing my best to form a smile. "Elaine's calling. Shouldn't let your fiancée go to voice mail."

And I shouldn't let myself forget there *is* a fiancée.

Chapter Four

GWEN

I'm doing a department store delivery, and my truck is full of shoeboxes. Should I swing by Green Valley, so Momma can rob me?

— POSTCARD FROM RYAN, NEW JERSEY

Dust floats into the air as I fiddle with the travel guides on my rarely visited bookshelf. They sit here patiently, pages yellowed with age, corners curved and crinkling from the many times my younger fingers flipped through the adventures contained within.

No doubt, most of the information is out of date.

A shelf higher, I have two boxes. One beautiful wood with a tiny golden latch my dad fashioned for me, the other a shoebox, courtesy of my mother. The second I dive into all the time. The first …

Heartache usually keeps me away, but today, I pick the heavier box up and settle on my bed with it cradled in my lap. The smell of old paper and ink wafts free when I lift the lid. Carefully, I run my fingers over the envelopes, all addressed to Maria, my grandmother. I note the return addresses and postal stamps. Last we counted, there were sixty-seven countries represented.

Gran always lamented about not having two more international friends, hoping to bring the total to a number that made me blush when she explained the meaning to fifteen-year-old me.

Maria Bowling was not a sweet, cookie-cutter grandmother.

She was so much better.

When I feel the pressure of tears, I quickly shut the lid and return the box to its home. Reaching into my back pocket, I pull out a postcard that arrived in the mail for me yesterday. The picture has a moose wearing sunglasses, and the post-mark says *Montana*.

Had to drive through a snowstorm the last two days. Happy spring. —Ryan

My brother's dry humor has me smiling, and I slip his latest correspondence into the shoebox. The country count for this container is one, but I've got almost every state represented twice over. I'll probably need another shoebox soon.

Following the scent of cinnamon and syrup, I trot down the wooden steps I've worn footprints in since I could walk.

"Mornin', baby girl. Two flapjacks or three?" Barry Elsmere greets me from his spot at the stovetop, where he pours batter onto the hot skillet.

"Good morning, Daddy. Three, please and thank you. Morning, Momma."

Anna Elsmere sits at the kitchen table, eyes on her book, brown hair up in curlers, hands wrapped around a steaming mug. She doesn't bother glancing up as I walk past. "Mornin'. Sugar's almost empty. Be a dear and grab more while you're in the cabinet."

I smirk but do as I was told, first sliding a plate from the bottom shelf, then reaching up to the top and picking out the half-full bag. Somehow, a man and woman who are solidly average height produced two offspring that would look right at home on a basketball court—not that my brother or I should be allowed on one with our abysmal hand-eye coordination. Momma claims her mystery father must have hidden the tall gene in her DNA. My parents haven't needed a step stool since Ryan and I hit puberty. My brother has four inches on me, but that still leaves me closer to the ceiling than the floor.

"One day, I'm gonna move out, and you'll have to drink bitter coffee and unsweetened tea for the rest of your life."

Carefully, I fill the porcelain jar that lives on the counter. Little bluebirds flutter around the word *sugar*, matching two other containers—one holding flour and the other brown sugar.

"It's rude to make threats first thing in the morning," Momma murmurs before sipping her coffee and smacking her lips, as if thoroughly satisfied with the sweetness.

"I'll borrow a pair of your momma's heels. Slip those on, and I'll reach every-thing in this house." Dad gestures toward his worn house slippers that are old enough to rent a car on their own. Pretty sure the soles are pure duct tape at this point.

A grin sneaks over my lips at the thought of my work-boot-wearing dad strutting around in the fabulous footwear my mother treats herself to.

"I think you'd look lovely."

"You keep your feet away from my shoes." There's no heat in my mom's warning.

Two Christmases ago, he gifted her a hand-crafted shelf to store her heels. There are lights in each compartment and everything. My dad knows he'd be sleeping on the couch for a month if his unpolished toes even brushed one of her coveted pairs.

As I settle in at the kitchen table with my hot pancakes and a glass of orange juice, I try to ease into my normal day-off, relaxing-morning mindset.

Problem is, that energy from yesterday's encounter and hospital visit is still buzzing through me.

When I got home last night, the gossip train had already made a stop by our house. Or more like the Piggly Wiggly while Momma was out shopping. I gave my parents a thorough rundown of what all had happened the moment I showed up at Mrs. Keen's, all the way to my trip to the hospital, only leaving out one detail.

A very big, very handsome detail.

Sebastian Kirkwood.

The two people I love most in the world are entirely too good at reading me. They would have known—seen it in my eyes or heard it in my voice—how much the man still affects me. The only way to hide anything from the two is by not mentioning it.

And I very much do not want them to know I still have a crush on Sebastian.

Not when he's about to be married.

Not when Momma held me while I cried the night I lost my one chance with him.

Junior year, Green Valley High's student council put together a Sadie Hawkins dance—where girls asked the guys—and I convinced myself there was a possibility I could land the guy of my dreams. That maybe—just maybe—my Biology partner might like me back enough to say yes if I invited him to the dance.

I planned every detail of how I would ask.

But I never could have predicted the embarrassing accident with a box of dead frogs that had me fleeing the school partway through the day.

Luckily, I made my escape before anyone important saw.

But by the next day, I was too late. Elaine Springfield had asked him while I was at home, scrubbing frog juice off my clothes.

And he had said yes.

Damn the dead frogs that stole what could have been my happily ever after. I'm not normally one to hold a grudge, but those amphibians will forever be my nemeses. No doubt, there's a host of froggy ghosts that haunts me to this day. The harbingers of all my bad luck.

Still, I envy that young Gwen. She had gumption. She longed for things and tried going after them.

"Do you ever think about going on a trip?" I ask between sips of orange juice.

"A trip?" Momma flips a page in her book. "To where?"

"I don't know. Alaska. New Mexico. Brazil."

"Why would I want to go to Brazil?" Her eyes stay on the words, even as her lips dip at the corners.

"To see something new. To have an adventure." My leg jiggles under the table as I imagine strolling down streets I've never walked before. It's been years since the urge pricked at me, the longing once in a hibernating state but now awake and hungry. "Eat different food. Meet people who live life in a different way than we do. To be a stranger in a strange land."

"I don't want to be a stranger." My mother shakes her head, setting her curlers to bouncing. "Everyone in Green Valley knows my name, and I like that. I never feel unsafe here."

Safety. That's all I wanted after Gran passed. To be *sure* of everything.

To know exactly what was going to happen when it was going to happen. To trust that nothing else would make an abrupt, devastating change.

I got hurt, and I curled into myself. Folded Green Valley around me, like staying here, driving the same route, eating the same food, living under the same roof would somehow keep any new pain away.

Now though, all I can see are possibilities. As if the incident with Mrs. Keen shoved me out of my comfort zone and reminded me about life. What it means to *live*.

A familiar voice, light and playful, whispers through my head, telling stories I haven't heard in years. Recollections I've shied away from, just like my travel guides.

Because the memory of her voice hurts.

But the hurt makes me feel.

When did I stop feeling?

"I'm going to plan a trip," I announce.

"Great idea." My father flips his pancake.

"To Brazil?" The horror in my mother's voice has me smiling.

"No, Momma. Not Brazil. Not yet at least. I'm thinking Nashville. Knoxville is the farthest I've ever been from home. And I haven't even gone there since high school."

Oh, high school Gwen. Such a different version of me. Somehow more scared of the world, but also braver. That girl had plans. Travel books stacked beside her bed and a map pinned to her wall with colored pins in a tiny box, waiting for her to pluck them out and plunge them into her visited destinations.

I took the map down a few years back. The single pin in Tennessee had mocked me.

"You could come with me." The trip blooms brighter in my mind with the thought of my mother at my side. "A girls' trip. You, me, and Nashville. We could listen to live music. See the sights. Go shopping." The last one is the largest carrot I could dangle in front of her nose. Oh, the shoes that must exist in Nashville.

"Sweetie." The smile she gives me, small and apologetic, is answer enough. "Nashville is so far. The Jam Sessions have all the live music I need. No big-city bar is gonna compare."

"But the *shoes*," I press.

"I'm sticking to a budget this year." She glares at my father when he snorts. "And I don't know anyone in Nashville."

"But wouldn't that be exciting? Meeting new people?"

She watches me over the rim of her mug as she sips her coffee, taking her time in answering. "Sometimes, you sound so much like Gran Maria that I could swear she stepped out of heaven to chat with me." This smile, while tiny and sad, also holds a shadow of understanding. "You're more like her than I ever was. If you want to visit Nashville, then I say, go. You don't need me there."

My eyes flick to my father, but he offers a smirk that says, *I love you, but no way am I driving that far with my sore back.*

I try not to sigh too loud as I tuck into my pancakes and play around with the idea of being a solo traveler.

One woman exploring the world.

I should. I could.

Why don't I?

Chapter Five

SEBASTIAN

Sometimes, I wonder why I never leave this place. You make coming and going seem so easy.

— LETTER TO MARIA

"If you hate these things so much, why do you agree to come to them?" I pull at the blue tie—the same color as my date's dress—that I must have knotted too tight. The air around me tastes stuffy as I drag a breath into my lungs.

There's no reason I should feel so confined. The event room at the Donner Lodge has plenty of space, even for the crowd of donors gathered.

But it's hard to breathe in here. And hot. My palms are sweaty enough that I'm worried if I pick up a drink, it'll slip straight through my fingers. Or maybe all the liquid will slosh out first because of my shaking hands. The second I stop tugging at my tie, I shove them back in my pockets, so no one sees.

This didn't used to happen. Once upon a time, I was a great date to large events.

Now though, everything is different.

"It's important to my parents," Elaine mutters against the rim of her wineglass before swallowing the rest of the dark liquid in one gulp.

"Just because the charity is important doesn't mean you should have to suffer through an event."

In the past, I never spoke these thoughts out loud. I accepted attending these occasions as part of our relationship.

But lately, I find myself testing every decision I took for granted.

The sight of Elaine's agitated shifting, paired with her desperate glance toward the bar, matches my internal restlessness. If this were a few months ago, I would put my arm around her waist and tell her we could leave whenever she wanted. Then, she would sigh, leaning into me, and we'd go grab another drink. Nothing would change, and I'd feel I'd served my role as the supportive partner.

But that's not us anymore, which is my fault.

"They expect me to be here." Elaine strides to the bar, and I follow.

"They expect it because you always come. Next time they send an invite, just explain that you don't want to go."

"We all have to do things we don't want to do, Sebastian," she snaps. "It's called being an adult."

"We have to do taxes or else we'll go to jail. We have to shower regularly or else become the town pariah. We have to shovel snow or else get entombed in our own homes. But you don't *have* to attend parties just because your parents are throwing them."

From the tight set of her jaw, I know she's clenching her teeth harder than is healthy. She wears a mouthguard at night to prevent the same thing from happening.

"I do if I want them to be happy."

"What about your happiness?" I keep my voice soft, trying to make her understand I'm on her side in this.

"Oh, have you started caring about that again?"

The young bartender's wide eyes jump between us as he passes Elaine a liberally filled glass of Cabernet. My date immediately turns her back to the guy before drawing in a deep gulp. As she wipes a stray drop from her bottom lip, she gazes off to the side.

And she doesn't understand. She doesn't know that every decision I've made, even the ones that hurt, I've agonized over because I hate the idea of making her sad.

That I'm scared of what her distress might mean.

"I'm sorry for pushing." The apology sounds like a lie to myself, but some of the tension eases from Elaine's shoulders, and I breathe easier.

"I'm sorry for what I said." She wraps a light grip around my forearm, tugging me toward a deserted corner. As we walk, I take a good look at her.

Today, she has on her professional face. This is not Elaine Springfield, not really. This is more her persona, Elle Fields, Channel 11 weatherwoman.

Elaine dressed herself to meticulous perfection, the way she always does when someone else expects something from her. Form-fitting dress made of stiff material. Nails perfectly polished. Heels too high to be comfortable. Honey-blonde hair framing her face in smooth, large waves.

When Elaine lets her hair air-dry, the strands opt for different styles. The parts that frame her face fall almost completely straight with only the slightest wave to them. But when you dive under, fingers finding the base of her neck, Elaine has a collection of blonde ringlets. They curl softly and always fall free of her ponytail.

Those are the first to be styled into submission.

Her makeup is carefully crafted to give her skin a glow and to highlight her eyes. Her lipstick is a muted color. The sight has me thinking of Gwen's makeup and the dark purple of the postwoman's mouth. I've seen Elaine put makeup on hundreds, probably thousands of times. She always has an air of resentment when she applies the products. She never does herself up because she wants to.

It's a chore to please others.

With Gwen though, I got a feeling the cosmetic touches were something she liked adding.

Stop thinking about the mailwoman. You're here for Elaine.

"Look at you two! Color-coordinated and everything. So charming." Mrs. Springfield floats up to us and presses a kiss to her daughter's cheek before wrapping me in a hug.

"Evening, ma'am. This is an impressive party." And I try not to let on how much we both hate being here as I hug her back.

The woman is a vibrant, loving presence, and I always wonder how she could be so clueless as to her daughter's discomfort at social gatherings. The elder Springfield is riding the high of a successful event. As a board member of multiple nonprofit organizations, she lives for these kinds of gatherings.

Elaine would rather peel her skin off than spend so long in a crowd. But I know better than most how good she is at putting on a show to keep others happy. I can do the same.

"Hi, Momma. Is the silent auction ending soon?"

"Yes! You should browse the bids." She clasps her hands in rapture under her chin. "This year looks to be the highest-earning one yet."

"That's great. I'm so glad." Elaine wears a soft smile as she takes in her mother's joy. This is why she comes.

Then, Mrs. Springfield rubs her temple—a subtle move—and Elaine's face falls as she homes in on the motion.

"Are you all right, Momma? Is your head bothering you?"

The woman immediately drops her hand and waves a dismissive gesture. "Oh, no. I'm fine. *More* than fine. The event is going better than I hoped." She scoops up Elaine's left hand, holding it up so the diamond ring sparkles in the light. "And seeing you here with Sebastian ... I think this would be a perfect venue for the wedding. Don't you think?"

Elaine makes a noise that could be agreement, and my insides twist with discomfort.

"Anyway, we'll talk about that later. Make sure to say hello to everyone. No one can see you over here. Mingle!" Mrs. Springfield blows us another kiss before strolling away to join an animated group closer to the live band.

"Do you want to mingle?" I ask.

Elaine immediately shakes her head, placing her finished glass on an empty table and snagging a full champagne flute from one of the passing waitstaff.

"One more hour." She twirls a long strand of hair around her finger, then gives it an agitated tug that has me wincing in sympathy. "Then, you can drop me off at home and go back to your life."

"You say that like I hate being around you, Elaine. That's not it, and you know it." My shaking hands go back in my pockets. *I'm too tired. I need to get more sleep.* "I'm just wondering how long you're going to keep pretending you like these things. And how long you want to keep doing *this*." I nod to the space between us, then glance toward the room full of people who don't know the truth.

The skin around her lips whitens as she pinches her mouth shut in a sure sign of stress. She flicks her gaze to her mother, then to the crowd, then back to me.

"This isn't a good time. Just a little longer. Then, I'll tell them."

I nod, not wanting to push her. Guilt already sits as a heavy weight in my gut. After making such a huge decision for both of us, I can let her have control over how this situation plays out. Elaine deserves at least that much from me. And a part of me needs her to sign off on this. To accept the end without too much force.

"I can be there when you do. If you think it'll help."

Elaine takes a long swallow of the bubbly alcohol before shaking her head.

"I'll do it." She tucks her hair behind her ear and pastes the charming smile I've seen her practice in the mirror. "If I'm going to be single, I might as well get used to doing things on my own."

Chapter Six

SEBASTIAN

I tossed a coin into the fountain for you today. I hope you felt the luck.

— LETTER TO MARIA

Needles stab into my back.

"What the fuck?" I groan, sleepily rolling over.

"Careful!" a familiar voice scolds me. A voice I'm used to ignoring. But the strong hand on my shoulder keeps me from flipping fully onto my back. "You'll squish her!"

"Who?" My room is bright, and I take a moment to blink the sleep from my eyes before meeting my sister's determined gaze. "Is there a *she* in my bed?"

"Yes." Kennedy smirks. "I brought you a lady friend. No need to thank me. Just being a good sister."

"Brat," I mutter. "Who'm I gonna squish then?"

"Your new best friend." Kennedy reaches over my shoulder, plucking the sharp needles out of my back a moment before shoving a furry ginger face into mine.

Green eyes stare at me with wide pupils, gazing unblinkingly into my soul.

"There's a cat in my face. Why is there a cat in my face?"

The thing mews, as if answering my drowsy question.

"Do you remember Cowbell?" My sister names our old family cat as she sits on my bed, legs crossed, holding the unfamiliar fuzz ball.

When I shift to sit up, she reaches out her arms and sets the kitten on the quilt next to me.

"Of course I remember him." Leaning back on my headboard, I watch as the orange menace pounces on a loose thread of my blanket. "But he died six years ago. Don't try convincing me he had some illegitimate litter that we're now responsible for. I won't fall for it."

"I'm not trying to prey on your notorious gullibility. Not today anyway." Before I can snipe back at her, Kennedy hits me with a vulnerable, pleading stare that has my big-brother instincts kicking in. "My friend is in a bad situation. I'm really worried about her, and I thought you could help. Can you? Please?"

"Of course." I lean forward to clasp her shoulder in reassurance. "Whatever you need."

She sags in relief. "Thanks. I knew I could count on you."

"How can I help?"

"You can clear out some space for a litter box up here."

"Uh …" I glance around the loft space in our parents' former barn, turned second garage and living space. For the past few months, this has been my temporary home until I can figure out the next step in my life. There's plenty of room, if you ignore the cardboard boxes that hold all my belongings. "Your friend needs me to watch her cat?"

"Nope." When Kennedy lets her *P* pop with extra gusto, I know I've been duped.

"Your friend is …"

"The cat." She scoops the kitten up again and deposits the creature in my quilt-covered lap. "She's a special lady. Fun fact: only one in five orange tabbies is born female. Her name is Curie."

38

What have I agreed to? But that's not the question I ask. "Curry? Like the spice?"

Kennedy glares as if the suggestion offends her. "*Cu*rie. Like the chemist. Marie Curie."

"So, you got yourself a cat, and you need me to watch it for a couple of days?" Hope hitches up the tone of my voice.

"Nope." She slides off the bed and makes a finger frame with her hands, putting me and the kitten in a portrait. "Curie and Sebastian. Looks like a *purr*fect match to me." Her hands drop, but her satisfied grin stays in place.

"This"—I wave at the Cheetos-colored feline—"is not happening."

Kennedy strolls around my room, gaze on the wooden rafters rather than me. "Let's review the facts. One, my apartment doesn't allow cats. Two, you loved Cowbell so much that you built a casket for him when he died."

"Cameron helped," I mutter while stroking the kitten behind the ears, surprised at how soft the fur is under my rough fingers.

A memory arises of the wooden box I cut and nailed together, then painted black. My younger brother lined the inside with a soft blanket and covered the lid with stick-on rhinestones he'd found at the dollar store.

Kennedy ignores my comment. "Three, you just promised to help me in whatever way I needed." She keeps tapping her knuckles against my boxes as she passes, using the muffled thumps to emphasize her points. "Four—"

"Four, you didn't tell me your friend was a cat."

"*Four*," she speaks over me, "you're already bonding with her."

Letting the terror dig her miniscule claws into my forearm does not mean I'm bonding with the silly thing.

"Five—"

"How long is this list?"

Curie fits easily in my palm as I hold her against my chest while scooting to the edge of my bed.

"Just a few more." Kennedy stops her meandering to face me head-on. "Five, you're a great caretaker."

Heat rises to my cheeks at the compliment, even as I scoff. "I'm barely taking care of myself right now. Twenty-seven, and I'm back to living with Mom and Dad."

"This is temporary. Better than living with your ex."

My sister has never been the kind to dance around a topic, and she's one of a handful that knows I broke off my engagement. If I hadn't told her, she would've interrogated the truth out of me, using all manner of creative psychological torture.

My sister, my brother, and my parents know. And no one else will until Elaine decides she's ready for the news of our split to be public.

That ill-advised engagement makes this breakup so much worse. The juiciness of the gossip is riper than a Georgia peach. And with Elaine having a small amount of celebrity with her Elle Fields weatherwoman gig, I can imagine the prying questions that would pop up on her social media feeds, dragging the pain of a breakup on until the vultures got their fill. A constant string of strangers taking screenshots of her ringless finger, the same way they homed in on the diamond when she first started wearing it.

The weird thing is, I never *officially* proposed.

At dinner one night, Elaine told me her parents were asking about when we *would* get engaged. That statement turned into the two of us visiting a jewelry store in Knoxville. A week later, the rock was on her finger, and our calendar had a date circled with the bold word *wedding* written in the square.

My wedding.

The word tripped me every time I passed through a doorway in our rental house. The hanging hook of the *G* snagged loose threads in my clothes. The points of the *W* scraped the insides of my eyelids until I wanted to cry from an exhaustion I couldn't alleviate, no matter how long I lay in bed.

Wedding.

Wrong.

But I didn't realize how wrong until I made another mistake. One so large that I'm not sure I'll ever escape the shadow that now lingers over my life.

At least I realized I needed to start changing things. Unfortunately, our relationship wasn't a broken item in need of repair. It was a ring we never should have bought from the store.

"You can't spring a cat on a guy when he's in the middle of rearranging his life."

The kitten vibrates with purrs that rumble past my skin and into my chest.

Does Kennedy have any supplies for her?

Keeping a firm hold on Curie, I use my free hand to search under my spare pillow for where I shoved my laptop before falling asleep.

"Change one thing, change a few things. What's the difference?"

My sister might as well be talking about a potted plant. And I'm not sure I could keep one of those alive right now either.

"The difference is a cat."

Is there a pet supply store in town?

Anything I order online will take a few days to arrive.

Will Gwen deliver the boxes? Is my parents' house on her route?

"Well, it's done now. I signed your name on the papers at the shelter, and I can't take her back. It's impossible. And remember, Cowbell always made Dad sneeze, so he'll stick Curie out in the woods if you try pawning her off. She's *your* cat now."

"Why?"

"Why what?" Kennedy looks everywhere but at me.

"Why did you get me a cat?"

She shrugs. "I like to think of it as the universe getting you a cat and I was merely the delivery minion."

"Kennedy." I try to appear stern, but I'm not sure I manage the proper level of intimidation when I'm holding a purring furball against my cheek.

She's *so* freaking soft.

"Because you're *alone*, okay? And I think breaking it off with Elaine was the right thing to do, but I can't stand the idea of you sitting in this creepy attic all by yourself, like you've been doing for the past few months."

Kennedy glares at me, but in the intensity of her stare, I see vulnerability. And I know what she's remembering. Another breakup, one with her first college boyfriend. Kennedy was the one to decide on the split, and she probably told him so in her normal blunt manner.

Two days later, she learned he'd taken a handful of sleeping pills and he never woke up.

Even though no one blames her, I know she still thinks that guy is gone because of her. I know that she watches people closer now, for signs something is wrong. Breakups hold a certain kind of anxiety for her.

And despite me repeatedly impressing on Kennedy that what happened with her ex wasn't her fault, I can't help mimicking her fear. Applying it to my own situation.

What if Elaine does something destructive because I ended things?

That terror lingers in the back of my mind whenever I see Elaine, keeping me from pressing her further. I know how bad things can go now.

But Kennedy doesn't realize that I'm not the one at risk.

"Momma comes by," I point out.

"Oh God. Stop talking. You're making it worse. Next, you're going to tell me you've made friends with a ghost and you two knit together."

I snort at the image. "So, you thought a cat was a better choice?"

"Than our mom and a ghost?" She eyes me in my pink boxers, sitting on a twin bed made up with Thomas the Tank Engine sheets. "Yes."

With a dramatic twirl she no doubt learned from our brother, Kennedy heads to the stairs, leaving me alone with a kitten I never agreed to keep. After the clunk of the door shutting echoes through my space, I notice the bags of supplies piled by the top of the stairs.

Glancing down, I meet Curie's inquisitive gaze. "I guess you're better than an unplanned ring."

Chapter Seven

GWEN

My buddy has a German shepherd that rides shotgun, and he named it Ned Jr.,
after his dad. Think I might get a weird little pug and name it Gwen.

— POSTCARD FROM RYAN, DELAWARE

There aren't many stoplights in Green Valley, and I don't know if that makes it more or less likely I'd end up at one, next to an ambulance driven by Sebastian Kirkwood. The emergency lights aren't flashing, and the boxy vehicle sits quiet as it waits for a green. The driver's window is rolled down, a tanned arm with the sleeve pushed up draped out of the opening. When I spot the pink hairband hugging his wrist, I know exactly what handsome face I'm going to see when I pull up beside him.

Sebastian sits, relaxed, with one hand on the wheel, gaze forward, not noticing me at first even though I'm right next to him. Literally. I drive in the right seat of my car.

The steering mechanism and pedal set up in my SUV allow me to sit in either the left or right seat. All to make mail delivery easier. When I got hired as a rural mail carrier, Stanley—a postman who retired two years ago and the mentor I shadowed—recommended I give my car over to the care of the Winston Brothers Auto Shop, so they could set me up with dual steering.

Unfortunately, my well-worn compact car with two-wheel drive crapped out on me after too many back roads. Hence my used, but new to me, Bronco. This one got the postal worker makeover the same week I bought it.

I lean one arm, all casual-like, out my window, leaving one hand resting on the steering wheel, mirroring Sebastian's pose.

"You boys lookin' for a race?" I rev my engine, as if we were two hot rods at The Canyon.

The paramedic jerks, whipping his head to face me, his melted-chocolate mane of hair swaying with the movement. And doesn't my heart want to pound right out of my chest when I watch that heal-any-hurt grin spread slowly across his mouth?

Oh no, I should've just rolled up my window and driven away.

But he's spotted me now, and I've made the decision to stop avoiding the scary, exciting things in life. Which is a category Sebastian firmly sits in.

"Well, hello to you too, Miss Elsmere. You think that little mail buggy can match this beauty?" The paramedic pats his dashboard, then leans full out the window. "Did you know your steering wheel ended up on the wrong side of the car? Want me to have a stern talking-to with your mechanic about that? I'd hate to hear the Winstons are playing a joke on my favorite postal worker."

"Don't try to distract me just because you're intimidated." Wiggling in my seat, I make it look like I'm ready to race. I've even got my hot-rod red lipstick on today. "I think you're too used to cars getting out of your way. You've never had a *real* challenge."

Something flares in his eyes, and I wonder if I've just signed myself up for a drag race. But the little pop of something disappears, and Sebastian's his normal, carefree, charming self. He combs his fingers through his loose, silky strands. I wonder if he'd look silly with his hair in a bun. Probably not. He would make the hipster hairstyle work effortlessly.

"You might be right."

Just then, I get a green arrow to turn left.

"Saved by the light." I shrug as I accelerate. "Another day."

"Come back, you coward!"

He waves a mock irate fist in the air as I pull away, and I let out a string of giggles.

What was shaping up to be an average day now has a golden glow around the edges, all from a minute-long exchange with Sebastian. I'm glad I decided to stop avoiding him even if my pesky crush stubbornly persists. He's the kind of man who can make even the surliest person smile.

He's so kind. And funny.

And damn it, I want to rip his work uniform off with my teeth.

I have a theory that Sebastian would be the optimal lover. A giver. And I'm not normally a selfish person, but if I were in bed with him, I would take like a greedy dragon hoarding treasure. The treasure that is Sebastian's naked body.

Before arriving at my next mailbox, I flip down the mirror in my visor to check my mouth and make sure I haven't started drooling.

Elaine had better appreciate every bit of him.

Chapter Eight

SEBASTIAN

Your stays are always too short.

— LETTER TO MARIA

E ven when Gwen is gone and I'm still lingering at the red light, I can't get rid of my grin. A few minutes in her presence, and my day is brighter.

The same thing happened in high school. I'd be having a shitty morning for whatever reason, but then I'd walk into Biology class and sit next to Gwen, and whatever teenage angst load I was carrying would suddenly lighten.

There's something about her smile. Or maybe it's her laugh. Could be the playful way her eyes crinkle when she looks at me.

Or all of it together.

The light turns green, and I accelerate absentmindedly, pointing us back toward the station, where we'll spend the rest of our shift unless we get another alert.

We got a call this afternoon about a woman going into labor a week early. I was fully ready to deliver a baby on the way to the hospital. Come to find out, she popped the kid out while we were driving over. We showed up, and the new mom was cradling her bundle of joy. Her husband was the one who needed medical attention, the guy looking ready to pass out.

We got some fluids in him, checked that baby and momma were healthy, and dubbed it one of the fastest deliveries Green Valley had ever seen. No need to even head to the hospital.

A good day in my book. And now, I can spend my time thinking about a certain postwoman. I rifle through more memories of Gwen and conclude there are fewer of them than I'd like. Plenty from high school, but mostly just time spent together in class. After graduation though, all I can think of are brief glimpses around town. A quick wave when I happened to catch her eye.

I let so many chances to chat with her slip by. Now, I'm hoping to catch Gwen on her route. Get her to stop and talk to me. She's obviously willing to linger and catch up, going by what Mrs. Keen said.

When I reach a Stop sign and glance to my right, I realize Grizz is staring at me. Staring with brows raised. The expression is the only warning that I'm about to get some shit.

"What?" I flick on my blinker and try to concentrate on turning, but I can't ignore him now that I know I'm under the microscope.

"You were *awfully* friendly with that cute mail lady." The man wears a smug grin, like he's solved a puzzle I was trying to hide the answer to.

And I imagine what my exchange with Gwen looked like.

Like an engaged man flirting with a single woman.

But even if I *were* engaged—which I'm not—that doesn't mean I'm not allowed to talk to women other than Elaine.

I clear my throat and tug at my suddenly tight collar. "Gwen and I used to be friends." *Did that sound defensive?* "We *are* friends." That definitely sounded defensive.

And also kind of like a lie. It's hard to say I'm only her friend when I'm dealing with a massive amount of attraction I did not expect to get hit with. But I'm not ready to admit that out loud. I can't, not when I'm still letting Elaine choose when to end our happy-couple ruse.

So, for now, the best explanation I have is that Gwen and I are friends.

No need to tell Grizz or anyone that I've watched every single one of Gwen's makeup tutorials. She's vibrant on camera. Smiling broadly in the glow of her ring light. Making silly jokes as she expertly transforms her face into a beautiful piece of art.

And the way she applies lipstick? Lips parted slightly, the stick tugging at the softer skin.

The sight should be a crime. Or an award-winning piece of media.

I'm a horndog, and I know it. But playing her videos while I'm getting ready for bed is the best part of my nightly routine. And the perfect way to make sure she shows up in my dreams.

"*Friends*. Of course." Grizz's voice jerks my thoughts away from a certain dream I had the night before.

"Of course, what?" I snap, then grind my teeth.

Grizz gives me a shit-eating grin. "I don't know why your briefs are in a twist. I'm *agreeing* with you. Just sayin' you two looked friendly. Real friendly. Giving her those gooey eyes that friends give each other. I mean, that's how you always look at *me*." My coworker chortles.

I'm not giving him *gooey* eyes. The exact opposite in fact.

"Shut up," I mutter, which only makes him laugh outright. We reach the station then, and I pretend to focus entirely on backing the ambulance into an empty bay, so I don't have to say anything else.

No doubt Grizz's ribbing was his roundabout way of calling me an asshole. Pointing out how dickish flirting with Gwen was.

Or at least how it'd seem to everyone in Green Valley if they found out.

Chapter Nine

GWEN

Met a roadkill taxidermist. How do you feel about a flat raccoon for your birthday?

— POSTCARD FROM RYAN, ALABAMA

W hile running my fingers over the selection of eye shadows, I mentally catalog the colors I have at home. If I could buy everything on this shelf —in this aisle—I would. But after a few hefty credit card bills, I realized I needed to set a makeup budget.

Unlike my mother and her shoe budget, I plan to stick to it.

Now, I only treat myself to new products every few weeks and merely a handful.

"*Mermaid's Song*," I read the label of a turquoise-colored eyeliner.

A mermaid look. Haven't tried that yet.

Visions of sequined scales and vibrant blues tease me, and my hunt focuses.

"Gwen?"

Jitters skip down my spine, which can only mean one thing.

Sebastian.

I turn and find the sexy paramedic wearing a pink hoodie.

The engaged paramedic, I remind myself. *The engaged paramedic who makes that man bun work far more than I ever dreamed possible.*

I was right. The hipster hairstyle looks mouthwateringly good on him.

"Hi!" My greeting comes out way too peppy. From that high-pitched note, no doubt, he can tell how huge of a crush I have on him. To combat the mistake, I intentionally lower my voice. "What's up?"

Crud, now, I sound like a Neanderthal.

Sebastian's lips curl at the corners. "Just restocking some necessities."

He indicates his basket, and I spy a bar of soap, floss, Band-Aids, and a bag of peanut butter cups.

No condoms. Wonder if they're trying for a kid.

"Oh God," I mutter. "No. Nope. Don't do that."

His brows rise. "Do what?"

If someone pressed a match against my skin, I'm certain the thing would immediately ignite.

"Sorry. I wasn't talking to you."

He glances around. "Who were you talking to?"

"Myself. My brain." Well, weirdness is one way to put distance between me and a man. "Do your thoughts ever go down a random track without your permission? All you want to do is shift everything in reverse and think like a normal person?"

Sebastian studies me, and I let him as I fiddle with my eyeliner pencil.

Do you see now? Soak up the oddness that is me and run for the door. We were better when I crushed on you from afar.

"My guess is, normal people's thoughts are boring," he says.

Oh. That's not the preamble to the quick escape I was expecting. "Well, my life is boring, so I must be normal."

Sebastian steps closer, and I catch a hint of crisp sandalwood. My eyes dip back to his basket and the soap, wondering if I should buy a bar for myself. Just … because.

Because I want to sit in my bedroom alone and sniff it, okay?

"I don't think you're boring."

He holds my eyes as he speaks, and my stomach flamingos wake up and start their awkward, enthusiastic flapping.

"I deliver mail," I point out. "You save people's lives."

Sebastian frowns. "So? You're telling me nothing interesting happens at your job? You go all over Green Valley every day. You've got to see some wild things."

Good point. Saying I *just* deliver mail is oversimplifying my job. I don't only stick envelopes in boxes.

"I might have seen a wild thing or two." I try for a mysterious voice.

Sebastian grins. "Oh yeah?"

"Last month, a black bear and her cubs wandered into the road right in front of my car. That was pretty wild."

"Shit. That's the perfect combination of adorable and dangerous." His smile tips to a concerned frown. "Do you carry bear spray?"

"Yep. Got a can in the front seat. I didn't have to use it though."

And I don't tell him I first put the bottle in my car when I realized how many Iron Wraiths were on my route. I wanted some form of protection, but I've never been quite comfortable carrying a gun, no matter how many times my dad takes me out to the woods to shoot cans for target practice.

I've got good aim but a lack of conviction. I'm just not sure I could use it.

But spray a guy in the face with stinging chemicals? Yep, I can handle that.

Sebastian opens his mouth but stops with a wince. And that's when I notice an odd bulge in the front of his hoodie.

"Is that bump moving?" I point to the protrusion on his chest.

After a furtive glance around us, Sebastian reaches to pull the zipper of his sweatshirt down a few inches, revealing a fuzzy orange face with wide, blinking eyes.

"Oh my God," I whisper-squeal. "You have a kitten?"

The paramedic grins down at the fluff ball like a proud cat dad. "Yep. This is Marie Curie—or Curie for short. I didn't want to leave her at home when I was just running a few errands." He winces again. "She's got some little needles in those paws."

The cat purrs and kneads Sebastian's shirt, her green eyes taking in our surroundings.

"Can I pet her?"

"Go right ahead."

He leans closer to me, and I scratch Curie under her soft chin. She rubs her head against my fingers, purring all the while.

When I glance up to thank Sebastian for letting me say hi to his kitten, I realize how close we've gotten. His face lingers inches from mine, the warm puff of his breath tickling my cheek. This close, I can see a light-green ring in the hazel of his eyes.

Is he staring at my mouth?

"Sebastian."

At the sound of the deep, stern voice, the paramedic straightens and re-zips his hoodie, and I shake my head to get rid of the ludicrous notion he might have been fixated on my lips.

"Father." Sebastian uses an overly formal tone that has me biting the inside of my cheek to stifle my laughter.

"I told you not to bring your cat into my store." Mr. Kirkwood, owner of Kirkwood Drugstore, stalks down the aisle toward us, a scowl on a face that's slightly rounder than his son's.

I'm used to seeing the man smile, and I get the sense he's more exasperated than mad.

"Gwen is a human woman, not a cat." The paramedic shakes his head, as if disappointed. "Do you need glasses?"

"You're impossible." Mr. Kirkwood turns on his heel, facing me. "Gwen, may I ask what you were petting when I approached?"

Not fair. He wants me to tattle on his handsome son and an adorable kitten?

The man puts too much faith in my integrity.

"Your son."

Silence descends.

"Excuse me?"

"I was petting Sebastian," I insist. "You know, just some friendly pats on his head." I reach up to give the younger man a couple of firm pats right on his noggin. "He gets antsy if you don't show him affection."

Mr. Kirkwood narrows his eyes as they flit between the two of us, and I pray I'm not about to lose access to my supply of cosmetics. Sebastian, meanwhile, grins as if he were at a carnival with a handful of ride tickets. His bump shifts again.

"The more you encourage him, the odder he gets. I hope you're aware of the monster you're creating, Miss Gwen." The man turns on his son. "Out. No pets. It starts with your cat, and then the next thing you know, that mechanic will be in here with her cursing parrot. Then, there will be customers complaining. Guess who has to deal with those?"

"The parrot?"

"Me! You see this?" Mr. Kirkwood points to the bald spot on the back of his head. "I used to have a full head of hair before you kids."

"Aw, Dad." Sebastian pats his father's shoulder. "I still think you're handsome."

"Just you wait." He wags a finger at his son. "One day, you'll wake up, and half of that man bun will be gone. You know why?"

"Genetics?"

"It'll be gone because I'll have shaved it off when you were sleeping!" He throws his arms in the air, as dramatic as his son. "See if I don't!"

"Dear."

At the chime of a sweet voice, we all turn to find Mrs. Kirkwood, who stands at the head of the aisle in her white pharmacist jacket.

"Are you threatening our son?"

"Of course not." Mr. Kirkwood straightens his tie. "I'm *promising* him."

I snort, then press my lips flat to keep more noises from sneaking out. Sebastian leans over to butt his shoulder against mine and gives me a mock glare.

His sweatshirt meows.

"Good idea, Gwen," Sebastian says loudly. "I *do* want to go look at the travel-sized shampoos."

Before I can respond, he has his arm hooked through mine, and we're escaping from the grumpy gaze of his father. When we stop a few aisles over —in front of the travel-sized items, like I apparently recommended—we share a snicker.

As my laughter fades away, I can't stop from picking up the cute little bottles.

"Did I accidentally tell my dad the truth?" Sebastian peers over my shoulder at the compact shampoo I'm fondling. "Are you stocking up for some summer travel?"

Thoughts of my bookshelf pop into my mind. All those never-used travel books.

"I was thinking I might go somewhere. A short trip. To Nashville maybe."

I turn the tiny shampoo over in my hands.

Maybe I could buy it. I just need to commit. Declare that I will drive out of Green Valley for an excursion.

"You should. Nashville is a fun place." He unzips his hoodie again, and Curie reappears, her whiskers twitching as she peers around.

"Do you take her everywhere with you?" I drop the shampoo in my basket and grab a conditioner, too, half-tempted to ask what brand he uses so I can attempt to make my hair half as lustrous as his.

"I wish. If I wasn't worried about her running off or getting stepped on, I'd take her to work. Maybe when she's bigger, I can convince the guys the fire station needs a mascot. But for now, she's on her own during my longer shifts."

A frown mars the man's normally smiling face as he tucks his chin and stares down at his kitten.

"What about Elaine?" I ask, forcing myself to acknowledge his fiancée's existence.

Sebastian jerks his eyes up, then clears his throat. "Well, we're in the process of moving out of our rental in Merryville. She's still there, but I'm in the apartment above my parents' garage. You know …"

He goes to finger-comb his hair but remembers halfway through the gesture that he tied it back, which leaves the configuration in disarray. He tugs out the hair tie, and the silky mass tumbles around his face like velvet curtains. I have to bite the inside of my cheek to keep from groaning.

"Staying here is easier with the new job. And easier to look for a permanent place in town."

"Mmhmm." The mumbled noise is all I can manage as I take in every endearing, sexy, rumpled inch of the cat dad with a head of hair stolen from some god of temptation.

Not fair. His existence isn't fair.

"So, yeah, Curie is alone for a while. My parents aren't really pet people."

Feline eyes blink at me, and I blame my next words on the way his long fingers scratch her chin in a gentle, loving gesture.

"I could check in on her."

Sebastian tilts his head, cascade of satin hair brushing against his cheek. "You could?"

"Yeah. Definitely. Of course." *Stop saying words that mean the same thing.* "It's just that summer tends to be lighter on the mail, which means my route goes by faster and I'm off earlier. I could swing by your parents' place and check on her. Cuddle her. All that fun stuff. Only if you want."

"That would be amazing! I could pay—"

"Oh, no!" I wave away the offer. "Please don't. I'm not trying to make money off you." No need to mention that breathing in his sandalwood scent would be payment enough.

"But—"

"Seriously, Sebastian." His mouth clicks shut when I say his name. "If you try to give me money, I'll just donate it."

The paramedic huffs out a laugh, then slowly smiles, the expression made for his face. "Okay. I can give you a spare key." He steps in close, draping one arm around my shoulders in a side hug that steals my breath. "You're the best." His large hand squeezes my bicep in another mini hug, then rubs from shoulder to elbow. A friendly caress.

"Sure." Somehow, I force the word out without sounding too breathless.

I swear, I am not going to snoop to find out what shampoo he uses.

Chapter Ten

GWEN

I saw a ghost. You'd better not be laughing. It was real, damn it! All spooky and glowing white and standing on the side of the road, waiting for me to pull over so it could steal my soul. Unrelated, I'm not listening to any more horror audiobooks while driving at night.

— POSTCARD FROM RYAN, LOUISIANA

Curie sprints across the floor in a frantic flurry, using every muscle in her tiny body to catch the little red dot. When I first played with the laser pointer, I worried that she might get agitated, never actually catching the thing. But she seems to enjoy the chase, making eager chirping noises whenever I pull the light out of my pocket.

After enough rounds of the room to have her panting, I tuck the toy away. Don't want to have to call Sebastian and tell him his cat passed out on my watch. Even if it was from having too much fun.

"Hey, sweet girl. Let's take a cuddle break."

Seating options are sparse in the studio apartment above Mr. and Mrs. Kirkwood's garage. A bed with a soft comforter beckons me, but I opt for the low-backed couch. Other than those two, there's nothing else. Not even a table in the kitchenette.

Does Sebastian mind staying here alone?

If I were Elaine, engaged to the man with the best smile on earth with a personality and body to match, I wouldn't want to spend one night apart from him. Much less however long it's going to take them to run out the lease on their place in Merryville.

A part of me is grateful this apartment is only a stop on Sebastian's moving journey. That way, I don't have to play with his adorable cat while surrounded by smiling pictures of the happy couple.

But the exposure would be good for me. With an unending bombardment of Sebastian's love life, this pesky crush might finally go away.

"I bet you love your momma, Elaine, don't you?" I stroke the soft fur along Curie's back. "I guess I can't blame you. We used to be friends, you know. Back in high school. Before the Sadie Hawkins dance."

Damn dance. Damn box of frogs I never should have been carrying.

Elaine and I weren't best-friend level, but we might have gotten there. Sometimes, she and I would hang out, just the two of us, during lunch. Playing card games, exchanging food, making bad jokes.

"You might not know it now—what with her being on TV and all—but your momma used to be *so* quiet. You had to pry words out of her with a crowbar. And even then, you'd only get a handful. Unless you're me, of course. Elaine talked to me. And I guess she talked to Sebastian too."

I rub my stomach, a queasy clenching starting up when I think of the girl I used to be friends with. That tentative friendship is one more reason I wish I could wipe out this crush. Elaine would be uncomfortable if she knew I harbored lusty stomach flamingos for her fiancé to this day.

The two of them are going to get married and build a long, happy relationship together that doesn't need to be soured by someone standing on the sidelines, saying, *What if that were me?*

Elaine and Sebastian are all set up to be a model couple. Fell in love in high school, stayed together for years, getting married in their hometown. They'll probably have two-point-five kids and live in a house with a white picket fence.

At the thought of their future home, I'm brought back to the loft. Why is Curie with Sebastian instead of Elaine?

Maybe the cat has an insatiable fixation on him too.

Spending more time around Sebastian isn't helping, like I hoped. The paramedic remains as sweet and funny as ever. The guy is a fine wine, getting more intoxicating with age. All I want is for him to be a wilted piece of lettuce. Some curdled milk. A moldy piece of bread.

I sigh and sink lower into my seat.

That's not fair. The world is better with a kind Sebastian in it.

It's only me that suffers.

I scoop up the kitten and hold her close to my chest as I stand from the couch and meander around the room. When I scratch behind her ears, Curie kneads her claws into my shirt like I'm a big ball of dough and she's ready to cook up some biscuits.

"Let's take a picture for your papa."

She's tiny enough that I can support her with one hand and pull my phone out of my back pocket with the other. The first few come out blurry, my fingers clumsy as I try to make sure Curie doesn't wiggle out of my hold.

Finally, I get a decent one with her fuzzy little head pressed against my chin.

"*Purr*fect." I chortle at my unoriginal joke as I send the image to Sebastian.

Me: I'm officially a cat person.

I toss my phone on the bed, then give in to the urge to sit down on the mattress, stroking Curie from head to tail all the while. She purrs a comforting hum against my chest, and the sensation travels straight to my heart.

"You're entirely too cute," I murmur to her. "I might steal you."

Another vibration, this time from my phone. When I look at the screen, I let out a gasp, then bite my lip to keep from moaning.

Sebastian sent me a selfie, which should be an innocent action—not at all gasp-worthy. But the man is in uniform! And I'm not panicking over a bleeding Agnes, which means I can observe him in all his handsome, professional splendor. Like the way that blue EMT button-up fits him just right, except for the sleeve that seems to struggle to contain the swell of his bicep.

Does he have an undershirt on? Or would sliding each of those buttons from their holes reveal—

"I'm hopeless," I groan, collapsing back on the bed.

Curie meows and leaps off my chest, and then, unfazed, she plops onto her side and starts cleaning herself.

And I commit to torture by gazing at the picture when I should delete it.

Sebastian stands in front of the ambulance outside, the sun soaking into his skin, turning him a tempting golden color. A set of pink-rimmed sunglasses sits on his nose, and he wears an overly exaggerated pout.

Sebastian: *I wish I were with you two.*

I read the message once. Then twice. Then, I take a screenshot and read the words on the picture to make sure they still say the same thing.

You two. Plural. As in I'm one of the things he wishes he were with.

I reopen the picture I sent to check if there's a third being in the photo. Maybe a ghost who lives in this garage apartment that Sebastian is buddies with.

But nope. Just me and his cat. And he wishes he were with us. Both of us.

"He was being nice. We're friends. It's perfectly normal to want to ditch work and hang out with a friend," I explain to an uninterested Curie.

If I were having a rough day on my route and Arthur or my other coworker Lance sent me a picture of them drinking beers together—which they never would because neither one is the selfie type—I'd text back, *I wish I were with you two.*

Because they're my buddies.

I'm Sebastian's buddy.

"And being a buddy is A-OK." I sound like a perky camp counselor trying to convince surly teenagers to be friends with each other. Only, instead of adolescents, I'm trying to convince my vagina and stomach flamingos to calm the heck down and be fine with friendship.

Having talked myself away from jumping off a lusty ledge into a free fall of disappointment, I snap another picture of Curie lounging on his bed.

Me: Curie misses you too. But she likes the extra mattress space.

Barely a minute passes before my phone lights up with a response.

I guess there are no active emergencies in Green Valley.

Sebastian: Oh, so ONLY my cat misses me? I see how it is ...

The flamingos are back, wobbling around in my intestines, jabbing my heart with their bony knees.

He's just teasing, I know. That's what Sebastian did in high school too. We would trade jokes all through class, sometimes whispering, sometimes writing in each other's notebooks.

I was the one who read too much into it. My innocent mind thought we were flirting.

I'm wiser now. Sebastian is a playful, affectionate person. Thinking this is anything more would be ridiculous. Especially when he's probably sexting Elaine right now. I'm just the hometown buddy he trusts enough to hang out with his cat.

She gets passionate kisses, late-night touches, and a diamond ring.

I get Curie's murder mittens poking holes in my polo shirt.

Me: So sorry.

Me: Your giant fort of cardboard boxes misses you too.

See? I'm playful and not serious. No way will I read more into these exchanges like last time.

Though it hurts to think about my gran, I pull up the memories of her. Specifically of how she talked about relationships.

"I've enjoyed so many people. I'm lucky. Most people insist on finding one person, loving them so entirely that they give up on the rest of the world. But why not explore? Why not sample all the passion out there?"

She was a free-spirited woman. My idol. The way she talked about the world had me wanting to see every corner of it with her by my side.

Gran gave me that romance insight when I asked about my grandfather. Apparently, she never learned his name. She called him Dublin because that was where she'd met him, and that was where they'd spent a passionate weekend together that resulted in my mother being born. And according to her, she *did* love him in her way. But she never wished for him. Never wanted their affair to last longer than it did.

Maybe that's how I could be. None of the men I've dated gave me the urge to stay with them longer than a few months.

And this crush on Sebastian? If I could give that an end date, my heart would appreciate the relief.

There are so many ways I want to be like my grandmother. Lively, adventurous, exciting. Why can't I be independent too? Choose to keep my relationships brief and passionate and ending without a broken heart.

Gran had an amazing life, and despite the discomfort of her treatments at the end, she was still happy. All she regretted was not having more time with me. To fulfill all the plans we'd made.

That's what I should focus on. The promises I made to her.

"You're going to live such a beautiful life. I only wish I were staying to see it." She gripped my hand tight when she whispered that a week before she passed away. *"Promise me you'll go to all the places we talked about."*

I promised her even though I couldn't fathom entering an airport without her by my side. But what could I say?

No, Gran. After you die, I'm going to spend the rest of my life in Green Valley. I'll hide all our dreams in a box on a forgotten shelf, and I'll pine for a man I can't have, and I'll pretend I'm happy until I can't remember what an adventure even looks like.

"Nashville," I whisper to myself as I stare out the window toward the road I've driven hundreds, maybe thousands of times on my mail route. A circle. The same stops every day.

I need to deviate before I get stuck in the same pattern for the rest of my life.

Chapter Eleven

SEBASTIAN

Please send me a picture with your next letter. I long to see your face.

— LETTER TO MARIA

While Jed, my partner for the day, fills up the ambulance with gas, I head into the convenience store, hunting for snacks for the drive back. We're in Merryville again today, having had to swing by the hospital to drop off a kid who had decided to go truck surfing.

And, yes, it's as dumb as it sounds.

Some teenagers tied a surfboard to the top of a truck and then drove that truck on the winding mountain roads surrounding Green Valley. When his buddy stopped too fast, he's lucky that he flew headfirst into a bunch of bushes instead of the pavement.

The branches might have slowed his fall, but if my initial diagnosis was right, the kid has a fractured collarbone.

Jed confiscated the surfboard and roped it to the top of the ambulance. I hope he's not planning to climb up there and ask me to drive him around.

"This it?" the cashier asks as I unload my armful of snacks and energy drinks.

I'll eat healthy another day.

"Yeah …" I trail off as my eye catches on a splash of color.

Beside the checkout is a rotating rack full of postcards. The one that stands out shows a gorgeous sunset over what must be a forest in the Great Smoky Mountains National Park. The sun lights up the sky in a wild range of pinks and oranges, which reminds me of the wall of cosmetics Gwen was exploring at my parents' store.

What if I send a colorful piece of mail to the mailwoman?

Could this inspire another makeup look?

She hasn't posted a new video in over a week. Not that I'm checking multiple times a day or anything …

"This too." I add the postcard to the pile and pay for everything, shoving the picturesque photo in my back pocket as I make my way out to the ambulance.

Just then, my phone buzzes. I juggle the food and drinks, eager to see a familiar name.

I'm not disappointed.

When I click on Gwen's name, a new text pops up with an image.

Gwen*: Find the cat.*

The shot is of my kitchenette area, and I scan every corner until I discover the sneaky furball.

Me*: That's not a cat. That's my new fridge gargoyle.*

Curie has perched herself on the top of my refrigerator, lording over her domain. Gwen sends back a simple *ha-ha*, and I try not to be disappointed the short conversation is over.

Every picture she sends me is torture.

Some only have Curie.

Some have Curie and Gwen.

The first has me wanting to see Gwen. The second has me wishing the sight of her didn't cause this strange clenching tug in my chest.

It's too soon for anything like this. Elaine and I were together for over a decade. Now, we've been broken up for a few months, and I'm already obsessing over someone new?

I'm not obsessed. I'm just ... interested.

And that's all I can be now anyway, what with the public still thinking I'm engaged.

Hell, *Gwen* still thinks Elaine and I are an item.

"Doritos, nice. You mind?" Jed holds out a hand, and I toss him the bag. The guy climbs behind the wheel and settles the chips in his lap, ready to snack for the drive back.

While he crunches away, I brood.

Is there a specific timeline I have to stick to? I'm single. It shouldn't be a big deal that I like someone.

And I like Gwen. A lot.

Lately, when my mind wanders at work, my thoughts find their way to Gwen. I'll wonder where she is on her route for the day or if she's finished early and hanging out in my living space with my cat. Every day when I get home, I breathe in deep, trying to catch the subtle floral scent of her perfume.

One time, when I lay down in my bed for the night, I got a strong whiff of the fragrance, which led me to think about her lying in my bed. And what I would do to her if she were still there.

I drag my brain away from that train of thought, not wanting to get hard when it's just Jed and me in this ambulance. No matter how comfortable I'm getting with the guys at the station, I'm not to the point where I can explain away a random boner.

After we arrive back at the station and restock the medical supplies, we each head to a desk to fill out the required paperwork. No matter how big or small the call, a record always needs to be kept. The process is tedious, and when I'm halfway through the forms, my mind drifts again. Back to Gwen.

I slip the postcard out from my back pocket, considering the blank side.

Before I can think better of it, I scrawl out a few sentences and tuck it away again.

Probably won't even mail it.

Chapter Twelve
GWEN

Whenever I see a post office, I think of you.

— POSTCARD FROM RYAN, WASHINGTON

"How big is the load this time?" The deep voice rumbles through the entire post office. At least, that's what it seems like to me when Jethro Winston speaks. The guy has a presence without trying.

Though he quickly fades to the background if his movie-star wife is around. She must be why he's at the post office today.

I'm back early this afternoon. The amount of deliveries was light, so I got through my route faster than normal. Fall and winter are the busy seasons, and I try to enjoy the leisurely days while I can.

I head to the front of the building in time to see Mrs. Holloway pass a crate of mail across the desk to Jethro.

"A few pounds," she says. "I can't believe we still get so much. Don't get me wrong; your wife is a talented lady. But doesn't everyone just tell her that on social media these days?"

Jethro chuckles, his dark beard creasing with a devastating smile, and he sifts his hands through a few weeks' worth of envelopes, all sent to the same PO box.

Fan mail for one Sienna—formerly Diaz—Winston.

"I want the ones that smell nice," a tiny voice proclaims.

Looks like Jethro brought one of his sons with him. He and his wife have three.

"Let someone check them all first. Then, we'll give you the nice-smelling envelopes." He leans an elbow on the counter, offering both me and Mrs. Holloway a conspiratorial smirk while dropping his voice low. "The perfumed ones are always the dirty ones."

I snort, imagining some weirdo out in the world thinking they could woo Sienna away from her gorgeous husband by applying the right scent to a bunch of hand-written naughty talk.

I guess it's nice to have dreams.

"Are all Sienna's assistants busy?" Mrs. Holloway asks, sounding a touch breathless. She takes her glasses off and cleans them with the edge of her shirt, as if the proximity to the Winston man fogged them up. "Are you filling in today?"

"That I am. A few on the team caught a stomach bug. And I promised Andy he could buy stamps." He sets his hand on the little one's head, and the kid grins up at Mrs. Holloway and me with almost as much charm as his dad.

"Do you have dogs? I want stamps with Pavlov on them." Andy names his uncle's dog.

"I don't think we have Pavlov stamps. How about Scooby-Doo?"

The boy fist-pumps the air—a clear yes.

"How're you doing, Gwen?" Jethro turns his full attention my way as my coworker spreads books of stamps on the part of the counter low enough for Andy to see.

"Oh, I'm dandy." And that's the truth. An adventure is on my horizon, and I've had some quality cat cuddles this week. "Delivered some oddly shaped packages to your brother this morning. I'll let you guess which one."

"Cletus," he says, tone flat, eyes sparking with laughter.

"Uncle Cletus is going to help me build a trap," Andy announces as he examines a book of stamps with ducks.

"A trap for what?" Jethro asks, a wary note in his voice.

"Uncle Cletus says it's a secret."

I bite on my inner cheek to keep from chuckling. That one's gonna be trouble, no doubt egged on by his wild uncles. I almost pity Jethro.

But I think he's enjoying every hectic minute of being a stay-at-home dad. I see him around town all the time with all his kids, and likely as not, he's smiling wide as he herds them like a group of disobedient, adorable sheep.

"I want the ones with frogs." Andy pushes his choice out of the bunch, and I barely mask a grimace.

Damn frogs.

But I keep my prejudice to myself and wave to the father and son after they pay and head off.

"Have you seen my son today?" Mrs. Holloway asks. "Sometimes, I swear we don't even work in the same building."

"We passed by each other this morning."

Lance is another rural carrier and one of my friends. At least, I'd consider him a friend. I've hung out with him and Arthur more than a handful of times. We don't talk much, but I figure that's because Lance isn't a chatty person.

"If possible, he seemed even quieter than normal."

She gives a dramatic sigh. "That's 'cause he's in a bad mood. His coffeemaker broke yesterday, and he hasn't had time to replace it." The woman pulls out a travel mug. "I brought him some of mine but missed him. He's gonna be angrier than a raccoon in an empty trash can. I hope he doesn't run into any silly people today. He'll bite their head off."

I fight a grin as I try to imagine the quiet, calm man ever giving in to a temper.

I love hearing Mrs. Holloway talk about her son. Half-loving, half-exasperated. Reminds me of Momma talking about my brother.

As if hearing my thoughts, Mrs. Holloway sends a smile my way. "I think I saw a pretty postcard for you this morning. Your brother still sending you those?"

Excitement has my hands clenching in my pockets, my fingers eager to seek out the piece of mail. "Yep. Whenever he sees one he thinks I might like."

Another addition to my shoebox full of correspondence.

Sure, we could easily text each other, but there's something special about receiving a physical piece of mail. Something magical. It was one of the reasons I applied to work at the post office when I saw the opening.

And other than the days I have to go out in freezing sleet or sideways rain, I'm pretty happy with my choice.

"Thanks for the heads-up! I'm on my way home now. Let me know if I need to bail Lance outta jail for pissing off the wrong person."

"Lord help me," Mrs. Holloway says to the ceiling, and I chuckle to myself as I make my way across the parking lot.

Instead of going straight home like I said, I swing by the Kirkwoods' place again to give Curie some more love and affection. It's funny, but I feel like I have a deeper relationship with the kitten than with her owner. I see her every day Sebastian works, but I never do more than send him a text or two, letting him know I stopped by.

He hasn't sent me a picture since that first day, which is probably for the best. My phone only has so much handsomeness storage capacity, and that single shot of him in uniform maxed the limit. One more, and I'm sure the device will short out completely.

Or maybe that's my brain …

Anyway, I fully expect our friendship to settle into the normal *wave at each other when we pass by* kind of relationship. Especially when Sebastian and Elaine straighten out their living situation. Whenever that happens, I doubt my cat-cuddling services will be required anymore.

After wearing Curie out, I refill her water and food bowl before pointing my Bronco home. The sight of my mailbox renews my good mood, and I pull up next to it, reach for the flap, and tug out the stack of mail. Once I park, I do a quick shuffle and sort, separating letters for me, my momma, and my daddy.

A pop of color has me shimmying a little happy dance in my seat.

Postcards are my favorite. It's as if the sender chose to share some of their well wishes with me, the message carrier. Every single one brings me joy. Just last week, Jessica James sent a beautiful image of the canals in Venice to her momma, and as I tucked the mail in their box, I knew I'd helped convey a message of love across the world.

My brother's cards, as ridiculous as they often are, each feel like a long-distance hug.

"What have you been up to, brother mine?" I admire the vibrant sunset on the picture side.

Ryan tends to pick the funny or weird postcards, but he'll choose a pretty one now and again.

When I flip it over, I pause, confused.

The handwriting isn't Ryan's. I've read enough notes from him to be able to pick his letters out of a police lineup—short, blockish, and extra dark from pressing down on his pen a little too hard.

But these letters are tall and slim, cramming eagerly together on the square of white.

Hey, Gwen.

Saw this at a gas station in Merryville. I thought this sunset would be fun makeup inspiration. Hope you're having a good day.

—S

The single-letter signature causes me to jerk my head up and stare out my car windshield, as if I expect an audience to be watching me. Spying on me as I read an illicit piece of information.

But I'm alone in my driveway, and there's nothing off-color or secretive about his message.

And yet the postcard feels entirely too personal. Like Sebastian whispered the words in my ear while palming my thigh.

And now, that image has the wild, horny flock of flamingos holding an orchestral symphony in my stomach.

Does he like—

"Married man!" I yell in my empty car, cutting my brain off before it goes any further. "*Soon*-to-be married man," I clarify at a more reasonable volume. But I need to speak the words out loud to quiet the instrument-wielding birds in my gut.

This is an innocent postcard. My brother sends me these, for Pete's sake.

So then, why, as I head inside, do I tuck the mail in the back pocket of my pants, away from curious eyes?

Chapter Thirteen

SEBASTIAN

You must return next year. And the year after that. And the year after that. I will never get enough of you.

— LETTER TO MARIA

I have half a taco hanging out of my mouth when Gwen walks through the front entrance of Green Valley Fire Department. Her eyes meet mine over the package she's carrying, and I watch her brows pop up as she takes in my caveman eating habits.

To be fair, I'm not the only one who's half-animal when it comes to the free food local restaurants drop off at the department. A couple of days ago, I swear I saw Jed Lawson swallow a whole piece of banana cake from Donner Bakery in one go.

Still, I'd rather Gwen have walked in on me doing pull-ups, or checking the official-looking medical equipment, or getting a medal of honor for bravery and general badassery from Chief McClure.

And then I'd want those images to linger in her mind as she went through her day, the same way I always seem to be thinking about her. I constantly have to fight an urge to pull out my phone and message her.

The quick texts we exchanged yesterday weren't enough.

Gwen: Just expertly cuddled your cat. Hope you're having a good day at work!

Me: You're the best. I was worried about staying late and leaving her alone for too long.

Gwen: Don't worry. She's watered and fed and a very happy kitty.

Me: You're seriously amazing.

Gwen: No problem. :)

That "amazing" bit was a slip of the thumbs, of course. Or that was what I told myself.

After rapid chewing and an uncomfortably large swallow, I grin and hope I don't have any food in my teeth.

"Hey, Gwen. You're here." *Wow, look at me. So observant.*

Her nose wrinkles with a smile, and I drag my eyes over her face, admiring every inch and cataloging her makeup now that I know how much work she puts into the look. Her lids have a dark shading that makes her green eyes vibrant, and she has a light-pink tint to her lips that reminds me of candy. I wonder if the lipstick has a flavor. What she'd taste like …

Stop thinking about licking her mouth before you get hard at work.

This didn't used to be something I struggled against multiple shifts a week.

"I'm here," she agrees, lifting the package higher. "Got a delivery for the chief. Want to escort me to his office?" she asks with a warm tone that makes me want to take her to my boss's office, then find a private corner, where I could thoroughly thank her for being such a friendly mailwoman. Do my best to make this her favorite stop on her route—

A twitch below my belt is another warning that my imagination is getting away from me.

"Sure!" I say way too enthusiastically. But when Gwen's pink lips curl higher in response, I don't regret my cheerleader-level energy. "Let me take that for you." I hold my arms out for the box.

"I can carry it." Gwen turns toward the stairwell, demonstrating that she doesn't actually need my help getting there. She's probably been delivering mail to the station for years now, and she might know the place better than I do.

"Of course you can. But if I carry it, then I get to flex my super-impressive muscles and hopefully make you forget about how I looked, breathing in a taco."

Gwen snickers as she takes her electronic scanner off the top and passes the box over. The thing isn't light, and now, I'm thinking about how strong Gwen's arms are and what they might feel like when wrapped around me.

"Sorry, I'll never forget that. You had chipmunk cheeks." *Her* cheeks flush with a pleased blush.

I groan, and she pats my shoulder, feigning an expression of pity.

"Don't worry. You looked *exactly* as ridiculous when you ate Pop-Tarts in high school. It's comforting to know some things never change."

We head deeper into the station, and I shoulder-open the metal door leading to the stairs to the second floor, where Chief McClure's office is.

"How's it going with Curie? I appreciate all this time you're spending with her. If you ever want to stop, I won't hold it against you." Even though I get an odd kind of comfort, driving back to my temporary home and knowing Gwen was there only a few hours earlier.

"I don't mind. We only ever had dogs, growing up. It's fun to get to know a cat."

Gwen mounts the stairs, and my eyes fixate on her body. She's wearing khaki shorts today, the fabric hugging her pert ass and showing off long, long, *loooong* legs.

I stumble, barely catching myself before face-planting.

Gwen doesn't notice, still chatting about my cat. "She's an adorably violent menace sometimes. Or maybe she thinks my hand is a toy."

"What do you mean?"

We reach the second floor, which I'm both grateful for and disappointed by.

"Oh, you know, just a casual mauling or two." The postwoman turns to grin at me. "Nothing worse than a few kitten scratches." She holds up her hand, showing off a Band-Aid on her thumb.

"Shit, I'm sorry." I set the box down and take her hand in mine, turning it every angle to see if there's any other evidence of injury.

Maybe I should go get my first aid kit. Put my paramedic skills to work.

Give her a full-body examination ...

"No big." Gwen seems more amused than hurt, her eyes twinkling as she meets mine. "She was going for a toy, and my hand got in the way. She was just being a cat."

Reluctantly, I let Gwen's hand slide from mine, noting the calluses on the tips of her fingers. I wonder if she got the rough edges from years of sorting mail.

My job has left different, less visible marks on me.

I bend over and heft the box up and push open the door to the second level, wishing the office were farther than ten feet away. In the lounge area, past the workout space, I hear the TV, where Jed is likely catching up on ESPN's high-lights of the Tennessee Titans—his favorite team.

Maybe I can take her on a tour of the station. Stretch this out.

"I guess you'll have to keep visiting her," I say as we resume walking, "so she doesn't pine away, waiting for her best friend to stop by." I mentally revisit the idea of asking my coworkers if they'd mind a feline mascot. If Curie became the official Green Valley Fire Department cat, I could convince Gwen to hang out here.

Although there's probably some policy against bringing pets to the station.

And infatuating women.

Gwen keeps smiling, but her eyes turn from mine, and I realize we've reached our destination. Fire Chief McClure glances up from a stack of paperwork and gives Gwen a broad grin.

"Afternoon, Miss Gwen. How's my favorite postal worker?"

After setting the box down, I duck out, but I can't make myself walk away. Instead, I lean against the wall near the stairs, waiting for Gwen to finish getting the package signed for. And also finish whatever animated conversation she seems to be having with the chief. From my post, I watch him chuckle and gesture and all-around enjoy the undivided focus of Gwen Elsmere.

I noticed back in high school how easily people engaged with her. Whenever Gwen talks to someone, more often, the other person is the one who does the chattering, and she always seems content to ask questions and listen. I bet everyone on her mail route loves when she stops by. No doubt, she has anecdotes about each one.

But, hell, I want to be more than another stop on her cycle through town.

I want to be her destination.

"You showing me the way out too?" Gwen appears in front of me, almost by magic, as I was so lost in thought about her.

"Wouldn't want you getting lost in this vast maze." I wave toward the wide-open floor plan, including the clearly marked Exit signs. "Did you get my postcard?"

Do you think of me at all during the day? is what I really want to ask.

"Yes. I loved it." She lingers at the top of the stairs, as if not ready to leave either. Her attention is back on me, her cheeks plumping as her candy-colored lips smile. "Did you know I have a collection? I mean, they aren't on my walls or in a scrapbook or anything. But I've got a box full. My brother sends me them sometimes."

"Well, look at that. I must've sensed it. Ryan works as a long-haul trucker now, right?"

She nods and teeters on the top step. "That's us Elsmere kids. Always behind the wheel."

Her foot drops, and she meanders down. I follow like the lovestruck puppy I am.

"You're not about to get yourself a truck, are you? Leave Green Valley in your dust?" A strange panic tightens in my chest.

Please don't leave. Not when it feels like I only just found you again.

"I don't think so." Gwen fiddles with the collar of her polo. "Green Valley is my home. Even if I left for a bit, I'd want to come back."

I breathe easier at her words. While I'm recovering from my mini worry session, she reaches the ground floor and faces me again.

"Actually, I *am* leaving soon."

My stomach bottoms out.

"I decided I'm doing it. I'm visiting Nashville in a few days. A little adventure." Anticipation sparks in her gaze as she tells me, and her teeth dig into her plump pink lip.

My panic calms, even as my lust spikes.

I wish I weren't a new hire—lowest on the ladder for time off—or else I'd offer to go with her.

"That's great, Gwen." I say her name simply to feel the shape of the letters on my tongue.

Side by side, we walk out to where her SUV sits. She parked on the road—a smart move so she's not blocking any of the vehicles in case we get a call while she's here. Not that it's likely. I've had multiple shifts where absolutely nothing happened. A cushy gig.

Just what I need after everything that went down in Merryville.

My mind shies away from the dark, anxiety-filled memories, and I focus on Gwen to bring some light into the shadowy corridors of my mind.

"Well, if I don't see you before you go, have a good time. And drive on the right side of the car." I tap a knuckle on the door of her Bronco with a smirk, which she returns.

"I already am." Gwen's response has a little sass that gets my chest heating up. Then, she's sliding behind the wheel and pulling away, waving her hand out the window. "I'll send you a postcard!"

Even as her car circles a bend, disappearing from view, I linger in front of the station. My body doesn't want to leave the space where she so recently was.

How did this happen?

When I ended my yearslong relationship with Elaine, I thought I'd go a while without wanting to be with anyone else. A year. Maybe more.

But then Gwen muttered, "Fuck a duck," and it was like my heart woke up from stasis.

The romantic notions I'd had for her, which I tucked away after high school, came crashing back, and they're here to stay. Every word and smile and laugh from her has this longing growing. I want to go stake out the post office, so I can be there when her workday is over, then catch her when she's leaving and invite her out for food. Next, a drink at Genie's. Then dancing to whatever music the bar is playing.

Does Gwen dance? Can she move her long limbs gracefully to the beat, or is she as goofy as her jokes?

Fuck, I want to know so bad. I want to find out how she dances and then press our bodies together and move with her. I want to hear all her traveling ideas, then plan a getaway with her.

But I can't do any of those things.

Not as long as the world thinks I'm engaged to another woman.

Gwen deserves better.

Chapter Fourteen

GWEN

I had a doughnut at a diner. Didn't taste great. Made me miss Daisy's.

— POSTCARD FROM RYAN, NEW YORK

I f doughnuts alone could make a girl happy, I should be in unmatched bliss. At the moment, a plate of three of the doughy circles rests in front of me, each one a decadent, delicious creation.

Who needs travel when I have desserts? Doughnuts are enough. They're all I need.

And yet the discomfort of dreams unfulfilled casts a shadow over my treats.

I bite into the blueberry cake one, forcing all my attention to the sweet, fruity flavor on my tongue, and for a moment, I forget my cowardice.

See? Doughnuts are all I need.

The glimmer of glaze and the rich color of the berries have my mind going to makeup. I'm in the middle of planning a doughnut-themed look when a flash of pink catches the corner of my eye.

Could it be ...

Sebastian.

My body fights a battle between waving like a wild woman and shrinking low in my seat so he won't catch me skipping out on my plans. But it seems my once-well-honed hiding skills disappeared the moment I decided to stop avoiding the man.

When Sebastian scans the diner, his eyes hook on me and stay there as that *should require a prescription from a doctor* smile creases his cheeks. His thick brows rise, almost touching the pink bandana wrapped around his head—a silent question.

With a gesture to the empty half of the booth, I invite him to join me, trying not to be thrilled at how quickly he strolls over.

"Hi!" I squeak. *Too high.* "Hello," I add. *Too low.*

Will I ever find a way to be mostly normal around this man?

"Fancy seeing you here, Miss Gwen." Sebastian settles in across from me, hazel eyes taking in my ever-so-slightly surly, slumped pose. "I gotta ask, what has you glaring at that collection of doughnuts? You can't tell me a Daisy creation has ever done you wrong. I won't believe it."

His teasing almost succeeds in drawing out my smile, but I'm wrestling with too much self-directed disappointment.

"No, the doughnuts haven't committed any crime." I take another bite and sigh as I chew, using the moment to decide if I want to admit my failings to him.

There's something about Sebastian that has me itching to peel back my layers and show him more of me. And not in the *hey, could we maybe take our clothes off together* way.

That's never going to be us.

"If it's not the doughnuts—" Sebastian gets cut off by the arrival of a waitress. He puts in an order for coffee and a few doughnuts of his own. When we're alone again, he turns back to me.

"Today was my Nashville trip." I cringe through the confession.

"Really?" He leans back in the booth, glancing around, as if I were hiding the entire city behind me. "Back already?"

"Never left." My fingers fiddle with my doughnuts, stacking them with the half-eaten one on top. "I cleaned my car instead."

Sebastian watches my doughnut architecture with a half-smile. "What kept you from going?"

"Well, there were the twenty or so granola bar wrappers. And about ten empty water bottles. A handful of half-melted ChapSticks. Plus, mascara marks on the mirrors and eye shadow powder stuck in the bottom of my cupholders. Then, the rugs were looking dirty, so I had to pull 'em all out and vacuum them. Then, I had to deal with all the fingerprint smudges on the windows and the dust on the dashboard. And I figured if I was cleaning the inside, then I might as well do the outside too. So I—"

"Gwen?" Sebastian saying my name, all soft like that, cuts off my rambling more effectively than if he shouted. "It wasn't about the clutter. Was it?"

I take another bite of doughnut, so I don't have to answer right away. But no matter how delicious the pastry is, it won't change the truth.

"No," I admit after a hard swallow. "I might have been just a tad bit uncomfortable." The vinyl seat squeaks as I sink lower in the booth in dejection. My knees knock against Sebastian's, and I shoot back up. "Sorry." A blush heats my face.

"No harm done."

There's a firm pressure on my knee, and I'm shocked to realize the sexy paramedic has reached under the table to squeeze my knee. The gesture is meant to be comforting, but all I can think about is how badly I want him to slide his hand up farther.

And I'm officially a horrible person. Lusting after an engaged man.

I drop my eyes away from his, refusing myself the wonderful comfort of his hazel gaze. The weight of his hand disappears.

"I guess I'm the kind of person who dreams about adventures but doesn't go on them."

There, I said it. Now, he knows the picture I tried to paint of myself was only words. I'm a small-town postwoman with great makeup and zero backbone.

There's no shame in that. But I shouldn't try to pretend I'm something I'm not.

"Gwen." Sebastian's tone, the pleading way he speaks my name, has my attention sneaking back to his face.

An emotion I can't interpret crinkles his brows, and I want to know what's going on in the brain underneath that luxurious head of hair.

But as he opens his mouth, a heavy weight drops next to me on my bench seat.

"Hey," Arthur says in greeting, slinging his beefy arm along the back of my booth. "You owe me a doughnut."

Then, my coworker picks up my chocolate-glazed one and takes a bite, all while holding intense eye contact with Sebastian.

Chapter Fifteen

SEBASTIAN

I've already begun to plan for your next visit.

— LETTER TO MARIA

The arm has a possessive air to it. Arthur is staking a claim on Gwen.

Is it a romantic one?

"Hey!" Gwen snatches the rest of her doughnut back and immediately shoves the remainder in her mouth, seeking to save the treat in any way she can.

The ease with which they share food twists my stomach.

Are they a workplace romance? The two postal workers falling for each other over bins of mail?

Adorable.

I fucking hate it.

Once she finishes chewing and swallowing and washing the doughnut down with a gulp of tea, Gwen starts on Arthur again. "I owe you a shift at work. Not my doughnuts. You're getting greedy."

She fake elbows him in the stomach, and he grunts, as if it hurt, but I see the smile twitch in his beard. The facial hair is a dark mass that was built to intimidate.

I scratch my relatively short scruff.

"How's it going?" I greet Arthur, trying to pretend I'm not a jealous asshole.

The mailman studies me. "Good."

Well, isn't he a chatterbox?

Still, I refuse to be intimidated, instead racking my brain for all the information I know about Arthur Kraut. He's a couple years older than Gwen and me, a senior at Green Valley High when we were sophomores. The guy left town after he graduated to travel or something. No siblings, but a bunch of cousins. He delivers mail.

And I'm drawing a blank past that.

If we were sitting alone at this booth, I could probably come up with more, but my mind only wants to think about Gwen. I only want to cycle through all the memories I have of *her*.

And I want to make more.

But first, I need to figure out what exactly Arthur is to her.

"You drove all over the country, right?" I ask.

He grunts a noise that I think means yes.

"Where were the best places? Gwen's looking to explore some."

Look at me, being friendly.

Arthur tilts his head toward his coworker.

Please let that be all they are.

"You thinking of heading out finally?" he asks, directing the conversation entirely to her, cutting me out.

Gwen shrugs, shoving another bite of doughnut in her mouth, which I'm guessing is her new tactic to avoid answering. Her face flushes as she chews, and both of us watch her.

"Um …" She coughs, then drinks more tea, the cup almost empty. A half-moon of peach lipstick stains the edge of the glass. "Maybe. I need to pee." She waves her hands in a shooing motion to get Arthur up and out of her way.

He rises with a grumble and sits immediately back down when she scurries to the restroom.

Leaving the two of us alone.

This is not the pairing I would have chosen to remain. *What do I have to do to get some alone time with Gwen?*

My blood turned molten hot when the mailwoman gave me her signature greeting of squeaking out a high note, then overcompensating with a too-low one. Hearing her affect a man-ish tone should not turn me on as much as it does.

Then, I touched her.

Mistake. Big, fucking huge mistake.

My palm still prickles with the sensation of her bare skin against mine. Maybe if she'd been in jeans, the gesture wouldn't have come off as intimate. But her Daisy Dukes gave me full skin-to-skin contact. And she backed away.

But, damn, I wanted to explore more. Lean forward and drag my fingers up the inside of her thigh. Find the frayed edge of her shorts. Push past them.

Fucking hell. I clench my fist on my knee below the table, trying to hide my frustration from the big postman watching me with eyes that see too much.

"Here you go." The waitress appears tableside with my doughnuts. She places my food in front of me, refills Gwen's tea, and takes Arthur's order of a burger before leaving us alone.

"So …" I lean back in my booth seat, picking up a pastry to keep from crossing my arms defensively over my chest. "How long have you and Gwen been together?"

Arthur stares me in the eye, giving absolutely nothing back. Not even words for a stretch.

Finally, he cracks his stony countenance. "Been friends for years."

The sludge clogging my lungs seeps away at the word *friends*. But the guy isn't done.

"You've been with Elaine since high school," he says, as if I need a reminder. "When's the wedding?"

Shame scrapes me raw, and I can't stomach taking a bite of my food yet.

There's no reason for me to be ashamed.

Except for how this looks. Me sitting here, alone with Gwen, resting my hand on her bare leg, no doubt giving her sex eyes. I look like a guy ready to cheat on his soon-to-be wife before I even go through with the ceremony.

Once again, I agonize over the promise I made to Elaine to let her define the timeline. How long will it be before she's ready to move on from us? I want to be able to flirt with a single woman without hurting anyone and looking like the biggest sleazebag in a hundred-mile radius.

I want to flirt with *Gwen*.

"There's no date." I relent, not adding the word *yet* because that would be a lie. "And Gwen and I are friends." *For now*, I silently—hopefully—add.

I want Gwen. She has me eager to make plans for the future even if it's just a dinner date later in the week. I feel like it's been forever since I thought about anything more than the present moment.

But Gwen deserves better than a guy still tied to another woman even if it's only in name.

"Friends," Arthur repeats my label, staring at me all the while.

Damn, the guy sees straight through me. I'm not even making it hard. I've never been good at lying. Kennedy used to love playing poker with me when we were teenagers because she'd clean me out.

Suffice to say, I'm still bad at bluffing, and my new coworkers are happy to have me at their weekly poker game at the firehouse. Sierra Betts, a park ranger, was at the last round and claimed she almost felt bad, playing against me. But not bad enough to stop her from taking the last of my money with a straight flush. Grizz had claimed all the rest before that with not an ounce of reluctance. Some of the guys muttered about him being a cheat, but there's no proof and even if he is, I doubt he bothered using his tricks on me. I'm that bad.

Still, no matter how abysmal my bluffing is, I'm not about to admit the truth to this guy. "Yeah, friends."

Arthur picks up Gwen's tea and sips from the rim.

Did he put his mouth where hers was? Does he have Gwen's taste on his tongue?

Jealousy spikes in my gut.

But what can I do about it?

"Gwen has a lot of friends in town." He sets the tea down with a thunk. "People who want their favorite postal worker to be happy." The guy's eyes go as dark as his beard. "You ain't her friend if you're gonna hurt her."

"That's not—" My growly denial gets cut off by the woman in question reappearing beside the table.

"I got you your own doughnut." Gwen plops a maple-glazed in front of Arthur. "Mouth off mine, or you're gonna lose some teeth." She shakes a not-at-all-threatening fist his way as she settles in beside her coworker.

I wish Gwen had sat on *my* side of the booth. Pressed her thigh against mine and leaned into my chest as I slipped an arm around her shoulders.

With a deep breath, I try to let my resentment go. Arthur didn't say anything like *stay away from my woman*. He warned me not to hurt her. How can I argue with that?

Hopefully, it's not too much longer until the world knows I'm unattached and therefore not trying to corrupt the beloved mailwoman.

My muscles tense with the need to do something about how I feel.

But I'm hit with a sudden realization.

Wooing Gwen is going to be fun.

Yeah, I want Gwen *now*. Right now. Like if she let me take her home this minute and kiss every inch of her, I'd be out of this booth faster than when we get an emergency call at the station.

But I'm also up for taking my time.

And, God, that feels fucking amazing. So different from the fluctuation of numbness and anxiety I was trapped in, living with Elaine in Merryville. These emotions—frustration, jealousy, longing—as bothersome as they are, they are as rich as melted dark chocolate.

Out of context, a grin spreads across my face.

Arthur's brows dip in distrust, and Gwen tilts her head with curiosity.

"What's so funny? Do I have doughnut on my face?" She grabs a handful of napkins, more than she needs, and gets to scrubbing her cheeks.

The sight is so endearing that I can't help chuckling.

"No, Gwen. Your face is perfect."

That earns me a full-blown scowl from Arthur and a ruddy flush from the gorgeous postwoman.

The timing isn't the best. My life is still tied up with Elaine's.

But my guess is that starting something with a woman—*this* woman—is possible.

I just need to wait a little longer.

Chapter Sixteen

SEBASTIAN

I never thought I'd have a friend a world away. Knowing you has allowed me to gaze past the horizon.

— LETTER TO MARIA

"I didn't know they made leashes for cats."

Gwen crouches beside my parents' mailbox, teasing Curie with a long blade of grass. The cat briefly forgets about her new pink harness as she swipes and pounces and overall dials up the adorable factor to ten.

"Yep. Only she's not great at the walking part. She keeps flipping over and trying to play with the leash. It's gonna take some work." I linger beside them, trying to keep from panting after basically sprinting out here when I saw Gwen's SUV heading toward our house.

And, no, I did not drag my cat along as a temptation for the postal worker to linger.

I *carried* Curie, of course.

"I believe in you." Gwen shoots me a grin, and a series of painful, pleasurable clenching claws through my chest.

I pity my past self for all the years I spent not around this woman. That life seems so dull compared to the last few weeks with these sparse but vibrant interactions.

If only I could spend more time with her. A long stretch where we don't have to worry about nosy townsfolk gossiping.

But that's impossible in Green Valley.

I glance around us now, half-expecting Karen Smith—the most notorious tongue wagger in Green Valley—to jump out of the bushes and shout, *Aha! I knew you were a dirty, rotten philanderer, Sebastian Kirkwood!*

If I keep trying to get close to Gwen while in town limits, people are going to give me the same glares Arthur did, assuming I'm seducing Gwen and cheating on my fiancée.

Or maybe he was mad for another reason.

"So, uh, you and Arthur seem close." *Oh god. What am I doing?*

"Yep. He's the best." Luckily, Gwen is fully focused on my cat, so she doesn't see the heat in my cheeks or the way jealousy has my jaw clenching.

"Are you ... have you ..." *Don't ask. Don't do it.* But the rational voice in my head is drowned out by a desperate pleading to know the truth. "Did you two date?"

"Me and Arthur?" She flicks her eyes to me then away. "No. Never have. He's like a brother."

Relief loosens my joints so much I almost sink to the ground.

Not that this changes things. Not really. By all accounts, I'm still taken.

Elaine needs to come to terms with the end of us and tell her parents our relationship is over. These past months, I've thought of it as her taking time to cope, but it's starting to feel like she's dragging out the painful part.

Leaving me lingering in a purgatory of wanting Gwen.

"Any headway on a new adventure?" I ask.

Gwen's brows dip with a rueful grimace. "I don't think I can plan a new one until I finish the one I chickened out on. Nashville or bust." She sighs. "I'll probably bust again."

I should go to Nashville soon too.

My brother, Cameron, lives there with his partner, Maurice, and it's been ages since I visited. At my last job, I never took time off. I worried if I stepped away from the work for too long, I'd never get the courage to go back.

But I've changed things. New job, new me. I don't need to run myself into the ground to blot out the images threatening to play on a loop in my mind.

"I'm going to go to Nashville to visit my brother," I announce, loving the way the decision fills my chest with exhilaration. When I glance down, I find Gwen sitting cross-legged in the grass with my kitten in her lap, her vivid green eyes staring up into mine. "We should go together."

I didn't think about the suggestion. I just said it. But the moment the possibility sits in the air between us, I love it. Gwen and me on the road together. In a new city together. Exploring. Laughing. Living.

"Yeah." I grin at the vision. "Let's go together."

Chapter Seventeen

GWEN

There's nothing worse than people who can't drive in the rain. I almost squashed a Prius today.

— POSTCARD FROM RYAN, CALIFORNIA

When my body freezes, Curie jumps out of my lap to attack a bug.

"What?" I study Sebastian's face, searching for a hint of teasing.

But he's all earnest sincerity.

"You could come with me," he repeats. "I'm too new to schedule vacation, but I have a three-day stretch off next week. If you can take a couple of days off, we could drive there together. See some sights while Cameron is working, then hang out with him in the evenings. He's got a big place, and he loves having guests." Every word out of Sebastian's mouth fuels his smile. The guy vibrates with eagerness as he talks.

He makes it sound so easy. So possible.

Take a trip with Sebastian Kirkwood.

Has he been peeking into my brain? Rifling through my secret desires?

Because, Lord, do I want this. Want *him*—bad. I crave having him all to myself, able to say and do anything I'm creative enough to imagine. At night, my thoughts are full of Sebastian. What it would be like to tangle my fingers in his silky hair. To have his lips against mine. To know the weight of his body pushing me deep into a mattress.

I have a very soft mattress. His body could entomb me in the cushion-top.

But those are fantasies. Even as I let myself revel in them, I know the truth. He's taken, and he has been since the Sadie Hawkins dance junior year. I had one shot, a single moment in time, and I let fermented frogs steal the chance of happiness from me.

But that doesn't change the fact that I know Sebastian is off-limits.

But why does this offer sound on-*limits?*

Within limits?

No limits?

That one, I think.

Whatever the wording, there's a single glaring question I both hate and need to know the answer to.

Where, in all of these plans, is his fiancée?

"Go to Nashville with you *and Elaine*?" I put extra emphasis on the last two words, like pinching the tender skin on the back of my arm to stay awake.

"Er, no." Sebastian twines Curie's leash around his fingers, then lets the strap slip loose. "Just me. You and me."

You and me.

Gwen and Sebastian.

But it's not us. It's Elaine and Sebastian.

My nerves jitter, my skin aches in wanting, my stomach flamingos try to square-dance and trip over one another.

But I refuse to pretend that the world isn't the way it is.

Where is Elaine?

"This is odd."

"What's odd?"

"This." I gesture around us, where it's just the two of us and a cat.

"My cat on a leash?"

"No. Well, actually, yes. That's odd too. But I mean … we can't go on a trip. You and me."

Even if I *really* want to, that does not mean I'm okay with an affair.

Not that I think Sebastian is offering *that*. But come on. Green Valley is a small town, where gossip is as valuable as a full tank of gas. Maybe more so. And two young people traveling together looks like one thing and one thing only.

"Sure we can."

Sebastian scratches the corner of his beard, and I can't believe he's this obtuse. But maybe he is.

"Not without consequences."

"Like having a good time?"

"Like having people talk. About you and me. Together. Alone. Traveling and leaving Green Valley. Everyone would say things because … it's *odd*." Anxiety at the idea of gossip and glaring townsfolk has me tangling my fingers together in an anxious wringing. "You're engaged, but you want to leave town with me. Why would we do that? Just you and me? No one would say, *Oh, because they're friends.* They'd say we're going to a motel to take our clothes off and get freaky and be sinful. They'd say I'm a home-wrecker. Even though I don't wreck homes!" I shove to my feet and pace and chew the inside of my cheek and imagine being alone in a motel with Sebastian. "But what evidence would I have that I *didn't* take a big ole wrecking ball to your relationship? Everyone would think we *slept* together. That we shared a bed, and you took off my clothes, and I took off your clothes—oh God." My imagination popped out of my mouth in the worst way because what I'm describing doesn't even sound bad to me.

But it is. It's *so* bad.

Remember that it's bad!

I meet Sebastian's wide eyes, and I wave my hands, as if to distract him from the last few sentences I let escape. "But I would *never* do those things with you. Never ever! Not in a million years." *In a million and one maybe.* "But that's what people would *think*."

"Gwen—"

"We can't do it." And I don't clarify *it* because I'm not sure which *it* I'm referring to. And I hate that even though we can't do *it*, I want to do *it*.

All of it. I always have.

"Gwen." Sebastian steps in front of me, stopping my pacing with the wall of his beautiful, tall body.

The look on his face is a bewildered mess, and I regret bombarding him with my anxious rambling.

"We can't—"

"I'm not marrying Elaine."

Chapter Eighteen

SEBASTIAN

Tell me about your granddaughter! Does she vibrate with life the way you do?

— LETTER TO MARIA

"You're not …" Gwen stares at me, expertly shaped brows raised almost to her swooshy little bangs.

She went and messed up her hair during her anxious rambling, and my fingers ache to comb the short strands back into place.

But I keep my hands to myself.

"I'm not marrying Elaine. We're not engaged anymore. Haven't been for months."

"Oh." She blinks a few times, as if her brain needs a moment to reboot. "I-I'm sorry. I didn't know."

"No one does. Just my family. And now, you."

Guilt joins a whole crush of emotions in my chest. Amusement at the way Gwen went on a ramble. Annoyance at the idea of town gossips. Disappointment that, apparently, I'm not someone she would be with in a *million* years. Shame that I wanted her to be interested even though Gwen thought I was unavailable.

"I broke it off, but I decided that since Elaine is in the public eye—you know, Elle Fields and Channel 11 and all that—she should decide when the information goes public."

"Oh," Gwen says again, and I wish I had a better read on her. That I could understand the thoughts not being said behind that single-syllable word.

"Yeah. End of an era." *What am I even saying?* "And could you maybe not tell anyone? At least until Elaine decides to."

Gwen's face crumples in confusion. "Of course I won't. But why are you telling *me?*"

"Well, you did just go into vivid detail about how the whole town would think we were philandering."

A blush steals over her cheeks, turning her skin a rosy color without the assist of makeup.

"True. But won't they still think that? Since I'm the only one who knows?"

You're the only one who matters. I keep that to myself.

"They would if people knew we were going to Nashville together." I dislike the next idea as it comes out of my mouth, but not enough to stop myself from saying, "We could keep it a secret."

Gwen steps away before crouching down and going back to teasing Curie with grass, which I take as a good sign.

"And besides, this trip wouldn't be romantic." As much as I want it to be.

The idea of spending the night with Gwen, our bodies tangled up together, fills my mind. There's not much else in the world I want more than that. But we're on different wavelengths. She needs to know I'm not coming on to her.

"I'm looking to visit my brother because I haven't seen him in a while. This would be two friends traveling together. I'll be the force that obligates you to go. I'll even pre-clean my car, so you have no excuses."

That earns the start of a smile. A hint at the corner of her mouth.

I'll take it.

"Come on. Nashville is amazing. Think of the music and food. Plus, we'll have a local to show us around." I have one event in particular in mind. Something I doubt many of the Green Valley residents would be up for. But my bet is, Gwen would love every second. "Take a trip with me," I press, hoping she doesn't hear the desperate note in my voice.

But this intense longing to be near her is getting harder to live with. Even if all we'll ever be is friends, I still want that.

The seed of a smile blooms into a full-blown grin as she gazes up at me.

"You're a good salesman, Sebastian Kirkwood."

"Is that a yes?"

But she's not looking at me anymore. Her attention has wandered into the distance, as if she could see past the woods and mountains to the vibrant city we're discussing.

"We could go to the Honky Tonk Highway. And the Country Music Hall of Fame. And Madame Tussauds. And eat hot chicken …" Gwen continues muttering a list of activities like a tourist encyclopedia.

The recitation has me fighting an excited grin. That's too many things for a single trip. Sounds like she'll want to go a few times. All I need to do is make sure I'm around for each one.

I start making my own list. The first couple of trips, we'll go to the big tourist places. Then, the next few times, I'll have Cameron show us where the locals like to go. Then, maybe we could plan another visit during a music festival. Gwen said she liked the idea of a city version of the Jam Session.

I like the idea of holding her hand while she sways to some live music. Maybe wrapping my arms around her from behind and resting my chin on her shoulder and kissing her neck as music plays …

Hold up. Stop. Just friends, remember?

I can do that.

"Is that a yes?" I ask softer this time and hold my breath as I wait.

Gwen refocuses on me. "All right. A secret adventure it is."

Chapter Nineteen

SEBASTIAN

When the world is boring, I think of you and wish you were here.

— LETTER TO MARIA

I'm in the middle of filling out reports when my phone buzzes. Paperwork is the most boring part of my job, so any reason to procrastinate is welcome.

When I see Elaine's name on my phone, I send up a silent prayer.

Please let this be the call. The one where she tells me her parents know. That everyone knows. That we're both moving on to the next chapter in our lives.

Tell me that nothing bad is going to happen to her because of me.

And I feel guilt at wanting to urge her along faster.

You see, I know I said I'd wait until you were ready to go public with the breakup, but remember Gwen Elsmere? Lately, I can't stop thinking about her, and whenever she's around, I can't help flirting with her, and even though she thought I was engaged and we're just friends, I still wanted her to be attracted to me because I'm a huge pile of cow manure.

I accept the call. "Hey, Elaine. What's up?"

"Hi. Are you at work?"

"Yeah, but I'm at the station. No calls to deal with."

You have plenty of time to tell me how you're ready for everyone to know we're broken up.

"Good. When is your next day off?"

"Uh"—I think about my stretch of three days I promised to Gwen—"Friday."

"Perfect. I think we should get breakfast or lunch at Daisy's that day. Or dinner at The Front Porch. Which would work best for you?"

I wonder if I got lost in thought for a moment and missed part of what she said. The invite doesn't make sense, not with how things are between us. "You ... want to go out for food together?"

"Yes."

"Why exactly?"

Even when we *were* together, going out for food was a rare event. Two reasons come to mind why we were homebodies. Elaine, no matter the personality she plays on TV, is an introvert. And I was exhausted all the time, my last job running me ragged.

"I think people have noticed we haven't been spending much time together lately. There might be gossip going around."

People. More like her mother.

I'm not annoyed with Mrs. Springfield asking about us. The woman is curious about her daughter's love life.

But this is not the way Elaine should be reacting to prying questions.

"Elaine ..." My chair squeaks as I lean back and make sure none of the guys are around, taking the moment to figure out how to approach this topic without hurting her more. "I said I'd hold off on telling anyone other than my family. I didn't mean ..." *God, this is a mess.* "I didn't mean pretending. Us going out on what equates to a date—that's more like keeping up appearances." The charity event was bad enough. "I'm not looking to do that anymore. I don't want to actively lie to people."

"Eating food with me isn't lying. It's just food."

Her words are hard, defensive, and I scratch my beard and hold my tongue to keep from saying something harsh. Instead, I wait. Because I know Elaine. This is how her temper works. Quick spark, then out.

"Sorry," she breathes the word on a sigh. "Are we never going to eat together again then?"

A sharp jab to my heart, and I rub my chest to ease the ache, knowing that I've hurt someone I care about. There was no cataclysmic betrayal that ended our relationship. Just me realizing we were holding on to something because it was the norm. Because we're two people who avoid conflict, and that's exactly what a breakup is.

Especially when someone isn't ready to let go.

"If you want to have food as friends, then I am all for that." *Not this Friday though. I'll be in Nashville.* "But that's not why you're asking me to go to The Front Porch with you, is it?"

A long pause.

"No. It's not," she concedes.

"Do you think now is a good time to tell everyone?" *The answer is yes.*

Another pause, but I don't think it's from indecision.

"There's a lot going on right now."

"A lot going on" could mean different things.

"Like"—I don't want to offer, but I also can't stand the thought of her drowning in stress—"things I can help with?"

"Not really," she says, and I try not to audibly sigh in relief. "Not exactly. I'm interviewing to move to a different station—Channel 5. Larger audience, better pay, all that."

"That's amazing!" A new job has to be good, right? This shows she's doing fine without me. "You deserve a promotion. I'm sure you're going to get it."

"Yeah. Well, there're other candidates. And we're all under the microscope."

Ah. There it is. As I find more reasons for us to step away from each other, Elaine seems to be finding reasons to keep up this ruse.

"Elaine, don't you—"

"Please, Sebastian. This job could be big. My parents are excited about it—especially Momma—and I ..."

There's a sound through the phone, a stuttering breath. Like someone breathing through the urge to cry.

Fear snakes down my spine. *What would Elaine do if our breakup came out, cluttered up her social media mentions, and lost her this job opportunity? Would that send her spiraling downward?*

How much is too much?

"It's okay," I reassure her, even as I tap my pen in an agitated rhythm. "I won't say anything. Just ... keep me updated."

"I will."

Silence stretches for a few breaths, neither of us knowing how to talk to the other anymore.

"I need to go," she eventually says. "I'm on-air soon."

"Okay." I try not to sound utterly defeated. "Good luck."

She hangs up without a good-bye.

Suddenly exhausted, I let my head drop to the desk, my forehead cushioned by the pile of papers I still need to fill out.

How much longer? When will she be ready to move on?

I know my family thinks it's strange I'm keeping silent about this, but I feel like I owe her. If I'd been honest with Elaine about how my love for her changed over the years—shifting from romantic to platonic—I would have ended things between us long ago. There wouldn't have been the promise of a future broken. I never should have gone into that jewelry shop with her to buy a ring.

The breakup felt like finally admitting I'd been lying to her for years.

Really, I'd been lying to myself.

When I ended things, it had been a while since we'd had sex. Even longer since we'd had a conversation not dealing with work, a family function, or a general scheduled item in our calendar.

The predictable pattern of our days was a strange sort of comfort in comparison to the high stress of my job. Our relationship was like a baby blanket I clutched long after it should have been folded up and stored away in the attic.

And that wasn't fair to Elaine.

She thought we had a future together. What does it do to a person to find out that's not the case?

Kennedy's tragedy festers like an infectious warning in the back of my brain. If I split us apart too fast, the worst could happen. But I can't help but think my easing into this break up—letting her parents, her fans, and the town believe nothing has changed—feels a lot like standing still.

When will we both move forward?

Chapter Twenty

SEBASTIAN

When is your next flight to Paris? I want to drink wine from your lips.

— LETTER TO MARIA

Gwen pulls her car into the garage under my apartment, parking the Bronco where no one in town will see and gossip about it. Step one in our secret vacation together, and already, the extra maneuvering we have to do makes me itch.

But she's all gorgeous smiles and thrumming anticipation, and I can't wait to tuck her into my passenger seat and drive out of Green Valley to a place where no one knows us. Where, for a short time, we can be free to do … whatever.

This is a friends' trip, I remind myself. *Gwen made it clear she doesn't want more than that.*

If only I could shut my feelings down the same way. Instead, I find myself eyeing the frayed edge of her shorts and the loose cotton of her T-shirt, pondering how, if I could, I would transform myself into a piece of soft fabric for the chance to caress her body.

"Is Curie coming with us?"

Gwen's question reminds me to get rid of those dirty thoughts and be a decent person.

"Nah. My mom said she'd fill her food and water. And Kennedy promised to drive over to visit with her, seeing as how she's the reason I have an animal that needs looking after in the first place."

Gwen nods and climbs into my car. "I brought snacks," she announces the moment I reverse out of the driveway. "And I'm really hoping your taste buds haven't progressed far past where they were in high school."

"They haven't. Same as my maturity."

We share a grin, and she opens a Piggly Wiggly bag to show boxes of Pop-Tarts and a few bottles of iced tea.

"Second breakfast!" I crow.

Our class schedule in high school shifted on a weekly basis, and one arrangement had Biology first thing in the morning. Gwen would always share her, as she called it, "second breakfast" with me.

"Did you have first breakfast?" I ask.

"Yep. All the healthy stuff is out of the way."

Same as when we were teenagers. Eggs and toast at home, Pop-Tarts at school. And I benefited from her sweet tooth.

As I drive, she hands me bite-sized pieces of the packaged pastry. True, they have nothing on the creations from the Donner Bakery or Daisy's Nut House. But there's an extra flavor to these. Nostalgia. With the first bite of Frosted Blueberry, I'm back in that classroom, sneaking snacks and brainstorming how to make my cute lab partner laugh. Like back then, I'm expected to keep my eyes forward, but all I want is to turn my head and gaze at the person beside me.

A lot and nothing have changed.

"You excited? Have a load of places planned for us to go to?" I grin over at Gwen, only to catch her smile dimming.

What did I say?

"Yeah. Of course. Only I'm trying not to get *too* excited. Don't want to build it up in my mind too much." She taps a finger on the side of her skull.

"Why not? Nashville is awesome!" I infuse my voice with enthusiasm, trying to get her spirits back up.

Gwen fiddles with the strap of her seat belt. "I know. But … haven't you ever had something huge you couldn't wait to happen? This thing you told yourself was going to be amazing, spectacular, life-changing. Then, it … it didn't work out that way. And all that expectation shriveled, and you felt so much worse afterward than if you hadn't gotten hyped in the first place."

I shift uncomfortably in my seat, thinking that's exactly the mindset I have for this trip, only without the shriveling expectation.

"Just because something can disappoint you doesn't mean it will," I point out.

"Yeah," she murmurs, staring out the window, and I wonder if she even heard me.

"Hey, Gwen?" I wait until she turns her head my way before continuing, "I promise that even if we get a flat tire halfway there or if we stop for food and a squirrel steals the car keys"—I pause for her adorable chuckle—"I will get you to Nashville, and we will have a great time. Maybe not the time you built up in your mind, but still great. Got it?"

"Got it." Her sweet smile is back. "Sorry about being a bummer. It's just"—she takes in a bracing breath and lets it out—"I made a lot of plans with my grandma. And, well, as you can guess, none of them panned out." She waves a hand vaguely out the window, as if gesturing to the world that no longer has her beloved grandmother in it.

Her worry about failed plans makes more sense to me now.

"You two were close?"

Gwen's entire face glows, as if she brought one of those fancy ring lights with her. "The closest. She was my best friend, and I don't even care if that makes me sound like a nerd. Because she was *so* cool." Another wistful sigh. "You know, you kinda took her job."

"What? Wait. Did I? When?" I grip the steering wheel tight as we pass the town sign, trying to think when I might have interacted with the woman and screwed her over. "Damn, Gwen. I'm sorry. I didn't know."

She snorts a laugh and pats a reassuring hand on my thigh that has the muscle clenching in response. "Calm down. I only meant, she was originally going to be my travel buddy."

"Oh?" I breathe in, relieved I didn't mess with her grandma, but still unable to relax with the memory of Gwen's hand on my body.

Put it back. Drag it higher.

Get your mind out of the gutter!

"Yep. Gran loved traveling. She worked as a flight attendant. I grew up on her stories of all the places she had flown to. Gran saw the world a hundred times over, and she wanted to take me to everywhere she'd ever visited. She said it would all be different with me. It would all be new." The last word comes out on a sorrowful note, and I hate knowing the result of all their plans was unfulfilled dreams.

"But she got sick?" I ask. "Before you could go anywhere?"

Gwen nods and throws me a sad smile. "I held out hope until the end that she'd recover, and we'd still go. But nope." She sighs and rubs her chest, like there's an ache beneath her breastbone. "She had friends from all over the world. We got mail from them, and when she was in the hospital, she'd have me read the letters to her."

"That's so cool."

"Yeah." She snorts a laugh. "Super cool until you get a letter from a horny Italian man who'd apparently been in love with your grandmother for decades and liked to describe *in detail* how he'd please her, if only she went back to him."

"Oh God." Good thing I'm not still eating a Pop-Tart or else I'd be choking while I guffaw. "That's more information than anyone needs about their gran."

"You're telling me. And she still made me read it, cackling the whole time. I swear, half the nursing staff crowded into the room to hear me recite a porno."

Oh hell. Now, I'm laughing and also devastated that I missed out on that experience. Plus, my mind can't help tying Gwen and porno into the same thought and crafting a new conclusion.

"Any—" I have to get through a few more chuckles before I can talk. "Any more interesting letters she got?"

From the corner of my eye, I watch Gwen grin wide, and I think my heart melts and reforms and takes on the exact shape of her plump lips.

"Loads."

She fills most of the car ride with her gran's stories, and when we start seeing signs for Nashville, I can't believe we've been driving for close to three hours. For most of that time, I've smiled so wide that my cheeks hurt.

But in my chest, there's a shadow of sadness. An aching regret.

Because Gran Maria sounds like a kind, vibrant, amazing woman, who Gwen obviously loved like a second mother.

And she's gone.

I'll never get to meet the woman who inspired so many people around the world to want to stay connected with her through the decades.

"We're almost there," Gwen whispers as she leans toward the dashboard to make out the approaching skyline.

I realize that beside me is the same kind of woman.

And if she ever decides to up and leave Green Valley for good, I'll be the pining man sending her explicit letters, hoping she comes back one day.

Chapter Twenty-One

GWEN

Barely avoided hitting a moose. The thing stared me straight in the eyes. If it had a middle finger, it would've flipped me off.

— POSTCARD FROM RYAN, WYOMING

Sebastian Kirkwood is the best traveling companion.

"It's Elvis. *Elvis!*" He jogs toward the next figurine in the wax museum. "Wow." The man gets his face as close as allowed. "How do they make them look so real?"

"My guess is, wax." I keep my voice light and teasing to cover up how much seeing him this enthusiastic affects me.

"You're a genius. Never would have thought of that." He tries to mimic the music legend's pose, and somehow, he pulls it off despite being in worn jeans and a T-shirt rather than an embroidered jumpsuit.

Sebastian has done this with all his favorite statues—tried to copy their poses, like that'll somehow bring them to life so he can chat with them. When there's a pair, he gets me in on the game too.

And I love every moment. Which only makes my heart think that loving *him* would be a perfect idea.

No, heart! Don't do that!

This is the exact opposite of my original aim. The whole point of getting to know Sebastian again was to get over my crush. If anything, I've amped my mooning up to ten thousand.

But is that a problem? Now that I know the truth?

I wanted to get rid of the crush to stop lusting after a taken man. As of now, he's not taken anymore. He's wide open.

Okay, not *wide* open. This is still a secret trip that I'll probably never be able to talk freely about because then it'll look like I was the mistress who broke up the happy couple.

If they even go through with it.

Face it, this is a separation for them. Not a full break.

The door people normally close when they end things is still cracked open for Sebastian and Elaine. Ending relationships, especially long-term ones, can't be easy, but to let it drag on for months? Sounds like they only need one knock on that door to patch everything up. Fixing their issues after some time apart.

Sebastian is only available temporarily.

Single or not—his status doesn't matter in the end. All my pining and debating is moot since Sebastian made it clear that we're just friends.

But I guess this means—at least for a short while—I don't have to feel guilty for making secret heart eyes at him. My bothersome crush can bother only me.

"Do I look like The King?" Sebastian asks, frozen in place.

"Hmm, let me see." I wander around him, inspecting him from all angles. He doesn't need to know where my eyes go when I'm behind him.

"Are you comparing my ass to Elvis's ass?"

Okay, I guess he could tell anyway.

"Whose is better?"

Yours.

"His. I think it's all the talent. Must have given him a perfect bubble butt."

Sebastian grumbles but doesn't move from his pose.

When I stop in front of him, I pretend to be sad as I shake my head. "I'm sorry, but you just don't measure up."

"Don't measure up?" The paramedic glares in mock offense, all the while holding his pose. "I am literally taller than the man. Go on. Get a ruler."

Leaning in, I give Sebastian a quick poke in the stomach. "Women don't need to carry rulers on them. We're not so concerned with comparing our *sizes* against each other. And if you ask me to unzip a wax superstar's pants to start measuring things, I will tell museum security you're trying to get naughty with Mr. Presley."

That finally breaks Sebastian out of his statue stance as he shakes with laughter. Then, he leaps forward and wraps an arm—a *friendly* arm—around my shoulders.

"I love your dirty mind." He chuckles as he says the beautiful sentence and steals my breath with his proximity.

Oh God, he's practically draped himself over me. How is a woman supposed to survive this? Is Elaine a ghost? She had his undivided attention for years. At some point, she must have perished from the pleasure, and I've only seen her zombie-strolling around Green Valley.

And it looks like I'm next.

Maybe we'll roam the streets together in our undead bodies, start a zombie pack.

Is that what groups of zombies are called? Maybe they'd be a murder, like crows. Or a band, like gorillas. Maybe a shiver, like sharks.

A shiver of zombies.

My stomach is full of an orchestra of flamingos as Sebastian's thumb teases against the bare skin of my shoulder.

That's it. It's official. I'm going to be in an orchestra of zombies.

Unaware that he's committing sexy, temporary murder, Sebastian tows me with him as he circles Elvis.

"Liar." The paramedic looks at me. Stares at me. Claims my eyes with his and holds them until I wonder if I'll ever be able to blink again.

He knows. I said I would never want to sleep with him, and he knows I was lying.

Still, I stutter an innocent response. "What?"

Sebastian leans in until his breath teases the short hair tucked behind my ear. "My butt is *so* much better than his."

And I'm dead.

Chapter Twenty-Two

SEBASTIAN

I love sharing my secrets with you.

— LETTER TO MARIA

"I'm going to need you to promise not to talk about this with anyone in Green Valley." I meet Gwen's eyes, trying not to get distracted by the hypnotizing green gaze.

We're stopped at a red light, two streets away from our destination. My hands have started sweating, sticking to the steering wheel.

Part of my nerves thrum with anticipation, but I have small, raw patches of worry. Gwen is about to discover a vulnerability of my brother's. He might not see it that way, but I know the sensitive core that exists under his take-no-shit exterior.

And something that hurts Cameron hurts me.

"Okay." Gwen stares at me, her brows rising. "I promise. You want to tell me where we're going?"

"It's a club." I bob my head side to side. "Kind of."

"Cryptic."

I shoot her a grin. "It's gonna be fun, I swear."

"Fun and secret. My mind is going so many places." Gwen taps a finger on her lower lip, which has my focus dropping to her mouth, which has the car behind us beeping their horn when I don't realize the light is green.

Since we're in the city, I end up in a paid lot, but we're close to the club, so I don't mind shelling out the few bucks. As Gwen and I walk down the sidewalk, I fight the urge to scoop up her hand and lace our fingers together.

She just wants to be friends. Accept that.

To move away from my randy thoughts, I reach into my back pocket, pull out a wad of cash, and hand the money to Gwen. "You're going to need this."

She stares at the rolled-up bills before turning wild eyes my way. "Are you taking me to a strip club? I haven't even gone to the Pink Pony. Hell, I'm too intimidated to try a class at Stripped!"

And now, I'm thinking of Gwen at the dance studio in our hometown, twining her body around a pole. Then on stage at the Pink Pony, the local strip club, with a G-string and sky-high heels.

Can I go five minutes without trying to peel her clothes off in my mind?

"It's not a strip club. But you'll want to tip the performers."

"Performers. Okay." The tension eases from her shoulders. "You keep giving me these clues, and I'll eventually figure it out."

We reach a brick building. The front looks unimpressive. Dark windows that give no indication as to what's going on behind them. I direct Gwen around a corner into a wide alley. There's already a line of people at the door, the mixture eclectic. Colored hair, tattoos, latex, feathers, lace, piercings in every body part a piece of metal can be stuck through.

"Am I underdressed?" Gwen fiddles with the stringy strap of her tank top. The color is a magenta pink, playing beautifully against her skin.

Every so often, I've noticed her rubbing her right arm, where there's the start of a farmer's tan. I imagine the sun kissing the skin just below her USPS polo whenever she reaches out her window for a mailbox.

I think her single tanned arm is beautiful. Whether in a runway-model gown or tank top and jean skirt, she's perfect.

"You look great. And no one wearing those boots could be considered under-dressed."

We both glance down at the one souvenir Gwen has bought for herself on this trip. A pair of bedazzled cowboy boots. The crystals are all swirls of pink, and she did a little excited line dance when she tried them on in the store.

"Momma is gonna be so jealous," I heard her whisper as she finally handed her credit card to the cashier.

When she'd first hesitated over the price, I was on the verge of offering to buy them for her. But I kept my mouth shut and tried to remember, *Friends don't buy fancy shoes for friends.*

Or do they? Is there a handbook somewhere? Maybe I should ask Grizz what he'd do if I bought him a pair of nice boots.

Probably give me shit for a year straight. But he might also wear them …

Doesn't matter because I've never had the urge to buy Grizz anything more than a fast-food burger.

I'm glad Gwen treated herself to the boots, and I try not to fixate on how they magically make her already-gorgeous legs stretch as long as the Appalachian Trail.

"Thanks." She gives my side a gentle nudge with her elbow. "Now, will you tell me what"—she peers around a man in a corset and mesh top to eye the neon sign above the door—"Stacked is?"

"Not yet. I want you to get the full effect when you walk in."

She bounces in her boots. "This is torture. Why are you tormenting me, Sebast-ian?" She groans the question.

Suddenly, my pants are entirely too tight.

Because I can imagine her gasping the same words in bed, after I've spent a leisurely time between her legs, using my fingers, my lips, my tongue to torment her in the best way.

Luckily, the line starts moving, and I'm able to tuck my hands in my pockets and discreetly adjust myself.

The bouncer is her first hint. They stand taller than both Gwen and me, which is a true feat. Their thigh-high boots are a shiny black leather that matches the rest of a scrappy getup straight out of a BDSM dungeon. A spiked collar sits just below an Adam's apple, and strong hands in fingerless gloves accept our IDs and cover charge.

"Have a lovely time." The bouncer winks at me with inch-long lashes, and I grin in return.

Then, there's the entryway—crystals on the walls and a chandelier reflecting light off picture frames that hold images of veteran performers. Even though we don't have coats, I still stick a bill in the coat check jar and smile at the attendant with a neon-green wig and black lipstick.

When we step into the main area and get the full effect of everyone in attendance, plus the stages waiting for performers, Gwen gets it.

"I'm not underdressed," she hisses, staring around. "I'm under-makeupped!" My postwoman pokes me in the side and tries to glare, even as her eyes spark with delight. "If I'd known we were going to a *drag show*, I would've put in more effort than this." Gwen waves at her face.

"You look great." I mean it.

She has some sparkly gold stuff on her eyelids and that same light-pink lipstick as the day I caught her delivering mail to the fire station.

She scoffs. "I might as well be barefaced. These queens are makeup goddesses!"

"Would a drink help you forgive me?"

Gwen pretends to waver but then nods with an ever-growing glow of eagerness. We maneuver through the crowd to the bar. And I get Gwen the tequila sunrise she asked for—quote, "Because if my face isn't colorful, then my drink damn well will be"—and a tonic water for myself.

I have the urge to stay sober tonight. I drove us here and plan to drive us home. Lately, I've felt like alcohol puts me in a weird mood. Kind of sad, but also my palms sweat a lot.

Better stick to virgin drinks.

We find a high-top table with a good view of the stage. There's a main platform, then a branch that extends into the crowd, giving the performers plenty of opportunity to strut and mingle.

"I. Am. So. Gosh. Darn. Excited." Gwen stares, riveted to the stage as she sips her fruity cocktail, lips puckering around the slim straw.

"Are you? Couldn't tell. We can head out now—"

"I will tackle you if you try to leave this bar before we see the show." She mock scowls at me, and I for real try not to forget how to breathe as I imagine Gwen smashing her body into mine and taking me to the floor.

A few more seconds, and I might have asked her to try, but the lights intentionally turn toward the stage, letting us all know the show is about to begin. The platform stands empty, but a husky voice with a hint of drawl fills the bar.

"Welcome to Stacked, the most fabulous bar in all of Tennessee. Did I hear we have a full house tonight?"

The crowd cheers in response to the hidden speaker.

"Well, dang. Sounds like they were right. Now, what I want to know is, are y'all ready to see some gorgeous Southern queens?"

There's a resounding, "Yes," and Gwen's at my side, shouting as loud as anyone.

"Oh, I love to hear that! Welcome, everybody. I'm your host … Brooke Enheart!"

An explosion of pink steps onto the stage. The drag queen wears a body suit covered in little hearts that glint under the bright stage lights. Two bigger hearts sit strategically on her chest and one at the apex of her legs. She has on a set of bedazzled boots like Gwen's, if Gwen's had gone out and robbed a jewelry store. On top of a wig of towering pink curls sits a rhinestone magenta hat.

"She's like a Cupid cowgirl!" Gwen stares up at Brooke with joyful wonder on her face.

The drag queen thanks the crowd's loud greeting with bats of her eyelashes and some suggestive shimmying.

"Now, I suspect y'all might be here to have some fun, let off steam after a hard week of toiling away at a boring desk job." The drag queen struts down the long stage until she reaches a pole. With a graceful move, she grabs hold and swings herself around, gazing out over the audience, wearing a bubblegum-pink smirk. "But your entertainers are on the clock and would greatly appreciate any and all tips." With a wave of sparkly nails, she gestures to the clearly marked tip buckets on the tables and bars. "Now, remember, this ain't no strip club," Brooke says while simultaneously dropping it low on the pole.

I have to shake my head at the level of showboating. *And people think* I'm *the class clown.*

"Y'all need to *hand* your generous tips to the ladies. Because if you stick your fingers into any crevices"—her voice goes deep—"you don't know what you'll find."

Everyone in the bar whoops with laughter, the sound ramping up when Brooke pops her generous-sized booty on the way up.

"Now, y'all get ready for a hell-raisin' show! We're here to *work*!" Brooke Enheart shouts just as a familiar beat starts rumbling from the speakers.

For the next few minutes, she lip-syncs perfectly with a classic country song. The amount of gusto Brooke Enheart gives the performance could fool anyone into believing the drag queen was truly the one singing about working nine to five instead of Dolly Parton.

I glance to the side to see if Gwen's enjoying the start of the show, only to find her with a flabbergasted expression on her face.

"Is that ..." Gwen stares up at Brooke, then turns to me, mouth wide in shock. "Is your brother a drag queen?"

Chapter Twenty-Three

SEBASTIAN

Try to come again for Holi next year. We can dance the day away, covered in colors.

— LETTER TO MARIA

After getting over her initial shock, Gwen gets right back into the swing of the show. When she asked her question, I braced myself to defend Cameron. But I should've known better. This is Gwen. From the moment she had figured out what kind of bar Stacked was, she had been nothing but eager. She didn't question why I might want to come see a drag show.

And that's one more thing I love about her. How she's curious about the world rather than judgmental when someone steps off what some might consider the "normal" path. I want to see everything with her because her eyes are the best view.

The night goes on, wilder than Genie's could ever hope to get. Acrobatics in gowns and heels. Glitter mixed into body hair. The scent of fruity drinks and alcohol. Sensual, deep voices doling out insults and sass to the laughter of the crowd.

And my brother is the ringmaster of this circus, commanding the stage whenever his alter ego of Brooke Enheart steps out from behind the curtain.

I never took Elaine to see one of Brooke's shows.

Not because I thought my ex would disapprove. Elaine knows what Cameron's secret passion is. But she's never been interested in loud, crowded places. Even the Jam Session could wear on her nerves. I knew she wouldn't find the joy in this place.

Not like Gwen.

"How many outfits does she have?" Gwen yells to me over the strains of Carrie Underwood's latest chart-topper.

Brooke now has on a latex dress and thigh-high boots. All pink, of course.

"And how the hell does she change so fast? I don't think I could get my jeans off as quick as she removes a skintight body suit."

Let's experiment. I'll be your assistant.

I want to bang my head against the table to get the dirty thought out of my brain before it's lodged in there for good, but I expect Gwen would notice.

"My guess is, three," a familiar deep voice says from over my shoulder.

"Maurice!" I turn to find a slender man with mischief in his smile stepping up to our table. The flashing lights spread pink and purple patterns over his dark skin.

After wrapping him in a quick hug, I pull the new arrival in for an introduction.

"Gwen, this is Maurice, Cameron's partner. Maurice, this is Gwen, my friend." And look at me, not even tripping over that word that doesn't seem big enough to hold the entirety of my affection for her.

"Hi!" Gwen extends her hand.

"Hello, Gwen." Maurice returns the shake, sharing a smile with her. "You enjoying the show?" His voice easily cuts through the pumping music, and I bet he's had a lot of practice with speaking in this kind of wildness.

"It is the best thing I've seen in my entire life. Which isn't saying much because I've barely ever left Green Valley. But still … sorry. I'm tipsy on tequila." She holds up her almost-finished drink as proof. "Do you come to all of Brooke's shows?"

The two of them chat as best they can in the loud room until a queen steals everyone's attention with her star-spangled bikini and rendition of "Party in the USA." Gwen and Maurice step away from the table to shimmy along to the catchy song and toss bills on the stage. I'd be happy, just standing and watching Gwen as she swings her hips and stomps her boots and grins like this is the best night of her life. But then she's grabbing my hands, leading me in a dance.

We stick to goofy, friendly moves. No bodies pressed tight together like in a nightclub. But as much as I want to feel her against every part of me, this—her, radiant with happiness—is better than anything.

Brooke Enheart reappears in—just as Maurice predicted—her third outfit of the night. This one makes me think of a call girl, cowgirl, and princess colliding. There are frills, deadly high heels, a corset, a crown, and a riding crop, tipped with heart-shaped leather.

All in varying shades of—you guessed it—pink.

"Attention, y'all! I have a special guest in the building!" she calls out in a high yet husky voice. "Wanna know who?"

The crowd roars, "Yes."

"My big hunk of a brother!" Brooke points directly at me, and all heads turn my way.

Up until this moment, I wasn't sure she saw me, but I guess I do stand taller than most everyone in this bar other than the men in heels.

"Get up here, Bass! Let's show these queens what they're missing!"

"I'll be back," I tell a gaping Gwen, and then I maneuver through the audience and bound my way onto the stage. I'm not the kind of guy to leave my brother hanging.

There're wolf whistles and catcalls, and I give the audience a wave and a bow.

"Tuck it away, boys! Sadly, my poor dear brother is afflicted with"—pause for dramatic effect—"heterosexuality."

There're groans from the crowd while Brooke presses a palm to my forehead and hisses into the microphone, as if my skin is fever hot.

"A terrible case. Incurable, the doctors told us."

"Take your shirt off!" a voice that sounds an awful lot like Maurice yells from the crowd.

"You hush." Brooke waves her riding crop in warning. "Or I'll have to take you over my knee." She slaps the crop against her thigh, and the crowd lets out more whoops of encouragement.

"Animals!" she yells at the raucous bar goers. "Do you think I brought him up here for your amusement?"

"YES!" everyone in the club hollers back, and the energy is intoxicating.

I can see why Cameron goes through his hours-long transformation each week, so Brooke can soak in this rabid adoration.

"Well … you're right! Get him, girls!"

And from the wings, drag queens storm the stage.

"This song is for my poor, unfortunate, *straight* brother!"

Katy Perry's voice blares from the speakers, and my gay brother starts lip-syncing about kissing girls and liking it. Suddenly, I'm sitting in a throne strewn with feather boas and flashing beaded necklaces, drag queens on all sides, some of them using me as a prop for their bringing down the house performance.

I ham it up, dancing in my seat. Through the pandemonium, I search out a familiar set of eyes. Finally, I find Gwen, right up against the main stage. Her hands are full of cash, she's shouting as loud as anyone, and the joy on her face hits me harder than a six-inch heel to the stomach.

If I could kiss *that* girl, I'd more than fucking like it.

I'd be destroyed by it.

Chapter Twenty-Four

GWEN

I drove past an air balloon festival today. Bunch of colorful balloons in the sky. It was a sight.

— POSTCARD FROM RYAN, PENNSYLVANIA

I always knew Sebastian embraced goofiness. He was often the class clown, even getting teachers to laugh along with his charmingly silly antics.

But this man, who is now giving his drag-queen brother a piggyback ride around the stage, acting as a goddamn Pegasus, has reached an entirely new level.

And. I. Love. It.

This night is a beautiful butterfly of an event I never expected to see. A shooting star across the sky, burning bright and hopefully never fading.

But it will, so I'd better enjoy every second while I can.

"Thank y'all!" Brooke shouts to the crowd over the last strains of the song. "You've been a lovely crowd. Tip the bartender, the waitstaff, and the queens, and have a gorgeous night!"

The roof is at risk of collapsing from the cheering getting so loud, and I scream my head off right along with everyone. Cash rains down on the stage, and a guy in sparkly shorts and a frilly apron comes out with a broom, sweeping up all the money and pushing it behind the curtain. I imagine piles and piles of bills back there.

Sebastian hops down from the stage, aiming for me, and when he's close enough, I grab his shoulders, jumping with the excited energy rattling in my veins.

"That was amazing!"

"Right?" He leans in to be heard over the music that started after Brooke sashayed off the stage.

"Has she ever called you up before?"

He's so near that I can smell the subtle scent of his sandalwood soap and a tinge of sweat.

God, I want to lick him.

"Nope."

There's a weight around my waist I belatedly realize is his arm. Sebastian pulls me closer as we converse in the loud room.

"That was the first time even though I've been to a few shows in the past."

His mouth is inches from mine, and I wonder if he tastes as good as he smells.

"Isn't this cozy?" a husky voice says over Sebastian's shoulder.

We both turn to find Brooke Enheart in all her pink goddess glory, watching us with a smirk.

"Oh my gosh." I shove Sebastian to the side to get closer to the queen. "That was *wonderful*! I've always wanted to see a drag show, but I never imagined it could be this spectacular!"

"You're too sweet. Stop, please." Brooke snaps open a magenta fan and flutters it near her face. "And by stop, I mean, keep going."

I giggle, then lean closer. "Your eye makeup—"

"Is horrendous. I know. I must have sweat it all off at this point."

"No, no! I was going to say incredible."

The drag queen used a pink liner to make a dramatic cat eye, and her false lashes have crystals on them. Paired with the starburst-patterned eye shadow? Perfection.

"Well, I learned from you, darling." She leans close. "Bass sent me your videos."

"Bass?" After a second, the nickname clicks. Bass, short for Sebastian. I turn to look at the paramedic, who has on an *aw-shucks* grin. "You shared my videos?"

His smile dims, worry creasing his brow. "Hell, should I not have? I figured since they were public—"

I cut him off by flinging my arms around his neck and squeezing as hard as I can. What a massively high compliment. I'm speechless, and I can only use my body to say *thank you*.

"Yes, yes. He's a big ole sweetie. So much sugar in him that you're bound to get a toothache."

Brooke waves her fan at us, and I end the hug. Sebastian keeps a hand on my lower back.

"Now, where is my man? I need to talk to him about trying to get my brother to strip onstage."

Maurice appears with apology cocktails, and as the music continues, the four of us dance and drink. At least, Brooke, Maurice, and I drink. Sebastian gets seltzer water all night.

Not that he needs alcohol. The man is wild, even completely sober. He takes my hands and twirls me around, as if we were in a ballroom rather than a drag bar. I'm a generally upbeat person, but I've never smiled and laughed so much as this night. When we eventually end up backstage, my abdomen aches from it.

I sit beside Brooke at her vanity and rifle through her makeup as she carefully removes her face and hair and slowly transforms into Cameron, a slim, sharply handsome man. But he shares genetics with Sebastian, so his hotness does not come as a surprise.

Meanwhile, Maurice and a drag queen named Sharon Smokes sit Sebastian down in front of a mirror and try a whole parade of wigs on the paramedic's head. The funniest part for me is when they first put the hair cap on him, covering up all his lovely brown waves. He still looks sexy as sin.

"Oh, this is pretty." I hold up an emerald powder with golden sparkles.

"Try it on. Try anything. We're going out after this."

He pushes some wet wipes my way, and I eagerly clean off my understated eye shadow.

"I'm Brooke's twin!"

Cameron and I glance over at Sebastian's exclamation in time to see him wearing a waist-length Pepto-Bismol-colored wig. The older Kirkwood shoots us a smolder across the room that has his brother snorting.

"I've got the hair; I've got the shirt." Sebastian gestures at his wrinkled pink button-up. "If Gwen lends me her boots, no one will be able to tell us apart."

He sends me a wink that has the flamingos twerking in my stomach. Who knew a man with Rapunzel hair could look so hot?

"Keep trying, old man!" Cameron jeers. "You wish you could be this beautiful." He does a series of vogue hands around his face.

The brothers exchange a few more lighthearted jabs before Sebastian insists he needs a green wig to really make his shirt pop. And so the faux hair roulette continues.

Cameron watches with a small smile.

"I always thought, one day, he'd stop with the pink," he murmurs low enough that only the two of us hear.

Satisfied with the new shade on my lids, I sort through the wide array of false lashes Cameron stacked in front of me. "Wearing it?" I ask. "Why would he stop? I figured it was his favorite color."

A beat of silence has me glancing at the younger Kirkwood brother.

"Maybe," he says as he plucks a pair of lashes with tiny gold butterflies from the pile.

When he picks up the small bottle of glue and carefully cups my chin, I give myself over to the hands of a fellow expert.

"Why would he wear it all the time if it's not?" I try not to move much as I ask.

"Because of me. He didn't tell you this story?" He smirks when I give a tiny headshake. "No, I guess he wouldn't. That's not my brother."

"What's not?"

"He's not … loud." When I snort, Cameron grins, both of us remembering his antics from the night so far. "Okay, yes, he's loud. But not about the way he helps people." He expertly adheres the false lash to my lid.

"When I was seven, Dad took Bass and me to the bait and tackle shop. There was this floppy pink camo hat, and it was the cutest thing I had ever seen in my little small-town life. I mean, *now*, I know it was a horrendous fashion choice. But at the time, all my whole heart wanted was that hat. So, I popped it on my head, ran up to Daddy, and begged him for it." The drag queen's hand is steady, but his lips are pinched. "He said I could get the green one. Or the gray one. But not the pink. 'Boys don't wear pink.'"

My heart breaks for young Cameron.

"What happened?"

"I put my treasure back. My glorious pink crown. And then I waited by the door for us to leave because the green? The gray? They were hideous. I wanted magenta or nothing at all. Then, Bass appeared and shoved the pink hat on my head, already wearing one of his own." A smile captures the corners of Cameron's mouth. "He gave our daddy this huge *I'm the firstborn son, and I can do no wrong* grin and said, 'Of course boys wear pink. I do it all the time.' " Cameron taps the second lash into place and sits back. "He'd used his allowance to buy the hats, and he walked me out to the car before Daddy figured out what to say. They were completely silent on the drive home. But I got to keep my hat.

"And every day—every *single* day—after that, Bass has worn something pink." Cameron sits up straight and reaches out to stroke his bubblegum-colored wig, where it rests on a mannequin head. "Because boys wear pink."

"Oh." *Is this makeup waterproof? Because I think I might cry.*

Suddenly, I miss my brother. Sibling love—it's an odd category, where one moment you want to shove their head in a toilet, and the next, you're researching how to hide a dead body because someone said the wrong thing to them.

"Look at that. Absolutely lovely."

Cameron gently pinches my chin and turns me toward the mirror, and I can't help a pleased smile. The butterflies seem to exist in a green and golden garden, the tiny terrariums on my lids. This is the amazing thing about makeup—how it can transform ordinary into artwork.

Maybe tonight, it can also make me into a woman who's as brave and carefree as I've always hoped to be.

Chapter Twenty-Five

GWEN

I can now say that I've changed a tire during a lightning storm. Can you? Scratch that. Don't try it.

— POSTCARD FROM RYAN, MISSISSIPPI

"He cheated on me!" The man wails, tears streaming down his face, full glass of wine in his hand. "Can you believe that bastard? And after I basically put him through medical school. And you should've seen this new boy. Barely old enough to get into a bar. He traded me in for a younger model. *Me!*"

When we got back to Cameron and Maurice's condo, they barely had time to pop a cork out of a bottle of wine before their friend Daniel called, needing a place to pour out his broken heart. Sebastian and I offered to hang out in another room, but Daniel waved our concerns away, claiming he wanted the whole world to know how his ex was a complete bastard.

And after hearing Daniel's side of the story, I'd have to agree.

"He's a piece of shit. We can key his car tomorrow." Maurice holds out his hand, and Daniel clutches it, offering a trembling smile.

"Thank you. You're good friends." Then, he chugs his pinot like it's the elixir of life. Or the blood of his ex.

We all share a look that says, *Wow, impressive.*

I sip my wine at a more sedate pace. In truth, I don't drink too often and rarely ever wine. My mom can't drink alcohol because it gives her headaches, and my dad prefers a cheap brand of beer I don't think is worth the calories. When I hang out with Arthur and Lance, they have better beer, and I'll have a can or two of those, but now, I'm thinking I need to see what the wine selection is like at the Piggly Wiggly. This one is tasty.

Hopefully, it makes good friends with the tequila already in my belly.

"I don't know what I'm going to do." Daniel stares out the dark window, voice forlorn. "I can't look at him. Can't be in the same room as him."

"Our home is your home." Cameron wraps the distraught man in a one-armed embrace, resting his chin on the top of Daniel's head to look at Sebastian and me. "We have two spare bedrooms. Stay as long as you need. Bass and Gwen can bunk together."

Oh. Oh God.

There's a weight on the side of my face, and I glance over to see Sebastian watching me with wide eyes.

"The couch is—" he starts, but I talk louder.

"Yeah. We can share a bed," I blurt. "A room. No problem."

This night has my adventure dial turned up to eleven, and a wild part of my heart demands I grab this chance while I can.

Share a bed with Sebastian Kirkwood.

Nothing more than that, of course. I don't have any illusion about us doing *things* in the bed together. But I want even the tamest version of the experience because it'll still be more vibrant than my vanilla life up to this point.

And I can answer some pressing questions like, *What does his face look like, fully relaxed?*

I remember once, in Biology class, he dozed off on his open textbook, his hair falling over his forehead. His mouth was slack and parted, and he might have drooled slightly on the glossy pages.

My teenage heart beat for that image, as if it were a masterpiece.

Could I have another one of those to store away in my mental library? There's a whole section devoted to Sebastian, and I want all the little pieces of info available to me. Ones I won't be able to get once he fixes whatever went wrong between him and Elaine.

My library has gone without new material for close to a decade, and I'm ready to restock.

"Yeah," Sebastian rasps, then clears his throat and gives a definitive nod. "We don't mind."

"Thank you," Daniel says. Then, he lets out a moan of despair, no doubt reliving some heartbreaking memory, and snatches up the bottle of wine to pour himself another generous glass.

"Let's get some carbs in you, sweetie." Maurice pulls out his phone. "Time for late-night pizza."

A half hour later, the five of us are halfway through two large pizzas and sloppily belting songs into a karaoke microphone Cameron pulled out because he claimed, sometimes, music was the only way to release pain in the soul.

I don't know about pain, but Daniel seems ready to get out some revenge with the way he's singing Miranda Lambert's "Kerosene."

After the man collapses on the couch, panting and cradling the vodka tonic he graduated to, Cameron escorts me to the spot in front of the TV and wraps my hand around the microphone. I opt for silly over sincere, bopping around to "Shut Up and Fish" by Maddie & Tae. And I feel the weight of Sebastian's attention on me the whole time. The grin he wears is a sunrise even in the middle of the night, and I want to bask in the glow.

We're going to sleep in the same bed tonight.

I can't fathom it.

Will we roll toward each other in the middle of the night?

Probably shouldn't. What if I throw elbows? Or if I sweat a lot while I'm sleeping? Or if I plaster myself all over him and he gets uncomfortable?

On second thought, this sharing-a-bed thing might be a huge, totally catastrophic mistake.

I'm going to need to build a pillow wall.

Or maybe, once Sebastian is asleep, I can creep down to the floor and sleep there for a night. If he wakes up before me, I'll claim I drunkenly rolled off the bed and just stayed where I was.

If that excuse is going to work, maybe I should drink some more.

Good plan.

Chapter Twenty-Six

SEBASTIAN

❧❀❧

You left your dress on my floor and your scent on my sheets. Then, you absconded with my heart. Please return, so we can exchange.

— LETTER TO MARIA

Gwen is drunk.

She's slightly sloppy and entirely adorable. Also, she fell asleep face-down on the couch about five minutes ago, and I've been agonizing over covering her with a blanket and leaving her where she is, or moving her to the bed we planned on sharing.

The bed is more comfortable, I reason. And I'd hate for her to wake up in a few hours and think I didn't want her in the room with me.

Hell, that's the only fucking thing I want.

But no fucking. Just two friends sharing a bed like friends do.

"I'm gonna carry her," I murmur quietly to the room, and Maurice gives me a thumbs-up while my brother smirks.

Daniel is too focused on the horror movie playing on the massive TV to pay me any mind, shoveling handfuls of popcorn into his mouth.

Gwen lets out a disgruntled huff when I roll her over and slip my arms behind her knees and back. She's not a small woman, but I've hoisted plenty of bodies larger than hers out of more difficult situations. The worst is when someone falls between their toilet and bathtub. No one wants to have a paramedic come save them, but it's even worse when your pants are down and your ass is in the air. But I pride myself on staying professional, in every situation I encounter at work, and I'm going to hold on to the professionalism now, no matter how good it feels to have Gwen clutched close to my chest.

In the bedroom, I manage to push back the covers with my knee far enough that when I set her down, I can finish the job, then tug them up to her shoulders. As much as I want to linger, I head to the bathroom instead.

When I'm done with a quick cold shower—which will hopefully dampen any hot thoughts I might have when I climb into our shared bed—I head back to the main area. The movie is off, and couches are empty, everyone having made the same choice to finally sleep for the night.

"I like how you are with her."

Cameron catches me in the kitchen, heating up water for chamomile tea. I have a cup every night before bed. A routine to tell my body it's time to wind down. Often, I have trouble falling asleep even if I'm already exhausted.

Guilt and anxiety gnaw at my brain whenever I try to relax. I was hoping the problem would go away now that I work in Green Valley, but sleeplessness lingers.

Cameron leans against the fridge, arms crossed over his chest, hair slicked back from his own shower.

"What's that supposed to mean?"

My brother loves to throw out cryptic comments and watch me struggle to figure out something he already knows. Normally, I respond with an *ah, yes, of course*, refusing to play his little game. But he said *her*, meaning Gwen, and I'm a sucker for that topic.

"You're exuberant. Jovial. Rambunctious."

"Are you hiding a thesaurus behind your back?" I make a point to peer around him.

"Some of us know these words without a reference book."

"Hmm. Sure." I fiddle with a tea bag. "Why do you assume Gwen has anything to do with my rambunctiousness?"

Cameron gives me a long look. In the pause, I realize there's a note of sincerity behind his teasing.

"Because you've been a zombie for years, it seems like," he says.

I flinch. I hoped no one I love had noticed.

"At least, in your relationship," he clarifies. "You and Elaine were so quiet with each other. Like you were high-strung horses, scared to spook the other."

"That wasn't her fault. We didn't fit. I know that. That's why I ended things."

"Have you?"

"Yes."

"But *have* you?"

"Hell, Cameron." I aggressively dunk my tea bag in the hot water. "*Yes.* I have. The important people know it's over."

"Elaine's parents know?"

That effectively cuts off my argument, but for once, Cameron doesn't seem pleased about having beaten me.

"If you spend all your time trying to take care of people, you're going to miss out on what's good for you." He grabs his water bottle off the counter and saunters away. "In other words," he calls over his shoulder, getting in a final jab, "don't fuck it up."

Since he's gone, the only person left to argue with is myself.

What does it matter if I'm different with Gwen? We're just friends. That's all she wants us to be.

But I know that's not what I want. It's what I'll take if that's all the affection she has for me, but if Gwen changes her mind, I'll be here. Pining.

That doesn't sound great. Like I'm just hanging around, waiting for her, only interested if I can eventually date her. But that's not my aim. I'm lucky to have

Gwen's friendship back in my life. I've missed out on years of it, and I don't know how I've gone without.

When I get back to the bedroom, I set the tea on the bedside table, untouched. I'm not ready to fall asleep yet. Just a few more conscious minutes of Gwen next to me. When I move to her side and set down a glass of water I poured for her, there's the rustling sound of sheets moving.

"Ugh."

The not-really-a-word is distinct enough to have me leaning in close.

"Gwen?" I keep my voice low and soft. If she's not already conscious, I don't want to wake her.

But she blinks bleary eyes at me.

"Bass?" she rasps, and I find the normally annoying nickname endearing on her lips. She can call me any type of fish, and I would love it.

"Hey. How are you feeling?"

She blinks slow a few times. "Are we on a boat?"

"Um … no. We're in Cameron's apartment. In one of the guest rooms."

"Why's it rocking?"

I grimace, imagining what her brain is telling her after soaking in all that alcohol.

"You're drunk, honey." The endearment slips out before I can stop it, and I hope she's drunk enough to disregard it. "I brought you a glass of water, and I'm going to grab you some ibuprofen. Okay?"

"Do I need to go in the ambulance?"

I chuckle. "No. I'll bring everything to you." I circle around the bed and head to the bathroom. The painkillers are in a drawer, and I shake two into my palm, then head back to the bed.

Gwen is sitting up and piling pillows, her movements both drunk and determined.

"Hey." I sit on the edge of the mattress on her side and offer the pills. "What's with the pillows?"

"Making a wall," she mutters.

"Gwen?"

She's more focused on her construction than me.

"Here're some pain meds. And why don't you drink this water?" I pick up the glass from the bedside table.

She turns my way and accepts the water, chugging half the glass, then takes the ibuprofen and swallows them and drinks more water. Some dribbles out the side of her mouth and drops to her shirt, making darker spots on the pink. When she puts the glass on the bedside table, she sets it down harder than necessary, making a loud thwack, and then the glass tilts precariously when she lets go. I save it before going back to examining her structure.

"Why are you building a pillow wall?"

She crawls out from under the covers to place another pillow farther down on the bed. I avert my eyes when I realize her skirt has bunched up around her thighs.

"So I don't attack you."

I can feel my face scrunching in confusion. "Do you have night terrors?" If so, I'm about to Google how to help someone with the issue. I can't remember if it's like sleepwalking, where you're not supposed to wake them, or what.

Gwen flops back, landing with her arms sprawled out on her now-pillow-less half of the bed.

"Nope." She pops the *P*. "I have horny dreams."

Good thing I wasn't drinking my tea or else we'd have a full-on spit take.

"Sorry. What was that?"

"I need to take off my face."

"Huh?" *How drunk is she?*

"So much makeup." Gwen reaches up and peels off one of her eyelashes.

In theory, I knew they were fake. No one has inch-long lashes where miniscule butterflies like to hang out. But witnessing her remove the piece of herself has me lunging forward to grip her wrist. There's a sudden panic in me she'll hurt herself. Try to take off an important piece that was meant to stay in place.

"I can help you take your makeup off, okay? Just let me go get something."

"You're—" Gwen blinks up at me and drags in a deep breath that shudders on the inhale.

"I'm what?" I ask, wondering if this is taking advantage of her. Finding out some truth with her inebriated.

"You're a good brother."

Ah. Yeah. Not sexy.

Is she saying I feel like a brother to her? I try not to dwell on the idea.

"Thanks. I'll be right back."

After retrieving a makeup wipe—which, of course, my drag-queen brother stocks his guest bathroom with—I resettle beside Gwen. And then, ever so carefully, I begin wiping her makeup off. After watching enough of her videos, I know that gentle circles are the best. Don't scrub. Massage away the product.

Gwen sighs, a small smile forming as I clean her face. I try to ignore how close we are and how her breath smells fruity from the wine and how she's settled a hand on my bicep as I work. All I care about is helping her get comfortable for the night.

When all the makeup is gone along with the second false eyelash, Gwen blinks up at me. I've seen her without makeup before. She never used to wear any in high school. I think she was self-conscious then because of her acne. After the first few days of sitting next to her, I never really noticed the red bumps. They were just part of her face. But I noticed her cute nose scrunching with laughter whenever I told her a joke and her full lips that I always wanted to kiss. I noticed her edgy hair with bangs she'd let fall over her right eye. Now, she has little swoopy bangs, and I finger-comb them to the side without thinking.

"You should get some sleep," I murmur.

"Sometimes ..." Gwen's eyelids flutter closed, and she turns her head to the side.

Sometimes what? But whatever she was going to say would just be drunken rambling. Still, I want to know.

I stand up, the mattress squeaking in relief. When I lie down on my side of the bed, I can't see Gwen because of her wall.

She said she has horny dreams. Are they about me?

Carefully, I take back one of the pillows and slide the cushion behind my shoulders, sitting up enough to sip my tea and try to calm my mind so I can fall asleep.

Sometimes, I wonder if I'd be able to sleep if I hadn't made that mistake. If this anxiety would have built in me anyway. Because it's not always my error that keeps me awake. When I lived and worked in Merryville, the things I would see on my emergency calls started to stick with me, playing over and over in my head.

There's less now that I moved to Green Valley. Not near as much horrible fodder for my brain to latch on to. But I still need help to calm my mind.

So, I drink tea.

Spend time with my family.

Break up with my long-term girlfriend.

Pine for a loveable postal worker who just wants to be friends.

Okay, maybe those last two aren't exactly soothing, but the former was the right choice, and the latter is inescapable.

Another pillow disappears from the wall, revealing a groggy Gwen face. She stuffs the puffy cushion under her head, blinks at me, and says, "Sometimes, you're my favorite person."

She falls asleep immediately after that.

I take a while.

Chapter Twenty-Seven

GWEN

A waitress left her number on my receipt. I thought you should know your big brother is a ladies' man. Do I get bonus points for her being sixty-plus? Experience is everything.

— POSTCARD FROM RYAN, KENTUCKY

Even in the morning, country music drifts through the Nashville air. Cameron brought us to his favorite brunch spot, claiming their chicken and waffles pair perfectly with mimosas. That combo gets no argument from me. Despite drinking more than normal last night, I feel surprisingly fine this morning. I have a vague memory of Sebastian making me drink water.

If only I hadn't passed out so quickly. I missed my opportunity to creepily observe him while he slept. Sebastian was awake and in the kitchen, making coffee, by the time I woke up. Maybe it's for the best.

We sit on the restaurant's patio, a large umbrella shielding us from the summer sun. As Cameron tells us about his boss's spray tan gone wrong, I notice the small, affectionate touches he and Maurice share.

Hands brushing, fingers fiddling, palms pressing. None of the PDA bothers me, other than how the little displays of love create a fissure in my chest, letting my longing slip out.

Wouldn't it be nice to have someone I want to caress like that?

Never mind. There's already someone I want. What would be nice is to have someone I *could* touch like that.

"And now, she can never wear the suit again. Two thousand dollars of snowy-white perfection down the drain. Let that be a warning to you, kids."

"Noted. I'll let the sun tan me and be extra careful with all my designer clothes." Sebastian grins, and the younger Kirkwood rolls his eyes before tracing an unimpressed stare over his brother's cargo shorts, wrinkled T-shirt, and worn pink baseball hat.

"You could benefit from throwing half your closet out. Your birthday is in a few months. I should buy you decent clothing."

"I'm completely decent." Sebastian spreads his arms wide. "These cover all the goods. Not a single indecent part of me showing."

"Yes, and we're all worse off for it." Maurice sends me a wink, and I take a long sip of my ice water to cool down the blush on my cheeks.

Ignoring the outrageous comment from his partner, Cameron continues to study his brother. "Huh," he says.

"What are you *huh*-ing about?" Sebastian shifts in his chair and reaches for his own water glass.

"Now that we're talking about your decade-long unaltered wardrobe, I just realized something about you."

"Had a revelation, did you? Should I be worried? What am I saying? It's you. Of course I should be worried."

"You never dated anyone before Elaine, did you?" Cameron asks.

Some of Sebastian's playful sparkle winks out, and he leans back in his seat, the move less relaxing, more distancing.

I try not to appear too interested in his response.

"No," he answers after a pause.

"Did you hook up with anyone before her?"

Now, Sebastian is the one blushing. "Why are you so fixated on high school Sebastian's love life?"

The server shows up then, handing around perfectly timed fruity morning alcohol beverages, which I'm not sure will help the situation but will certainly assist my nerves. She places a basket of biscuits in the middle of the table and leaves, not realizing she's escaping an intensely awkward exchange.

"Elaine is the only person you've ever kissed," Cameron declares.

And it just got worse.

The table goes silent.

I wait for Sebastian to deny the claim. But he doesn't.

"So what?" The older Kirkwood grabs a biscuit and starts buttering it. "It's not a crime to have only kissed one person."

"I might argue that point," Cameron says. "How do you know if you're any good at it? My bet is, Elaine's never kissed anyone else either. Nothing to compare it to. You, my dear brother, might be a terrible kisser."

"Whenever my ego gets too big, it's nice to know I can talk to you for a few minutes and have the thing instantly deflated." Sebastian speaks with dry humor, and he keeps his eyes firmly fixed on his biscuit. "You're providing a wonderful service."

Cameron continues talking, as if he didn't hear his brother. "How many people have you kissed, Gwen?"

Oh no, now, I'm in this?

"Uh …" I sip my cocktail to give myself a moment. After swallowing, I confess, "I don't really keep track."

"That many?"

"No!" I yelp. "Six, I think. That sounds right."

Cameron nods, as if he approves of the number. I get the feeling he would have approved of one hundred. Or two. Anything other than one or none.

"So, you've been able to compare. Perfect." He raps his knuckles on the table like a judge coming to a decision. "You should kiss my brother."

"Cameron." Sebastian growls the man's name in a chiding tone I've never heard him use before.

Is the idea of kissing me enough to make him angry?

The thought has me squirming in my chair and reaching for my mimosa again. I guess I should be grateful to Sebastian for shutting the talk down. Who knows what I'd do if I got free access to his mouth?

But I guess I don't know Cameron well enough because the censure in his brother's expression only fuels his determination.

"You're friends, right? What's a kiss between friends?" He waves between us, his pink nail polish glittering with the movement. "Come on. Get some practice. Get some feedback."

Yes, please.

And I'm suddenly anxious for Sebastian to give in. *Is this the only time I'll have a chance to taste him?* If so, then I want it. Every little scrap. A memory to tuck into my back pocket and take out to examine and cherish like an old letter from a lover. I want to fulfill at least one of the goals younger Gwen had in her heart.

"Stop putting Gwen on the spot." Sebastian glares at his brother. "She doesn't—"

"I'll kiss you."

That cuts off whatever my friend was about to say, his hazel eyes finding mine, wide with shock.

As he comes to terms with what I just said, I take a bracing gulp of mimosa and hope the champagne bubbles will fuel my courage and drown some panicking flamingos.

"You will?" Sebastian asks, eyes still wide.

"Sure," I say, trying with every molecule in my body to sound casual.

Sure, I kiss guys for practice all the time. No big deal.

With a little shuffle, I scoot my chair around to face his and indicate he should do the same. *Look at me, taking charge.* Or maybe it's my vagina calling the shots. Turns out, she can be a girl boss in the right circumstances.

Sebastian follows my example until we sit, facing head-on, our knees weaved together. With both of us being so tall, all that needs to happen is a little lean forward, and we'll be in range. I do, and he mirrors me, but his hands grip the arms of his chair so tight that he might as well be dangling off a cliff face.

Is he nervous? Or is it that he doesn't want to kiss me?

"Talk him through it."

Cameron's direction tugs me out of my doubtful thoughts.

"Sorry?" I glance his way to find the drag queen wearing an almost-academic expression.

Maurice hides his mouth behind a napkin, but his eyes tell me the man wears an evil grin.

"It's instructional." Cameron points at his sibling. "Move his head where you want it. Tell him what makes a kiss good."

"This is going far past helpful brotherly advice," Sebastian mutters, even as his focus stays on my mouth.

"Is it?" The younger Kirkwood smirks. "You made me walk you through every step of doing your taxes."

Sebastian's eyes flick to the side, then back to me. "This is not the same, and you know it."

If I don't take hold of this situation, I'll lose my chance.

And then the frogs will win again.

"Here." I reach up, pressing my palms to either side of Sebastian's face, cataloging the scrape of his stubble against my palms to be remembered later when I can melt into a puddle of goo in privacy. "I tilt right, which means you tilt to your right too." I adjust him just so.

Someone else might have to spend a moment figuring out what makes a kiss good. But someone else hasn't spent as much time as I have imagining exactly how they would kiss Sebastian Kirkwood.

Even though I want to dive in and consume his mouth, I stick to the teacher script.

"Get consent," I tell him, thinking of all the times guys dived in when I wasn't expecting it. *And please consent to kissing me, so I don't feel so bad about doing this.*

"Uh …" He clears his throat, and I watch his Adam's apple bob. "Can I kiss you?"

Yes. But you can do better than that. "Don't ask like you're filling out a work-sheet." I search for a way to describe how to make consent sexy. "There's a *yes* or *no* checkbox. But make me *want* to check yes."

Something flares in his eyes, and a surge of confident power infuses him. The hesitancy disappears, leaving his hand reaching up to cradle the back of my head.

"Tell me to stop," he rumbles low in his throat, quiet enough that only I can hear, "before I can't."

A shiver rolls down my spine.

Well, that's one way to get a massive check mark in the yes column.

"Don't stop," I whisper.

He doesn't.

Chapter Twenty-Eight

SEBASTIAN

There will always be a seat for you at my restaurant.

— LETTER TO MARIA

There are times when my brother is the most annoying person on the face of the earth.

There are times when he's a genius.

This is a perfect combination of those two.

But I forget his existence the moment Gwen's mouth touches mine. All that registers is her warm, soft lips, tangy with a drop of orange juice and the sting of champagne.

At the gentle, intimate pressure, my brain trips over itself, trying to find balance when the world is suddenly awash with tipsy joy. Gwen could be her own brand of liquor, bottled and sold for an outrageous amount of money. Because who wouldn't pay to imbibe this flavor? She's savory and sweet, and she burns so good.

I get drunk on her.

I want to ask if I'm kissing how she likes. If this feels even a fraction as good for her as it does for me. But her firm hand tangles in the hair at the base of my neck, keeping me pressed close to her.

That must mean I'm doing something right.

This kiss has a purpose. Learning. And that's all I want to do. Learn more of Gwen and what'll make her eager to do this whenever she sees me. I memorize the exact tilt of my head, the firm push of her mouth, how close her body is and could be. She seems fascinated with my lower lip, sucking on it just enough that I feel the gentle press of teeth.

Somehow, I stifle my groan, all the while taking initiative.

Even with need raging in my chest, I keep the pace slow. A languid kiss for our first one. Drug her into submission with my passion and convince her this spark between us is more than just friends.

With my mouth, but without words, I speak to her.

Can't you see how good we are together?

How I'd worship every inch of you?

As if hearing me, Gwen's mouth parts with the tiniest, sexiest of gasps.

"And there's our food!" Cameron announces loudly, his words—his presence—crashing down between us like a broken garage door.

We both jerk back into our seats, and I feel a guilty flush heating my face. A similar shade spreads over Gwen's cheeks as she grabs her drink and takes a determined sip.

The sight only makes me want to dive back in, lick the mimosa off her universe-altering lips.

That kiss was powerful. So monumental that it established a new timeline.

BK. Before Kiss.

DK. During Kiss.

AK. After Kiss.

I want a time machine to get me out of AK and back to DK, and I want to live in that time period for the rest of my life even if I only ever exist for moments and survive off the air Gwen breathes into me.

But she's already turning her chair back to the table. I'm slow to follow, as if waiting in the same position means we can start all over again.

But I don't want to make Gwen uncomfortable, so I reset my chair at the table, stare at my buttered biscuit, and try to remember if anything in the world could taste as good as the lips of the woman next to me.

"There you go, Bass." Cameron leans over to clutch my shoulder, giving me an impish grin only younger siblings are capable of affecting. "Now, you've kissed two people." He turns his attention to Gwen, and I'm tempted to tip his chair over to stop whatever comes out of his mouth next. "How'd he do? Hopeless case? You can be honest. We're all family."

I'm going to kill him.

The closest weapon is a pink plastic flamingo stuck in the ground beside our table. Those spindly legs will do. And when the cops arrive, I'll tell them the lawn ornament did it. Totally plausible.

"Good. Great. Top-notch kisser." Gwen clears her throat and takes another drink. "Don't think he needs any instruction."

"Hear that, Bass?" Amusement spills off Cameron in silent waves, all conveyed in his overly large grin. "No lessons needed! Guess you never have to kiss Gwen again."

My fingers itch for the flamingo.

"Thanks so much," I say to Cameron through gritted teeth. "You've been a big help."

And Maurice, thank the Lord, changes the subject from my romantic abilities to our plans for the day. Our last day in Nashville.

Tomorrow, Gwen and I head home to Green Valley.

Back to the place where I'll be seen as a cheater if I spend too much alone time with her even though we're *just* friends.

I want to curse.

I want to kiss Gwen again.

Then, I want to put her in my car and drive north. Or south. Or west. Any direction but east, where home lies.

Can't it just be the two of us for a little while longer?

I guess it is. For one more day.

And then I have to give Gwen up until Elaine is ready to accept the break.

But I'm starting to wonder if that day will ever come.

Chapter Twenty-Nine

GWEN

Your latest video isn't working. How am I gonna figure out contouring now?

— POSTCARD FROM RYAN, OHIO

With a full face of makeup on, Daniel is finally smiling.

"I love it. I wish I could wear this every day." He turns his head left, then right, showing the camera every one of his angles.

Over the past half hour, I gave him fierce red-and-black eye makeup, lips to match, and contouring that brings out his magnificent cheekbones. Truly, his bone structure didn't need my help, but now, he looks lethal.

I hope he posts a picture on social media and his ex cries himself to sleep over losing such a gorgeous man.

I click the button on the computer to stop recording. "Well, I can send you this video. Watch it a few times, and you'll be a pro."

"Good. Yes. But you won't post it, right? Not until I'm sure?"

"Cross my heart." I make the motion, and he gives me a sweet, sad grin over the expanse of beauty products at Cameron—aka Brooke's—vanity table at Stacked.

Brooke Enheart had another show at the club tonight, and Sebastian and I came for the second half. A local bluegrass band had been playing live at a nearby venue, so we'd decided to take in something new first.

The whole day has been new. My lips are still buzzing from that kiss.

That kiss.

I might never wear lipstick again, for fear it'll dampen the memory of the sensation of Sebastian's mouth against mine.

The man on my mind appears, clutching multiple drinks as he finds us backstage. Maurice and Brooke follow behind him.

"Daniel, darling, you look fabulous." Brooke air-kisses her friend before glancing toward the camera. "How did my laptop work for you?"

"So great. Thank you. I just like keeping track of all the looks I've done even if I'm not going to publish the video." I save the file to my cloud drive before turning back to the group. "Are things dying down out there?"

"On the contrary, they're getting ready to heat up. We warm the crowd up, and then it's all dancing and drinking for the rest of the night. The party never ends."

"Time to show off your look." I give Daniel an encouraging smile.

He glances toward his friends. "I'm not looking to meet anyone," he says. "It's still too raw."

"Of course it is. Let's just dance and show the world your lovely face." Maurice pulls Daniel up and tugs him toward the doorway to the main area of the club.

I'm about to stand and follow when a big body plops down in the stool Daniel vacated.

Sebastian stares at me, seeming as surprised to find himself sitting as I am. But a hand with pink manicured nails holds him in place.

"It's Bass's turn. I *cannot* keep telling people we're family when he looks like this." Brooke waves at what I would consider the handsomest man alive.

Clearly, we're not on the same page.

"What are you talking about? I trimmed my beard this morning. And my shirt has buttons." He gestures at his chest, as if to prove the point. "I look great."

"You look like a loaf of white bread. Boring. Let Gwen spice you up."

Sebastian sends me a pleading look, but I'm suddenly feeling inspired.

"I can do that." From the collection of beauty supplies, I snatch up a tiny glass jar. "In fact, there's a new style I've been wanting to try."

"Couldn't you maybe do it on Maurice?" Sebastian squirms, but his drag-queen brother keeps him in place.

"Nope." I bite the inside of my cheek to stifle my laughter. "Maurice doesn't have a beard."

His eyes narrow. "What are you planning to do with my beard?"

Leaning forward, I hold his eyes, and I remember the heat that flared between us —or at least from me—during our breakfast practice kiss.

"Do you trust me?" The question comes out huskier than intended, and I watch Sebastian's Adam's apple bob as he swallows.

"Of course."

"Then, let her work and stop complaining." Brooke leans between us to check her face in the mirror, then steps back. "I'll see y'all out there. And my brother had better look fierce!"

I barely keep a gleeful chuckle at bay. "Do you mind if I record? I want to keep track of how looks turn out."

"Uh, okay." He rubs his palms on his jean-clad thighs. "Yes. Good. Okay."

I pause with my finger over the button, glancing his way. "Does makeup really make you uncomfortable? We don't have to do this if you don't want to."

Sebastian shakes his head, then reaches over to press the record button himself before smiling into the camera. "So, what's the plan to make me beautiful?"

I hold up the glass jar with its shimmering contents.

"Two words. Glitter beard."

"Oh hell."

The first step involves oil. I find a jar of coconut oil that works and lather my hands with it, then massage the slickness into his beard. Let's just say, I am *very* thorough.

Despite his initial curse, Sebastian is game throughout the second step, where I coat the lower half of his face in the sparkly substance. Meanwhile, I try to be professional and focus on the facial hair rather than the tempting lips it surrounds.

By the time I'm done, we're both giggling like we're back in high school, passing silly notes. I'm not sure if this is what Brooke had in mind, but when you leave the room, you lose your chance to object.

Sebastian leans toward the camera, examining the result.

"I look like I just made a clown *very* happy."

That sets me off again, and I snort with my laughter, my abdomen aching as I try to subdue myself. "Or Tinker Bell," I offer between chuckles.

Sebastian grins my way. "You really think she has fairy dust down there?"

"That's the thing about fairy dust." I lean close, as if we were sharing a scandalous secret. "It gets *everywhere*."

Sebastian scoops up my hands as he laughs, then tugs me to my feet. "Come on, makeup queen. Let's show off your masterpiece."

"Someone thinks highly of himself." I remember to reach over and stop the camera, and then we make our way to the club.

Everyone loves the beard. Or maybe everyone loves Sebastian, and the glitter has nothing to do with it. Whatever the case, we all dance and joke and accept the praise from everyone who sees the self-proclaimed masterpiece.

And through it all, I try not to remember that this is our last night before heading home.

That when we cross the town line back into Green Valley, this will all go away.

Chapter Thirty

GWEN

I tried avocado toast. That shit is good. Don't tell anyone I said that.

— POSTCARD FROM RYAN, VERMONT

"In hindsight, this was a bad idea. Glitter is like a sparkly infestation. Cameron will never get rid of it all," I babble as I wipe a wet cloth against Sebastian's beard in the guest bathroom.

My friend is acting odd. Quiet. I'm not used to the paramedic keeping his mouth shut. Normally, he's throwing around goofy comments like they're free flyers.

But once we walked through the door of his brother's loft, it was like someone dialed down his animation switch.

"Was it ... okay?"

Maybe he's regretting acting as my makeup model. I should've stuck to the drag queens.

"It was great," Sebastian says, smile soft. "You're really talented, Gwen."

I pinch my lips to keep from grinning. "Thank you."

"Would you ever do makeup professionally?"

I shrug. "If someone I know asks me to do their makeup and offers to pay, sure. But I don't want to be some kind of entrepreneur. I like my job. Working at the post office isn't glamorous or perfect, but most days, I enjoy it. Plus, I don't think there's a huge call for makeup artists in Green Valley." My fingers press harder at the corner of his jaw, where there's a pesky patch of green glitter that doesn't want to leave. I sympathize. "Seems like everyone is turning their hobbies into side hustles these days. But I'm happy with just doing it for fun. Attaching money to it would put on all this extra pressure. Makeup has always been like … meditation, I guess. Something I did—" I cut myself off, realizing what I was about to say.

"Something you did …" Sebastian leads me toward the end of the thought.

I clear my throat, re-wet the washcloth, and decide to be a little bit vulnerable. "Makeup was something I did with my gran. She bought me my first kit. She taught me how to use everything. I'm not sure if you remember, but I had pretty bad acne in high school." I meet his eyes, and he just tilts his head, neither agreeing nor disagreeing. "Makeup helped with my confidence."

Self-consciously, I brush my fingers over my cheeks, feeling the shallow ridges of a few scars left over from that time. I tried every product until a dermatologist prescribed me a medication that finally cleared up the breakouts. Mrs. Kirkwood was the one I saw each month when I went to pick up the little pills that did what makeup couldn't.

"You're beautiful. With makeup and without it."

A natural blush infuses my cheeks. "Thanks."

"I'm serious, Gwen. Hey, look at me." His finger presses to the bottom of my chin, tilting my eyes up to meet his burning ones. "I had the biggest crush on you. Biology was my favorite class because you were there. I failed half the tests because I couldn't stop staring at you. Trying to think of something funny to say just to hear your laugh. If I ever noticed your acne, I forgot about it the next second because you were so fucking cute and hilarious and … perfect. You still are. All those things and more."

His confession sucks all the air out of my lungs. I stand silently, reeling as the words play on repeat through my brain.

Cute. Hilarious. Perfect. Cute. Hilarious. Perfect. Cute. Hilarious. Perfect.

Oh my God. Oh my FUCKING God.

Did Sebastian Kirkwood just say he had a crush on me? Was I right all those years ago?

But I don't want to let my mind fall into the past to reexamine every interaction we had. I want to be here. Now. In this moment, where he's looking at me like *that*.

Oh no. I'm about to do something that could be a total heart-obliterating disaster. And I'm not even drunk.

Still, I fist the front of his shirt and pull Sebastian in for a kiss.

This one isn't for practice or educational. This is all desperate questions.

Do you see now? How much I crave you? How bad I am because all I've ever done is want you?

And now, I'm finally taking what I want.

But is it truly taking if he's kissing me back?

Sebastian's mouth crashes into mine, hot and seeking, just as his hands grip my hips and drag me against his body. Everywhere is touching. I drop the washcloth to tangle my hands in his silky hair because it's all I've ever wanted to do. Whenever he tucks the strands behind his ears or shoves them out of his eyes, I want my fingers to take over. To claim ownership of this velvety mass. Braid it into the shape of my name.

But I don't have that skill set, so I settle for a gentle fist at the roots and a soft tug that has him moaning into my mouth, the sound sinking into my soul until I'm reshaped by it. Nipples hard, skin covered in goose bumps, spine loose and threatening to spill me onto the floor.

Instead of sinking down, I'm held up by arms that engulf me.

"Gwen," he rasps against my mouth.

Is he reminding me? If so, I want to thank him because my mind melted along with my spine and I forgot who I was for a moment.

We break apart, only far enough to stare into each other's eyes, as if we both need to check in and make sure this is all good.

"Okay?" he asks me through a series of pants.

"Yep," I squeak, the word too high-pitched, so I drop my voice low. "Okay."

Damn, too low again. I'll get it one of these days.

But then Sebastian is grinning down at me, and his thumbs are stroking my cheeks, and I have the notion I could do or say anything and he'd still look at me just like this.

"You should see your face," he murmurs.

"Why?" I turn my head, finding the mirror, then choke on a laugh.

Sebastian isn't the only one with glitter.

"Now, I'm the one who looks like I went down on Tinker Bell." I giggle.

"Hell," he grunts. "Am I weird if I tell you that makes me hard?"

"Yes." And I'm back to kissing him because I love when Sebastian is weird with me. When we're a set of oddballs together.

My fingers untangle from his hair to seek out the buttons on his shirt. I love the buttons because I don't have to remove my mouth from his to take his shirt off. He helps me by shrugging out of the fabric. Then, he returns the favor, whipping my camisole over my head so fast that I think he might have turned me into a lust ghost and simply ripped it through my temporarily incorporeal body.

"Chest," I say when my gaze drops south to take his in. I don't know why I have to say the word, but it's a blaring Hollywood-sized sign in my mind as I scrape my nails over his bare abdomen.

Sebastian Kirkwood has no shirt on, and I'm touching him.

"Um, yeah." He chuckles, dipping his head to meet my eyes.

But then he loses me because I lunge forward to kiss my way along his collarbone, over his pecs, nipping the taut skin, getting a taste of every inch I can.

"Holy hell, Gwen."

The chest I'm kissing shudders under my attention, but I keep on worshipping in a grid formation. If Sebastian Kirkwood were ever to go missing, I want to be able to describe him in perfect detail to a sketch artist, using only the feel of his body against my mouth.

"If you don't stop, pants are coming off. Yours. Then mine." He growls the words like a threat.

Does he know what a threat is? Obviously not because my hands are already at my fly, ready to help him follow through.

"You're gonna kill me," he mutters when I shimmy my shorts to the floor.

"I know CPR," I tell him, proudly smiling at the paramedic.

He laughs and tears his own pants off.

Let the record show, I am now in a bathroom with Sebastian Kirkwood, and we're in our underwear.

This monumental realization has me pausing. I need to slow down and savor this. If I go at this in a frantic honey-badger style, I'll miss the important parts. And all the parts are important because it's Sebastian, and I don't know if I'll get another chance at this.

So, I brace my hands against his broad shoulders, holding him back for inspection.

"Are you okay?"

Sebastian stays still, even as his hands clench and release and his eyes keep dropping to my floral cotton bra. I like this one because it has little pink roses on it. I'm wearing pink, just like he always is, only mine is secret.

"I want you so bad," I confess. "But I don't want to rush."

Sebastian's nostrils flare as he sucks in a deep breath. Then, he lets the air out slow, his body losing some of the intense tension from a moment ago. Well, not all of him …

There is one place in particular that is still very—deliciously—tense.

"Got it." Sebastian's hands rest against my rib cage, his thumbs tracing my underwire. "No rush." He leans down and presses a kiss at the base of my throat, then licks the warm spot. "I plan to take my time with you."

Chapter Thirty-One

SEBASTIAN

Do you think about that night? I do.

— LETTER TO MARIA

When I move to step back, give Gwen a little more space, she digs her fingers into my shoulders. Holding me in place.

"Where are you going?" She gives me a wide, pleading stare that threatens to buckle my knees.

"We can slow down. I won't push you."

Gwen lets out the most adorable growl I've heard in my life, and the sound somehow makes me harder.

"I didn't mean not to rush in general. I meant, I don't want to rush through this, right now, what we're doing." She lets go of me to reach behind her back, and a second later, her bra hangs loose on her shoulders. When she shrugs, the delicate underwear falls to the floor.

Fuck. She's just ... and I'm here ... and gah!

"If we go slower, I won't miss anything," Gwen clarifies as she strokes my chest, her fingers playing over my skin as if I were a fragile, precious thing to her.

"I can do slow." My voice cracks, betraying me because how the fuck do I slow down when it's Gwen, close to naked, in front of me? I'm greedy. I want to grab and taste and rub and suck.

But for her, I'll reset my pace.

"Back up," I command.

She blinks at me, surprised, but then she follows my instructions, moving until her butt hits the bathroom counter. From the way she shivers, I wonder if the granite is cool.

Can't have my woman cold.

I step forward, crowding her with my body, leaning my head down until our breaths meld together. With the slightest move, I could have her lips. Instead, I tilt my head to the side and kiss up her neck.

Real slow.

"Is this too fast?" My hands settle on her back, spanning the bare flesh.

"N-no." She trips on the word.

I grin.

Her hard nipples press against my chest, begging for attention. Luckily, Gwen is tall enough that they aren't too far. When I cup her breasts in my palms and drag my mouth to the first peak, she makes this noise—a choke mixed with a gasp mixed with a groan. A man could get addicted to that noise.

For the next few minutes, I make sure to suck her at a leisurely pace, earning that sound a hundred times over.

"Sebastian." She says my name like a curse. "I need more."

I lick her tender nipple with the flat of my tongue, and her hips jerk in protest. At some point, Gwen tangled her hands in my hair, holding me to her. But now, she lets go and shimmies her body. I'm so drunk on her that it takes me another few sucks to realize she's tugged off her underwear.

Completely bare to me.

Now, I'm the one groaning. I rest my forehead on her collarbone, staring at the curls on her mound, wanting to dive down and explore.

But she asked me not to rush.

"Can you touch me? Please?" Gwen slides one foot to the side an inch or two. Opening herself.

When I raise my head, I find her eyes have gone hazy and needy, begging me for what I'm longing to give her.

"Yes. God." Following her request my own way, I grip Gwen's thighs and boost her onto the lip of the sink. With a palm on each of her knees, I push her open until I see the slickness of her intimate lips.

I kneel.

Luckily, the bathroom has some thick mats to cushion my knees, but I would have dug them into the hard tiles if it meant I could get a taste of Gwen.

Again, I ache to charge forward, but I pause close enough that she'll feel my words and nothing more.

"Okay?" I ask.

We meet eyes over the expanse of her bare body. Gwen's flushed face stares down at mine, something like wonder lighting her eyes.

Is this as unreal to her as it is to me? Is that why she wants to go slow?

That's the exact reason I want to go hard. I want Gwen to make marks on my body. I want to be physically changed after this experience, so I'll never doubt every moment was real.

"Okay." Gently, she combs her fingers into my hair, but not to tug the strands or pull me close. This gesture is caring. Almost loving.

Or maybe that's how my heart wants to interpret the motion.

Whatever her thoughts, I'm determined to go above and beyond. I want to wreck Gwen in the best way.

I want to remember this night, yes. But I want this to be a preview of what's to come because this cannot be the only time I have her.

"Hold on, honey."

Before she can respond, I've already had my first taste.

If I thought her pleasure noises were addictive, I never had the hard stuff. Everything about Gwen is sweet, but her pussy is decadent. Heady with a tang of arousal, and fuck, I have to dip my tongue into her, hungry for more.

She writhes and whimpers, doubly so when I drag my mouth up to her clit, giving the nub of nerves as much care and attention as I gave her nipples.

At some point, Gwen wraps her legs around my head, and I clasp her thighs, spreading them farther apart, even as I pull her closer.

"Oh God! I'm—I'm going to—" She doesn't need to finish the sentence for me to feel the answer against my mouth, her pussy clenching, her fingers curling in my hair, a ragged sob coming from her throat.

When her legs loosen, I give a final lick, then stand, loving how red the skin of her chest grows as she pants for breath. I slide my arms around her, gathering her close to me.

In the mirror, I find a new angle of Gwen. The slope of her back, the dip of her spine. Gwen's ass pools in plump mounds on the marble counter, and her soft skin dimples where I dig my fingers in, kneading her pliant muscles.

So many parts of her to see, to catalog. At the touch of her lips against my neck, I'm hit with a wave of need, frantic to take in every detail of her, suddenly terrified this is my one chance. That we'll wake up tomorrow and find none of this happened.

I'm not dreaming. My mind could never come up with something this good.

Slim fingers sneak into the waistband of my briefs, fiddling with the elastic.

"Can you take these off?" she asks between kisses.

I leave off staring at Gwen in the mirror, cupping the back of her head with one hand and tilting her to face me.

"You want me naked?" I manage a playful smile, even as the weight of this night engulfs my body and demands I take all I can.

Gwen grins. "It's only fair." She sneaks a quick press of her lips against mine before leaning back. "I swear I won't coat your dick in glitter. Unless you ask me to."

The laughter surprises me. The noise barks out deep from my chest and lightens the air in the bathroom.

She's always able to do that. Brighten the world around us.

"Maybe next time." I shuck my briefs off fast, and my erection bobs in an unapologetic jut, happy to be free.

Gwen encloses my shaft in a firm grip. The pressure is ecstasy. Then, she gifts me with a long stroke, and I have to clutch the counter on either side of her hips to keep from sliding to the floor.

"Would you want to do more?" she asks. "I mean, have sex. Of course, we *did* just have sex. Or you sexed me with your mouth." Gwen lets go of my dick when she starts to babble. Her hands flutter, as if trying to catch the rapid-fire words from spilling out. But there's no stopping her when she's on a roll. "I don't want you to think that I think that oral isn't sex. I do. I mean, it's not like we have a bunch of virgin lesbians running around the world. Oh God, that makes it sound like I think lesbians run in packs. I don't. I'm sure there're plenty of lone lesbians out there. Oh no." Her face drops. "That sounds so sad."

And as Gwen sits on my brother's bathroom counter, completely naked, flushed from an orgasm and yet upset because she realized there are single lesbians in the world, I realize one undeniable fact.

I need Gwen Elsmere.

When did that happen?

Maybe it was years ago in Biology. Her dorky, endearing teenage self planted a seed in the back of my brain, and now, fed by time with the grown woman, that seed has burst forth in a wild, blooming vine of need that's twined around my brain. My body. My heart.

My entire being is a lush wall of ivy obsession for Gwen.

My mouth opens to tell her, to blurt that I want her to be mine.

Luckily, one thorn of logic keeps the declaration at bay.

Everyone still thinks I'm engaged to Elaine.

I can't ask Gwen to commit to me. Not now. Not when I'm in the slowest breakup in existence. It wouldn't be fair.

Besides, we kissed for the first time today. Even if Gwen wanted to be with me one day, I doubt that day is right now, when she'd be a secret.

So, instead of telling her, I lean in and claim what I can. Her mouth. Her little noises of pleasure.

And maybe …

"You're saying you want me inside you?" I ask, my voice rough with what she probably thinks is lust but is so much more.

"Yes. That. Sorry." She strokes her hands from my shoulders and up to my neck before plunging them into my hair.

Gwen likes my hair—take note.

"You don't need to apologize," I assure her as I leave off kissing long enough to search for a very important item.

This is Cameron's bathroom. He's got to have—

Second drawer down, I find the condoms.

Chapter Thirty-Two

GWEN

You have an emergency kit in your trunk, right? You need to be prepared, just in case.

— POSTCARD FROM RYAN, NORTH DAKOTA

Something about Sebastian holding up the foil packet makes this real.

Real in a really good way.

Real in a *I'm only now realizing I shaved my legs and am super happy about that fact* way.

He tears the condom open, and I watch as he rolls the latex down his length, fisting the root of himself when he's done.

The next thing going on that dick is me.

"Gwen?"

"Hmm?" I was so busy staring at his hands that I'm surprised to find his eyes on me when I look up.

"You want to take the lead on this?"

"Me?" I slap a hand on my chest, the flesh-against-flesh sound overly loud in the tiled room.

Sebastian nudges my palm to the side and leans in to kiss the handprint forming from the accidental slap.

"Yeah, you. Tell me what you like." He teases his lips across one of my nipples, sending flutters all through my body. "I want to know what gets you going."

"You do?" I ask without thought.

He straightens, giving me his goofy, medicinal smile, and I'm ready to melt backward in the sink, straight down the drain.

But then I would miss out on this next part, and I can't have that.

There's a beautiful little V at his hip bones, and I let that lovely letter be my guide, tracing my hands along the impressions, moving upward and around until I find the slopes of his ass.

"Like two firm stress balls," I murmur as I palm and squeeze the globes.

"Comparing me to office supplies? That's what gets you going?" The words are teasing, but Sebastian's voice is ragged, and his hips thrust gently with my kneading. Each little thrust bringing his cock closer.

I flex my arms, drawing him in, pressing him against my core. Heat against heat. I moan and bury my head in his neck, rocking my sensitive skin against his hardness. My sneaky hand finds a path between us, gripping him, guiding him.

Sebastian slides into my body with a grunt, the animalistic sound sending my pussy clenching around him. He mutters curses and praises, each one accompanied by a shallow thrust.

On the long strokes, he says my name.

I almost wish this weren't so good. That the pleasure didn't surpass my expectations. Where's the disappointment? The awkward angle that gives me a leg cramp and tones down my arousal?

If only he were a little bad at this, I could start convincing myself I won't miss this when it's over.

But, damn it, I will.

I'll miss the rough pads of his fingers dragging along the skin of my back, only to end in a powerful grasp at the base of my spine. I'll miss the way he holds me in place for each penetration. I'll miss the way one of those callous fingers seeks out my clit and circles and strokes and makes me moan and bite his neck and taste his sweat and—God, how will I ever survive—

"Come on, Gwen. Come for me, honey."

No, don't do that, I want to sob. *Don't make me feel all of this and call me sweet names and take it away. Oh God, I can't, I can't, I can't ...*

And still, I do. I come around him, pressing my cries into his skin to silence the raw emotions.

"That's it," he croons to me, one hand cradling the back of my head, the other pressing fingerprints into my thigh. "I-I'm there too," he gasps.

I'm the one grasping now, wrapping arms and legs and heart around him as he groans, settling deep inside me when he finishes.

What a horrible, amazing idea this was.

At least I've had practice with painful endings.

Chapter Thirty-Three

GWEN

Knock, knock. Who's there? Giant hail that dented my roof and cracked my windshield.

— POSTCARD FROM RYAN, OREGON

The closer we get to Green Valley, the quicker my sense of adventure dissipates. In Nashville, I was a different version of myself. Almost an imagined one.

I was Nashville Gwen. The woman who eats hot sauce that burns the roof off the top of her mouth, befriends drag queens, and sings karaoke in front of strangers.

Nashville Gwen fucks her lifelong crush on a bathroom counter. Twice. Then in a guest room bed a few more times.

Not to say that Green Valley Gwen is worse than Nashville Gwen. I like Green Valley Gwen.

I just wish she got to kiss every part of Sebastian Kirkwood too.

But Green Valley Sebastian is still engaged to another woman as far as everyone is concerned.

When the town sign appears around a bend in the road, Sebastian slows down and pulls off to the shoulder. Gravel grinds under the tires, and a cloud of dust rises up and settles as he quiets the engine.

His mouth sits in a tight line that looks wrong on his normally smiling face.

This is it. This is where Nashville Gwen disappears.

Where Nashville *us* gets tucked into a corner. To be remembered, but never revisited.

"These last few days have been amazing." He roughly finger-combs his loose hair out of his eyes. The gesture is almost cruel because *I* got to do that for one night, and now, I won't be able to again. "I don't want this to end." His words have my heart thudding a hopeful beat. "But I promised Elaine I'd give her time. That she could decide when we tell people."

No more hopeful thuds. Sebastian's words trickle over me like a bucket of mucky water dumped on my head. My understanding stains with the discomfort of truth.

A truth I should never let myself forget.

Their breakup is temporary.

I know that's not what Sebastian is saying or what he even believes in this moment. I'm sure, right now, he thinks they're done.

But I've spent enough of my life wistfully watching their relationship from afar to know that someday, maybe in a few weeks or a few months, they'll talk and smooth this rough patch out. They'll get back together.

Sebastian gave Elaine the power to decide the end date. He left that door wide open for her. And he's about to shut the door on us. He might not see it that way, but I can already predict his next words.

Maybe we could try when everyone knows. It won't be long, and then we can date.

But that time won't come. This brief break from his future is all we have. All *I* have.

And I want whatever small amount I can get while I can get it. The end of us will hurt, but I'll live through it. I've survived worse.

I'll be like Gran. Have a passionate affair, then move on to the next adventure.

My longing for Sebastian doesn't feel temporary now, but this will be a relief.

This can be perfect.

Knowing there's an end means I can prepare for it. Like taking a trip, I know I'll enjoy the time away, but I also know the vacation won't last forever. The adventure will still be worth every moment.

"I don't want to do this wrong," Sebastian says, unaware of the decision I'm solidifying.

From the concerned crease between his eyes, I know he's mulling over how to word the next piece he has to say. A suggestion to wait. He thinks there will be a future when he is not with Elaine and the whole world knows. And he thinks that'll be the time for us.

But if I wait for that time, it'll be like I'm back in high school at that Sadie Hawkins dance, waiting for sixteen-year-old Sebastian to finish another dance with Elaine, find me in my pink dress, and ask if I'll join him for a song.

But he danced with her for every one.

If I don't take my dance now, while Elaine is sitting out for a short break on the sidelines, I'll never get another chance.

"I can keep a secret," I announce.

Sebastian blinks at me, his lips parted in surprise. The expression has me wanting to lean over and kiss him. Since we're still outside of Green Valley and I'm still Nashville Gwen, I do. A quick snap of my seat belt, and I'm free. Plunging a hand into his hair, cradling the back of his skull, I draw him in and kiss the hell out of him, cataloging every curve of his lips, the way his hot breath puffs out in a surprised gasp just before he groans and kisses me back.

After a stretch of time, where we taste each other and steam up the windows, I finally break away enough to finish speaking, needing to sell him on my idea.

"I was going to keep the secret anyway. Of our trip." I drag my nails gently over his scalp and enjoy the way he shivers in response. "Easy to add something else to the list. I won't tell anyone that we were together." I swallow to get the bad taste of those words out of my mouth, refocusing on the musky, minty taste of his tongue that I was just sucking on. "And we can still be together right now. Just … carefully."

And that's all I'll ever ask from him. A brief vacation.

One with a return ticket. Him going back to Elaine and me going back to …

Being his friend.

Chapter Thirty-Four

SEBASTIAN

A part of me wonders if you'll even get this letter. A PO box? Where is this Green Valley? Is it a hidden gem in the heart of your country?

— LETTER TO MARIA

Gwen gazes at me with her lovely, wide eyes, and I can't imagine continuing with what I was about to say. A decent guy would. He would open his mouth and say the right thing. Tell her that when things are officially over and done with his ex, he'll ask her out on a proper date.

Not hide her away like a dirty secret.

Gwen doesn't deserve that.

I always thought I was a good guy.

But then I prove that notion false.

"If you're okay with that."

Her cheeks plump with a grin, and she scoops up one of my hands from the steering wheel and presses an excited kiss to my palm. "Definitely okay with it."

I swallow a few times and nod once or twice before I can get my brain functioning well enough to get the car out of park and back on the road. The panic that hit me when I saw the Green Valley sign ebbs. The force was so strong that I had to pull the car over and breathe and remind myself that leaving Nashville didn't mean leaving Gwen.

We're doing this. Whatever this is. Gwen and me. Me and Gwen.

I keep glancing her way, making sure she's where I left her. Not that she could get out of the moving car. If she was desperate enough, maybe.

We take a back road to my parents' house. A more direct route would have us driving straight through town. In view of all the Green Valley residents out and about. I ignore how this detour has my stomach churning.

And then Gwen starts fiddling with my free hand, and I find it easier to shove the guilt to a back corner of my mind, never to be explored if I can help it.

I'm a selfish bastard.

She kisses my palm again, and I pull off to the shoulder of the road, so I can steal a taste of her lips. A stroke of her tongue. A few minutes later, we're panting, and I'm cursing the fact that I can't just pull her into the backseat.

But then I'm driving, parking my car in my parents' garage, pulling her upstairs to my loft.

When we get in the door, things slow down. Mainly because Curie starts twining through our legs and threatens to trip us if we don't pay attention to where we're walking.

"Let me feed her real quick."

"Okay." Gwen gives me a kiss on the cheek before strolling across the room and sitting down on my bed. "No hurry. I'm not going anywhere."

For a moment, I stare at her. She's exactly where I've wanted her for weeks. My bed.

Curie lets out a wail that says, *Feed me this minute, or I will die.*

"Yeah, okay. Such a needy little chemist," I mutter, giving up the view of Gwen on my mattress as I scoop out dry food and refill the kitten's water bowl.

My hands washed and cat happy, I make my way across the room.

Gwen bounces in place, her movements nervous. And I get that. On our trip, we hooked up late in the evening, high on Nashville nightlife. Now, we're Green Valley sober in the middle of the afternoon.

But if anything, I want her more.

"How're you doin'?" I ask as I settle beside her, keeping my hands to myself for the time being.

"I feel like there's a bunch of birds flapping around in my stomach." She grins and blushes at the same time, owning her embarrassment. "Sorry. That's not sexy."

"False." I lean over, cupping her jaw with my hand, tilting her just right for a kiss, like she taught me at brunch. "Everything you do is sexy." I pause with only a breath between our lips. "Tell me to stop."

"Don't stop," she whispers back.

I swallow her gasp, pulling her torso flush against mine, and then I fall back on the bed and draw Gwen's body across mine until she drapes over me like the sexiest blanket ever quilted.

She pops her head up, eyes hazy with my kisses, staring down at me. "Did you just call me a sexy blanket?"

"I said that out loud?" My head drops back as I grimace. "My dirty talk leaves a lot to be desired."

Gwen giggles and climbs higher on me until she's sitting with her thighs straddling my hips. And, fuck, if this isn't the best view.

"We can work on it," she announces.

Then, she whips her shirt off, revealing a blue cotton bra that cups her boobs to perfection. The sight has me groaning, and next thing I know, I've tugged one cup down, and I have my tongue dragging over her nipple.

"Oh God!" she yelps, digging fingers into my hair, holding me to her chest, encouraging every lick with a rock of her hips.

My jeans get too tight as I harden under her.

"Too many clothes," I mutter against the soft skin at the valley of her breasts.

"Then, take them off," Gwen suggests.

I don't need a further invitation. As much as I hate setting her to the side, I have to, so I can rip off my shirt, pants, and briefs, tossing them across the room as if each piece offended me. Then, I turn on Gwen, who has a look of shocked wonder after watching my speed stripping.

"So, that's how Brooke switched outfits so fast," she says.

With a playful growl, I tackle Gwen onto the mattress, looming over her as she smiles up at me, one boob out, shorts still covering her bottom half. "I love my brother, but please don't talk about him when I'm trying to get us both naked."

"Sorry." She doesn't sound remorseful, snickering as I pretend to glare at her. "Think you can get my clothes off that fast?"

"Faster." Then, an idea pops into my mind, and I give her a mischievous grin. She's not the only one who can tease. "But I think I need to use a different technique with you."

"Huh?" She gets the wordless question out just before I flip her onto her stomach and gather her wrists with one hand, pinning them to the bed above her head.

"I think I want to go slow again," I announce.

Gwen lets out a groan. "Why did I say that? I never should have. I was lying. I do that a lot, you know. I'm a dirty liar who lies!"

She squirms, and I'm fascinated by her hips undulating on the bed.

"You're definitely dirty." With my free hand, I unclasp her bra and kiss the slightly indented skin where the elastic gripped. Then, I move to her shorts, sliding a hand between her belly and the mattress to undo the button and fly. I'm impressed with myself that I'm able to get all of her clothes off one-handed.

Gwen gasps through the process but doesn't try to escape my hold anymore.

Naked.

We're both naked in my bed, and my hard cock is begging to plunge into her pussy. But Gwen isn't a fast fuck. At least, not right now. I'll throw a few of those in. Slow sex, fast sex, moderately timed sex. Every position, every place. Morning, afternoon, night.

Gwen is everything.

Still keeping ahold of her wrists, I let my other fingers play in her wetness. She coats my skin with her arousal. Gwen whimpers when I slip my thumb inside her and stroke her clit with my pointer and middle finger, one on either side of the bundle of nerves. Curling my thumb, I search out that special spot. The one that'll make her—

"Oh my God!" Gwen's body goes tense, trying to curl inward. "Oh …"

"That's it." I stroke inside and outside in measured motions, memorizing the position of my hand and the pitch of her cries. "Want me to stop?"

"No," Gwen sobs, her slickness gathering in my palm until, suddenly, she's pulsing around my touch. Finding pleasure while completely at my mercy.

And her orgasm is so hot that I'm a second from turning into an animal and rutting into her.

Condoms. I need to find a condom.

I stole a box from my brother, but I left it in my bag, which is in my car downstairs.

"Gwen?"

She makes an inarticulate noise that has me chuckling and leaning down to kiss her shoulder.

"Honey?" As I slip my fingers from her, she lets out a sound of protest, which has me grinning wider and eager to complete my errand. "I need you to stay right here. Exactly like this. Can you do that for me?"

She mumbles something that sounds like, *Wheryagoin?*

"Condoms are in the car. I'll be right back."

Even though I hate leaving her in such a delectable state, I'm positive I can do this in less than a minute. With the right motivation, I'm fast as hell.

I don't bother with pants since the stairs are interior. I jog down the old steps, my cock bobbing along, wondering why the hell I'm moving away from the tempting woman.

"Just a minute," I mutter to it, pushing through the door to the garage and leaping toward the trunk of my car. Just when I have the zipper of my duffel bag pulled open, I hear a door open.

The outer door.

Oh no.

"Look who's home," Kennedy's voice rings through the space, and I freeze. "Sebastian?"

I hear her footsteps coming toward the trunk, where I'm bare as a newborn babe.

With a quick jump to the side, I maneuver the SUV between us, meeting my sister's eyes over the roof, cupping my junk, and hoping she can't see anything damning through the windows.

"Hey! Look, can I get a moment? Meet you at the house? It's been a long drive, but I'll tell you all about it in"—*Is Gwen still waiting for me? Can we finish what we started?*—"a half hour?"

Kennedy stares at me, squinting her eyes. She can always tell when I'm hiding something. My bad poker face betraying me once more. Her focus drops to my bare chest, the top of which she can clearly see. Sometimes, it sucks to be so tall.

"Are you just shirtless over there? Or are you in this garage, butt ass naked?"

I try not to growl in impatience. "Which one will get you to leave faster?"

That was the wrong thing to say.

She crosses her arms over her chest, scowling. "Is that any way to thank the sister who's been taking care of your cat all weekend?"

"Sorry. Thank you so much. You're the best. Now, *please* go away."

Kennedy does not leave. Instead, she peers at Gwen's SUV, which sits just over my shoulder. "Whose car is that? I've been walking past it, thinking, *Looks like Sebastian got himself some new wheels.* But then I thought, *If this is Sebastian's, how'd he get himself to Nashville? Did he take a bus?* But, no, you drove in your old car." She pats the hood of the only thing keeping me from flashing her. "So, whose car is that?" And because my sister is a smart lady, it takes her no time at all to put the naked puzzle pieces together. "Do you have a *girl* upstairs?"

"A woman," I correct, then cringe because I've ratted myself out.

Kennedy's mouth drops open. "You're *dating* someone? How? When? Who is it?" And I watch her stare harder at the Bronco, trying to place the owner.

And here's a major problem: what am I going to say to my family?

I hate that it's even a question. This is the exact issue with Elaine and her family. She's not being honest about what her relationship status is.

I'll tell them the truth. I decide I'll tell them I'm seeing someone. But that doesn't mean I want to parade Gwen past them every time she wants to come over.

"Yes, I'm dating someone. But until Elaine tells her parents about the breakup, we're going to keep things quiet, okay? Now, will you go away?"

Kennedy leaves off her detective work, moving back to studying me. "You *are* naked, aren't you? Gross. Fine, I'll leave, but only so I don't get scarred by seeing way more of you than any sister should."

She steps toward the door, and I sigh in relief. Too soon though because she turns back.

"This woman, whoever she is, you like her?"

Again, a conversation I'd rather be dressed for. "Yeah. I … a lot. I like her a lot."

"And she makes you happy?"

"Happier than I've been in a while."

That earns me a smile, and I feel a little bad for rushing her off. But not too bad.

"If you don't introduce me soon, I'm going to make it my mission to find out who she is on my own—fair warning," Kennedy calls over her shoulder as she leaves, reminding me a lot of our brother in the moment.

My siblings both enjoy giving threats.

When I get up to my room, condoms in hand but dick no longer hard, I find that Gwen has rolled herself up in a quilt and my cartoon train sheets and passed out. Curie is curled up next to her, kneading the blanket and purring.

"Yeah, yeah. Happy to see you too," I mutter to the cat as I carefully climb into the twin bed behind Gwen and pull the postwoman into my body, making her my little spoon.

I need to get my own place and a bigger bed.

Chapter Thirty-Five

GWEN

Had a drink at a bar, and there was a guy singing. Surprisingly good. Made me miss the Jam Sessions. I'll have to swing through town on a Friday.

— POSTCARD FROM RYAN, WEST VIRGINIA

"How was your trip?"

Arthur's question has me choking on my beer. Some of the carbonated liquid comes out of my nose, thoroughly burning my sinuses.

Arthur and Lance stare at me from across the campfire, the former's eyebrows dipping low, the latter's gaze assessing if I'm going to need some kind of rescue.

Can you even Heimlich someone who's choking on liquid?

Sebastian would know. Sebastian is also the reason I'm drowning in an IPA right now.

Because I promised I would keep what we're doing a secret, but I've never been great at lying, so how do I tell my friends about my trip without also revealing I was there with a sexy paramedic who everyone thinks is engaged?

"Good," I gasp once I can breathe again.

Smooth.

"You okay?" Lance asks, still looking ready to save me if I need it.

"Yep. Just"—I clear my throat again—"took too big of a sip. Went down the wrong pipe."

He nods, face clearing, and goes back to tuning his fiddle.

I remember when Mrs. Holloway first told me her son could play. I begged Lance for weeks to hear him, but he always refused. Then, one Thursday, Arthur invited the two of us over to his house after work for happy hour. When we showed up, he had a fire going, a cooler full of beer, his guitar, and a fiddle that turned out to be Lance's, which his mom had dropped off, saying she didn't want him to forget it for his playdate. My coworker's face went redder than his hair, but after a beer, he chilled out, and the two men started playing together.

I—who never progressed past the recorder in elementary school—am happy to be their audience and master of the fire.

"What all'd ya do?" Arthur's query sounds casual, and he settles his guitar in his lap as opposed to watching me with a suspicious glare.

Apparently, I'm the topic of conversation tonight in addition to being the fire master.

"Oh, um, I went places." *Could I sound any more like I'm lying?* "Like the wax museum." *With Sebastian.* "And to see a live bluegrass band." *With Sebastian.* "Oh, and a drag show." *MC'd by Sebastian's brother.*

Both men look to me then, faces curious.

"How was that?" Lance asks.

"Amazing," I gush but also pay very close attention to how much I share. Even if Sebastian and I weren't a secret thing, he asked that I not tell anyone about Cameron's second job. "I mean, the makeup alone was spectacular. But every drag queen was gorgeous and so talented. You'd think lip-syncing wouldn't be too impressive, but they take it to another level. I went two nights in a row, and I'd go back again."

Lance wears a half-smile, and Arthur nods.

"I went to a drag brunch," he offers.

Lance and I share a wide-eyed, *Seriously?*

"You did?" I ask.

"Yeah." Arthur strums a chord. "In Atlanta." Another chord. "Was fun." Another chord. "Good food."

A chuckle sneaks out as I imagine the big man eating bacon and eggs while a drag queen struts around his table.

I wonder if Cameron does drag brunch.

Before they can ask me any more questions, the post office's most recent hire appears around the side of the house. Morgan strolls up to our circle and offers a casual wave. The firelight plays off her red hair, the color a shade or two darker than Lance's. She has it gathered in a messy bun on top of her head, exposing a pale neck, made darker by intricate tattoos. She's *covered* in designs. Seriously, I think only her face and the palms of her hands are free of ink.

"Hi!" I greet her, exuding excited energy while Arthur and Lance opt for stoic nods.

"Hey." Morgan settles her long limbs in a folding chair and accepts the beer Arthur passes her way.

Morgan moved to town not long ago, and word is, she came to help her pregnant sister take care of the soon-to-be-arriving baby while the father is deployed. The rest of the postwoman's life is a mystery. I'd love to learn more, but Morgan is as quiet as my other two coworkers. Like everyone at the post office decided to take a class on how to be aloof and forgot to invite me.

Conversation doesn't pick back up, partly because three-quarters of the group isn't chatty, but mainly because the guys start playing. After Lance's mom basically forced him to show off his skills for us, the experience must have broken through whatever had him hesitating. Now, the two men often play together at the Friday night Jam Session at the community center.

As I enjoy the mini concert, my mind meanders, thoughts wandering toward Sebastian. He's at work right now, and I imagine him lounging at the station or maybe out on a call, saving someone's life. Before coming over here, I stopped in to say hi to Curie. I wish I were going back to his place after happy hour. Then, I could be waiting in bed when he got done with his shift, and he could tell me about it and then kiss me deep and peel off my clothes and—

One of the logs cracks, shooting off sparks that don't leave the stone circle but startle me nonetheless. Enough to pull me away from my erotic thoughts that I'm not sure if I should feel guilty about or not.

Elaine is not gone from the picture, I remind myself. *This is like a separation more than anything.* I need to keep acknowledging the inevitable end, so I don't build this thing too big in my mind.

Arthur grunts and nods his head, and for a moment, I'm worried I spoke aloud and he's agreeing with me. But then I realize he just liked something Lance played and was showing his appreciation.

Why can't I have an inescapable crush on one of them?

Arthur and Lance are both handsome, unattached men. But when I stare at their faces, try to force my heart to beat faster, all I can think is how they remind me of my brother. How I enjoy their friendship but don't ache for more.

Not like with Sebastian.

Stop it! You can't compare every man in the world to him.

I need to be more like Gran. Have this brief, passionate affair, then explore more of the world. Things between Sebastian and I will end, but since I know the ending, the pain won't be as bad. I'll properly brace for it, then move on.

This won't be like high school when I built his flirting up to more than it was and got crushed by him choosing Elaine.

And it definitely won't be like losing my grandmother after I hoped so hard for her to survive.

You know it's coming. You can bear it.

For the next hour, I practice. As my friends play, I sip my beer and envision the future, where Sebastian and Elaine are living in a house together—hopefully one I don't deliver mail to—and I'm taking my days off to drive or fly far from Green Valley. I'll reach out to some of Gran's old friends, make memories with strangers in different cities.

And maybe I'll meet someone handsome and sweet who makes me laugh, and I'll have a fling, and I won't think of silky hair between my fingers and rough whispers about going slow.

It'll hurt. But I'll be fine.

"Getting close to my bedtime," Arthur announces soon after I throw the last piece of wood on the fire, which is his nice way of saying, *Thanks for coming; get the hell out.*

Lance and I share a smirk. Our coworker is notorious for his inflexible sleep schedule. The man is not a night owl. His rowdy crowd of cousins often stay at Genie's until closing time, but Arthur will head home at nine thirty to make sure he's in bed by ten.

They've tried to bribe, threaten, and trick him, but he always barges his way out of it. His cousin Daren once sneakily stole his phone, then paid the bartender to turn all the clocks in the bar back an hour.

Still, Arthur found out and left in a huff at nine fifty-five, going full grumpy bear. There's no fooling him.

After tossing our empty cans in the cooler and banking the fire, Arthur walks with us around to the front of his house, where we parked.

When Lance and Morgan climb into their respective cars, Arthur stops me with a touch on my elbow. "Hold up."

I face him, curious.

Arthur's beard bunches, as if he's trying to force away a frown. "You okay?"

"Of course." The squeaky pitch of my voice gives me away, obvious by the dramatic dip in his brows.

"You were quiet."

"So were you and Lance and Morgan," I point out while trying not to fidget with my car keys.

"We're always quiet. You chat most times. Not tonight though."

When did he get so observant?

I seesaw about what to say, not wanting to worry him, but unable to break my promise. Also, I have a strong urge to talk to someone about the turmoil in my head and chest.

"Did it ever hurt?" I blurt, and when his eyes widen, I hurry to clarify. "When you traveled and you left a place. I mean, you visited so many. So, maybe not. But I'm just … you can't vacation forever, you know? You've got to return to the real world."

"And the return hurts," he says, not like a question. Arthur plants his fists on his hips and stares into the distance at a random stand of trees, taking a few seconds before he answers. "Traveling was my norm for a few years. It *was* the real world. Then, I went to India. Visited my mom's family." He clears his throat, and I wonder if it's because this topic makes him emotional or if he's just not used to speaking so many words in a row. "That hurt to leave."

"Why didn't you stay?" My voice is hushed.

He shrugs. "They wanted me to. But as amazing as it was, it wasn't home. Not like Green Valley."

"How did you deal with the pain?"

His smile is small. "Remembered I could always go back. And I realized leaving here permanently would have hurt a whole lot worse. This town has always felt like home."

If I was hoping he'd solve my problem for me, he hasn't.

What if the vacation feels like home?

Chapter Thirty-Six

GWEN

I found the best burger. I don't know what magic they used, but my mouth was in heaven. I ate five. Do I share this knowledge with the world? Or keep the glorious secret to myself?

— POSTCARD FROM RYAN, MAINE

"Do you like it?" Sebastian stands in the small front hall of the house he's decided to rent.

I wondered why he'd texted me the address of a house that barely ever gets mail. And, yes, I have a good idea of the quantities of mail every home on my route gets. That's what happens when you drive to them almost every day for years.

"It's cute."

A little outdated maybe, but the place has charm. The hardwood floor is only slightly scuffed up, and the walls have a new coat of cheery yellow paint.

Will he paint a room pink?

"So, that's a yes?"

LAUREN CONNOLLY

Sebastian steps in close, pressing his chest against my back and settling his hands on my hips. I shiver at the contact, then grin as he rotates us both, as if we were standing on a display platform.

"Take it all in. Don't be shy."

"Yes, fine. I like it a whole bunch. So, you're really renting this place? No more bachelor apartment above your parents' garage?"

You're really renting a place without Elaine? Not about to move back to Merryville with her?

"You'd better believe it." There's a warm puff of breath against my neck, then the soft touch of his lips as he kisses the juncture of my neck and shoulder. "And you, my sexy mailwoman, need to get ready for some sleepovers."

The flamingos in my stomach are sipping mimosas and toasting each other at the thought.

I love the idea of spending an entire night wrapped up in Sebastian, just like in Nashville.

Well, maybe not *just* like. We weren't sneaking around on vacation. But I don't let that fact ruin my excitement.

"Sleepovers? So, pillow fights and movie marathons?" I suck in my lips to keep from groaning as he nips my skin.

"Sure. As long as you're not wearing anything during the pillow fights and I'm licking your sweet pussy the entire length of the movie."

"Oh my God!"

He laughs at my gasp and wraps his arms around my waist from behind, lifting my feet off the ground and carrying me to the empty kitchen. When he sets me down, my hips press against the tan counter, and Sebastian presses against my back.

"That's the bedroom." He waves toward an open door, showing an empty room. "Since I don't have any furniture, this'll have to do for now."

"Wha—" A gasp cuts off my question as he reaches around to unbutton my shorts and tugs them and my underwear down, exposing me below the waist. "Sebastian!"

He pauses. "Do you want me to stop?"

"I—" *Never.* I just need a moment to confirm this isn't an early morning fantasy, where I'm half-asleep and imagining perfection. "No. Touch me."

"Good." There's a growl in his voice, and he presses my palms to the counter. "Stay like this. Don't move. Okay?"

"Okay." The word quivers, and I wonder if I might cry from wanting this so much.

Who knew the class clown would become the gruff commander during sex?

Who knew I'd like it so much?

Sebastian presses his body against my back, holding me to him with an arm across my waist. His breathing, the expanding of his rib cage, rocks me, and a hardening ridge against my ass demands attention. But for a stretch, all he does is hold me, our bodies fitting together as he traces kisses up and down my neck.

Then, his free hand cups between my legs in a possessive gesture.

"Okay?" he asks again, low and rough against my ear.

"Okay," I breathe out.

Another small bite, telling me my answer was the right one and he's proud of me. Then, callous fingers comb through my intimate curls, spread my folds, and stroke in my wetness.

"Oh—okay," I gasp the words as my nails scrape the laminate. "You really like counters, huh?"

Sebastian makes a happy humming sound in the back of his throat, still playing with me as his body envelops mine. As a tall woman, being held by Sebastian provides me with the elusive sensation of feeling small. Feeling precious. As if he could break me, but would never want to. Instead, he'd break anyone who tried to harm me.

Any other time, my inner independent woman would scoff at the notion that I want a man to protect me. But now? In this sensual moment? It's the hottest thing I can think of.

Then, a thick finger slips into me the same time his thumb presses firmly against my clit. My hips jerk forward, slamming against the counter, and I might be bruised tomorrow, but I don't care.

I hope I am.

"I like you pressed against a counter," he murmurs, sliding his touch in and out of me. "You like it too. Don't you?"

I manage a strangled noise of assent.

"Do you want more?"

More could mean anything, and that's what has me nodding like a broken bobblehead. Whatever his definition, I want it.

Then, his hands and body are gone, and I'm reconsidering my decision.

"Sebastian," I whimper, desperate for the heat of him and his touch.

"Wait for me, Gwen."

And that's when I hear the zipper. A quick glance over my shoulder shows Sebastian with a condom in his hand and his fly undone. Fascinated, I watch him pull out his hard dick, that part of him ruddy, as if blushing. He tears the foil open, pinching the tip and sliding it on. When he tilts his head up, burning eyes meet mine.

Somehow, I'm able to hold his stare while also spying his one hand circling the base and the other cupping his balls. I swallow hard, wanting my hands where his are.

"Want me to stop?"

And in the curious tilt of his brow, I see the playful side of this man mix with his aroused one. A part of me wants to tease back, but I'm also aching for his touch everywhere.

"Don't stop."

And I turn away from him, knowing Sebastian. That if he has an audience, he'll drive them wild with his teasing. If I keep my eyes on him, he'll stretch this out until I'm a needy puddle on the ground. But I want his touch *now*.

When hands grasp my hips, I smile, pleased with how I'm figuring him out. Or remembering what I already knew.

Then, all coherent thought melts out of my ears when he drags a hand under my shirt up to my chest, the other going back to my clit. There's the wall of his chest against my back and the erotic invasion of his cock finding my slick opening.

He takes me hard from behind, fucking me against the counter in his new home. I hope he thinks of this every time he's in here. One second, he'll be frying an egg at the stove, and the next, he'll see the ghost of me reaching back to tangle my hands in his hair for something to hold on to as his hips thrust. The slap of our thighs colliding is officially at the top of the list for sexiest noises I've heard. Turned away from him like I am, sound and touch are all I have in this moment.

His breath—deep, tinged with groans—caressing my ear. The slick rhythm of him entering me. My gasps and begging. The full pressure inside me mixing with the hot, wet drag of his mouth on my skin and the pinch of his fingers finding my nipple.

But it's his index finger more than everything else, insistent and firm against my clitoris.

Did his paramedic training cover this part of the female anatomy?

Is there a medical emergency requiring rescue orgasms?

Oh, look, here it is.

"I'm going to die if I don't come," I whimper to the peeling white paint of his kitchen cabinets.

"Don't worry." Sebastian nips my neck and stays buried inside me as his fingers put in the work. "I'll save you."

And he does. Or maybe he doesn't, and I die, and this pulsing cloud of pleasure that envelops my mind is heaven.

This is why people go to church, isn't it?

As the haze of ecstasy dissipates, there's a rumbling against my back, and I take a while to realize it's laughter.

"What's so funny?" I mumble, still working through my post-orgasm bliss.

"You just compared sex with me to church, and I have no idea how to take that."
He chuckles while he talks, still hard inside me.

And, wow, does that feel good.

"A compliment," I gasp, then moan as he starts thrusting again.

My arms are spaghetti soft, and I sink to my elbows, eliciting a curse from
Sebastian. His heavy palm spreads wide on my back, holding me in place.

As he chases his own release, I can't help smiling at his muttered words.
There're lots of curses mixed with endearments. Apparently, I'm gorgeous and
delicious, and he can't get enough of me.

That's what a woman likes to hear.

Then, he has his hands between my legs again, playing my body like I'm a banjo
at the Jam Session.

"Come on, honey. I need you here with me."

I bite on my lip to keep a vulnerable sound inside me at his words. They're too
perfect. Too much like a dream for me to believe them. But my body takes them
anyway, and as I come again, his movements lose their steady pace. He thrusts
fast and hard and groans deep in his chest before draping his body over mine.

The weight of him bears down on me, but I like it. I crave it.

And for a moment, I believe it means he'll always want me here.

Chapter Thirty-Seven

SEBASTIAN

When I read your last letter, I could not believe the words. I wish I could take away every bit of your pain.

— LETTER TO MARIA

Being a paramedic in Green Valley was supposed to be better. Small-town problems.

But I should've known a town with a drug-dealing biker gang could never be some pristine haven where nothing big goes wrong. We had a call today. Patient unresponsive. He was well on his way to being gone by the time we got there. I lost him halfway to the hospital.

Overdose.

He didn't look anything like the man I'd failed before. But the way his face went slack, eyes half-open, chest still …

I can't stop thinking about it. Can't stop overlaying their face.

Where did I go wrong?

That question pricks at me, sharp and unrelenting for the rest of my shift until my brain is a tender, jittery mess.

I'm tired. So goddamn tired.

I don't register driving home from the station. Suddenly, I'm in my parents' driveway. And then I remember I don't live here anymore, and I have to back out and drive to my rental.

As I'm unlocking the front door, my phone vibrates in my back pocket. Hoping to see Gwen's name, I reach for it.

Elaine.

I shut the door and lean against the wood. This day has been long. All I want to do is shower and zone out in front of the TV with Curie in my lap.

Maybe she's calling to tell me she's ready for it to be over. Officially.

That's the only thing that gets me to answer the call.

"Hey." The greeting comes out flatter than I intended, and I try to inject my normal positivity into my tone. "What's up?"

"Hi." Elaine has her terse voice going, which doesn't bode well. "Are you busy? Can you talk for a minute?"

Talk as in lay out the game plan for us going public with our breakup? I have all the minutes in the world for that.

"Yeah. I just got home from work." I toss my bag into the corner of the hallway to be dealt with later, then head to the kitchen, finding Curie lounging on the windowsill above the sink. She likes watching the squirrels that climb the tree just outside the glass. "Talk away."

"Okay. Good." A hesitation. "So, here's the thing ..."

Oh no. Not the thing.

That's Elaine's go-to phrasing whenever she tells me something she knows I won't like.

So, here's the thing. They discontinued your favorite cereal brand.

So, here's the thing. I found a great rental, but it doesn't allow pets. Let's hold off on adopting that cat.

So, here's the thing. We don't have enough time off for a vacation with your family and for the wedding.

So, here's the thing ...

"My parents want to have a dinner. A memorial dinner."

She doesn't have to speak the question for me to know what she's asking. Annoyance condenses in my chest, then melts quickly into guilt.

"You know I'm always here for you, Elaine."

I can hear the relieved smile in her sigh through the speaker, which has me tensing for the next part.

"I'm here for you as a *friend*," I clarify. "Do your parents know that yet?"

Silence.

I pace around my kitchen, all exhaustion gone. Instead, my pulse picks up, as if I were in the middle of a sprint.

"This isn't a good time to tell them," she says.

You've had months, I want to press. *When is a good time? When they're sitting at a church, waiting for our wedding to happen, but no one shows up?*

Still, I don't say that because I know Elaine, and I can hear the weak quiver in her voice. Elaine does not show vulnerability if she can help it. This isn't just a bad time for her parents. It's a bad time for her. The anniversary coming up guts her every year.

What will piling the pain of our breakup on top of that annual misery do to her?

Will it be too much for her to handle?

Will she do something drastic to escape the hurt?

"Okay. What are the details of the dinner?"

She rattles off the time—next week—and place—her childhood home. She tells me it's okay if we arrive separately—we have the excuse of work. No reason for them to wonder.

That's the problem with Elaine's parents. They love their daughter, but they also love the idea they have of her, which makes it hard for them to see when something is not exactly what they expect it to be.

When we hang up, I try to breathe but find the act difficult. My throat's tight. So is my chest. And my heart is doing that fast-paced battering that feels like a fist is squeezing it over and over.

"Fuck," I gasp, trying to blink, trying to focus, but the room is blurry.

As my back hits the counter, I wonder if I need glasses. Then, I wonder if I need to be hooked up to oxygen because my lungs are malfunctioning. My whole body screams at me to do something, but I don't know what, so I slide to the floor and grasp at the vinyl tiles as I try to breathe.

Breathe.

I can't. I can't. I can't.

Just breathe.

I can't ... I can't ... I can't ...

The panic and suffocation stretch on and on until I'm sure I'm going to die.

But I don't.

Eventually, my heart stops trying to batter its way out of my rib cage. I realize my lungs have been gasping in full breaths this entire time. My eyesight loses the fog that obscured the world.

Panic attack, I tell myself. Remind myself.

First full-blown one since moving back to Green Valley.

I stare at the wall for a long time, tracing the floral pattern on the old wallpaper. There's a set of vines that extends from a chair rail all the way to the wooden molding. My eyes work up and down the printed plant in a broken-record rhythm. Slow and pointless.

Small pricks through my pants jerk me out of the stupor, and I glance down to find Curie using me as a scratching post.

"Stop that," I murmur, carefully detaching her claws before scooping her up and holding her close to my chest. Some of her hair sticks to my sweaty palms when I set her back on the kitchen windowsill.

Like a robot, I work through my evening routine—pouring her food, refilling her water bowl, cleaning her litter box. When I make it to my bedroom, I strip off my sweat-drenched clothes and step into a cold shower, barely noticing the temperature when every part of me aches.

When I get out, I forget if I shampooed. Doesn't seem to matter. I stand in the middle of my bedroom for a time, trying to remember what I was doing.

Getting dressed.

There's a laundry basket on the foot of my bed, conveniently containing a shirt and sweatpants. Good. Searching through my drawers seems like too much work.

When I'm dressed, I find my way back to the kitchen, intending to make myself dinner, only to find myself standing in the middle of the room, the idea of opening the fridge too daunting.

I grab my phone and lie on my couch, flicking on the TV.

I'll get takeout.

But I can't think of any places that deliver.

There's got to be something. I could look it up.

But that's too much work too.

I'll get food later. When I'm really hungry.

And when my jaw isn't sore from clenching my teeth for so long.

I'm on my second episode of a drag-queen reality show when my phone buzzes.

If it's Elaine, I'm not picking up.

Even the idea has me flinching, as if she'll start up another episode. I can't do anything more for her. Not tonight.

But the name on the phone is the one I hoped to see earlier.

"Hey." My greeting comes out on a rasp, like I've taken up smoking. I realize I'm thirsty, but the water is all the way in the kitchen.

"Hey! I just finished shooting a video, and I have fire on my face. Wanna see?"

"Yes, please."

My phone pings with a new text message, and I open it to see Gwen's gorgeous face with skillfully drawn flames seeming to erupt from her eyes. She's so talented.

"Very cool." The words are true. The sentiment is true. My voice is flatter than farmland.

"I thought so."

I can hear the hesitation in her voice, and some part of my brain knows I should have a more upbeat response, but I struggle to manage the energy it takes to hold my phone to my ear.

"Are you okay?" she asks. "You sound off. Not that you have to be excited about my fire face makeup, but I'm just wondering."

My initial urge is to reply with a monotone, *I'm fine*. But I don't want to lie to Gwen. "I'm not feeling great."

"Do you have a fever? Or are you just worn out?"

As worn as a wet, old dishcloth, wrung too many times. "Door number two."

"Hard day at work? Never mind. If it wiped you out, no need to go into it. Are you heading to bed?"

Bed. The piece of furniture seems so far away. The only thing that would tempt me to heave myself up and stumble to it would be if I knew I'd find Gwen there. God, I want her here.

"I'm watching TV." I should stop there. "Want to join?"

Part of my mind reminds me I don't normally seek people out after a panic attack. I wait until all traces are gone from my face and my voice and my body. I wait until I'm the me that everyone enjoys being around.

Not this raw, exhausted shell of myself.

But for some reason, I want Gwen here, no matter what I look or sound like. I need her close.

"Of course! Have you eaten? I could grab some burgers for us from Daisy's."

"Burgers sound good." *As long as you're the one carrying them.*

"Great. I'll bring food, we'll watch TV, and if you pass out within five minutes of me getting there, I won't be offended in the least, okay?"

My throat gets tight again, but this time not with anxiety.

"Okay," I manage.

Chapter Thirty-Eight

GWEN

I stopped at the Grand Canyon today. It's the most beautiful hole in the ground I've ever seen.

— POSTCARD FROM RYAN, ARIZONA

Sebastian smiles when he greets me at the door, but there's a droop to his eyelids that gives me the sense he's only half-awake. I don't push him to talk to me. His exhaustion was clear on the phone and is even more pronounced in person. Even his hair looks tired, dangling around his face.

I'd be surprised if he stays awake five more minutes.

"Whatcha watching?" I ask as I set the bags of food on his coffee table and glance at the TV. The first things I spot are brightly colored wigs and outrageously creative makeup. "Oh! Perfect."

I want to ask if Sebastian watches reality drag shows because he misses his brother. But that question can wait for another time. After he sinks onto the couch, I open the Styrofoam container with his burger and set it in his lap before going to the kitchen to look for ketchup in the fridge. Returning to his side, I pass him the bottle and dig into my own food.

And for the next hour, we watch trashy TV together.

Sebastian manages to stay awake and musters enough energy to laugh at the funny parts of the show. The evening might not scream brief, passionate fling, but I enjoy every second. Knowing he wanted me here even if he wasn't up for talking or sex is all I need from him.

When our food containers are empty, I lie back against the armrest, settle a pillow against my chest, and pat the cushy square. "Lie down. Head here. It's okay if you fall asleep."

He follows my directions as if that's all he can do—obey orders.

Seeing such a vibrant person so out of it is both disconcerting and fascinating. Like I've peeled back a layer to discover a lesser known version of the man.

Sebastian is too tall for his couch, his legs dangling over the other end. But he lets out a sigh that sounds content when he rests his weight on me. I enjoy the press of his body, anchoring me to the couch. As we keep watching the show, I leisurely comb my fingers through his silky tresses, letting my nails drag along his scalp every so often.

Sebastian snuggles deeper into the cradle of my body, and I try not to let myself fall in love with this simple moment.

"There was a teenager," he says, the comment abrupt, as if wrenched from his throat without his permission. "He OD'd. We weren't able to save him." Sebastian says the most words he has since my arrival, and the stark list of events hurts my heart.

How much death has Sebastian seen?

This man—always the goofy, positive life of the party—has to deal with the darkest parts of life more than most.

How many people has he tried to save but couldn't?

"That's horrible. I'm sorry you had to go through that." I don't know what else to say. If there are any words that could help or comfort.

If only I were some kind of crime-fighting superhero who could eradicate the Iron Wraiths, who no doubt distributed the drugs to that misguided kid. But I'm an ordinary postal worker. My heroic acts are going to have to be the smaller ones. Like comforting the man who does his best to save the sick and injured in Green Valley.

"Thank you for coming," he says after another quiet stretch.

"I'll stay as long as you need me." *Even longer if you let me.*

Don't go down that road.

Sebastian reaches up, taking hold of my hand that's been fiddling with the ends of his hair. He pulls my palm to his face, pressing my skin against his cheek.

Suddenly, I realize my danger. There were so many warning signs I blatantly ignored because I wanted moments like this. I longed for intimacy with Sebastian despite knowing there was no avoiding an obvious conclusion.

I'm in love with Sebastian Kirkwood.

Chapter Thirty-Nine

GWEN

When taking a bathroom break in the desert, check for snakes.

— POSTCARD FROM RYAN, NEW MEXICO

Donner Bakery is crowded, but I don't mind waiting in line. Today, I've decided to treat myself to something decadent. A decision I seem to be making in a lot of areas of my life.

Ignore long-term consequences. Be happy in the moment. Deal with disappointment later.

Enjoying Sebastian is an easy thing to do. Even when he was in a bad space a few days ago and all I did was hold him. Being there for him, supporting him, made me happy. Not a bubbly *vibrating out of my skin* kind of happy. But a muted *this is exactly where I should be* happy.

Then, there was the middle of the night, when he woke me up with kisses on the back of my neck, hot hand on my belly.

"I want to take care of you," he whispered, voice rough against my ear, fingers playing with the waistband of my sleep shorts.

When I guided his hand lower, he didn't wait. He knew exactly where—how—to touch me to break every bit of me apart. Then, he held me close and kissed the skin of my shoulder until I put myself back together.

That night was perfect.

I'm too wrapped up in the memory of Sebastian that it takes me more minutes than it should to realize who exactly is standing in front of me in line.

Elaine Springfield.

My entire body tenses, rigid with guilt.

A voice in my head whispers stark, scolding words. *You were in bed with her fiancé! He touched you when he should only be touching her!*

I shut my eyes hard and try to focus on a logical, reasonable voice.

We did nothing wrong. They aren't together.

At least, not right now.

And yet I still feel twisted up about everything.

Through this mini freak-out, Elaine doesn't acknowledge my existence, and when I blink my eyes open, I realize her mother is with her and holds her attention, chatting about a dinner she is planning.

Breathing slowly through my tight throat, I take the moment to study Elaine —this woman who had Sebastian's heart for years but somehow lost hold of it.

Only for a moment, I'm sure, but still.

She's the weatherwoman version of herself, which is to say, cheery-colored clothes with a professional air. Blonde hair down and in waves that would make the ocean jealous. But these aren't rough and wild. Every strand is smoothed into a sculpted shape.

And those heels. Momma would love the purple velvet pumps. I wince at how high her arches must stretch. She's almost as tall as me in them.

This version of Elaine has always confused me. She's like a doll version of herself. Something she crafted in high school around the time she started competing in pageants. Not that there's anything wrong with wanting to put effort into certain parts of your appearance, as attested by my extra-intricate eyeliner today.

It's just that there's another version of Elaine. A *hair in a haphazard ponytail, men's boxy Carhartt jacket, worn jeans, and dusty work boots* version. That's how she dressed most of high school, and I'll see that version of her around Green Valley sometimes.

She walks different based on how she's dressed. More than stepping out of the heels and slipping on boots. Elaine in jeans and an old T-shirt is loose, shoulders relaxed, smile—still small—coming easier with a genuine tilt.

Elaine in a blouse and pencil skirt has the tense bearing of a woman on her way to a job interview, where the competing candidate has ten more years of experience and a family connection with the boss. It makes me want to pull a chair up for her and insist she take a load off.

Even now, when I'm dealing with a churn of agitated flamingos in my stomach about my relationship with her currently ex-fiancé, I also want to assure her that no one in this bakery is judging her and she can kick off her heels if all that subtle shifting back and forth means they're hurting her feet.

But I bite my bottom lip and avoid talking to her, like I did in high school. At least, like I did after the Sadie Hawkins dance.

"Hello, you two." Tempest, Donner Bakery's muffin expert, stands behind the counter, her beautiful red hair pulled back in a braid. "What can I get you?"

"We'd like to put in an order for double chocolate cupcakes to be picked up next Wednesday," Sebastian's ex says in her normal, careful tone, as if she thinks about each word before she says them.

"Of course. How many would you like?"

"You know your daddy and Sebastian eat more than their share of desserts," Mrs. Springfield says. "Better make it eight. Just in case."

For a moment, I'm sure I misheard the woman. But then my ears play back the dialogue, and I can't deny the truth.

Sebastian.

The Springfields are getting together with Sebastian. Their future son-in-law.

A little happy family.

Could he have ... lied to me?

Isn't this how it happens sometimes? A guy tells you he broke up with his girl-friend, but in reality, they're still together, and you're just the gullible other woman who believed him.

But after barely a moment of thought and a deep breath, I remind myself that what happened between Sebastian and me hasn't been isolated. We stayed with Cameron and Maurice. They all talked about the relationship with Elaine as being in the past.

So, things are as Sebastian described them. He and Elaine are only over as far as a few select people know, and this is just more of that cracked-open door. A dinner together, just like when they were engaged. I can see a steel-toed boot shoving its way into the opening, keeping everything from shutting up completely.

Suddenly, I'm sure I smell frogs and formaldehyde. My stomach churns.

As I work through my shock, Elaine and her mother order a few more pastries, and Tempest boxes them all up. Then, the weatherwoman is turning, and I want to hide, just like I used to from Sebastian. But short of ducking under a table, I have nowhere to go.

"Oh. Gwen. Hello." Elaine's voice is stiff.

Is it the version of herself that she is today, or is it because she knows about Sebastian and me?

"Hi, Elaine. Hi, Mrs. Springfield." I manage to keep from sounding heartbroken or guilty.

Because I have no reason to be *either* of those things. Not yet anyway.

"I wanted to thank you."

As her words permeate my brain, a creeping dread coats my stomach. Is this it? Is this where she says ...

Thank you for amusing Sebastian while we were apart.

Thank you for showing him a fun time, but he really wants to be with me.

Thank you for helping get that wildness out of his system.

And I'll thank you to stay away from my fiancé—soon-to-be husband—in the future.

"For the makeup videos you post," she clarifies. "I would have left a comment, but you have them turned off." Elaine holds the pastry bag in one hand and taps her cheek with the other. "The makeup artist at work always complains about my dark circles, but I used that brightening powder and concealer you suggested, and she complimented me the other day. So, thank you."

"You watch my videos?" *Did that come out too squeaky?*

Elaine shifts in her heels. "Yes. I was never very good at applying it myself."

Her mother wraps an arm around the weatherwoman's shoulders. "Oh, yes. I always had to apply it for her before pageants. But I can't rightly drive to her house at the crack of dawn every morning before she leaves for work." Mrs. Springfield gives her daughter a loving, exasperated smile.

A flush creeps up Elaine's neck and over her cheeks. "True. So, thank you."

"Of … of course. No problem. Glad they could help." Just grand. My hobby is making Elaine even prettier.

Immediately after that thought, I get sick with shame. Elaine has always been a quiet, kind—if reserved—person. Just because it's a matter of time before Sebastian falls back in love with her doesn't mean I feel great about resenting her.

"Have a good day." She gives a slight wave as the two step around me. The gesture causes a small glint of light to reflect off her finger.

No, not her finger.

The diamond of the engagement ring still sitting on it.

Chapter Forty

SEBASTIAN

I would rather send you an email than write all this down. But I guess there is a certain romance to the written word.

— LETTER TO MARIA

The leash didn't work out, but I have high hopes for the backpack.

Gwen's lips—bare of color today—curve in a broad smile when she meets us at the trailhead and sees Curie's little face watching her from the window in the back of the bag.

My furry companion will be an adventure cat if it kills me.

Despite her initial excitement, Gwen grows quiet fast once we head into the woods.

Maybe she's too mesmerized by my cat to talk to me.

I wish Gwen were the one in front, but she told me to lead the way, and I couldn't figure out a way to say I'd rather forget the scenery and spend my day looking at her round ass and long legs. Gwen has on some army-green shorts that fit her just right and a tank top, showing off shoulders I want to kiss. But since we're in an arguably public space, I hold off.

Turns out to be a smart choice when we round the first bend and run into a game warden.

Drew Runous strikes an intimidating picture in his uniform. He's got the build of a Viking and the long blond hair and beard to round out the image. But the locals know he's a big softy. Word around town is, he writes poetry. A lot of it for his wife, Ashley.

I bet Cameron would like him.

That's how I measure a lot of people. How well would they get along with my brother?

Gwen got a ten out of ten.

"Hey, Drew." I shake hands with the man, and Gwen offers a wave, getting a nod in return. "Any trouble on the trail?"

My eyes fall to the chain saw in his hand, and I notice the sweat stains on his uniform. This only adds to his whole *I could conquer your tiny village* look.

"Rainstorm blew over some trees. Needed to clear the hazardous ones near the trail. You're good to go." His shrewd gaze falls on the pink straps of my backpack.

"Oh yeah." I turn and offer my back, so the man can see the third in our party. "Say hi to Curie. This is her first hike." I grin over my shoulder at the man whose normally stoic face has a hint of surprise.

"You're hiking with your cat?" Drew says this with an underlying question of, *And you think that's a good idea?*

"Yeah!" I keep my enthusiasm high, so I don't start doubting the decision. I face him again. "You're telling me this is the first cat you've seen on the trail?"

Drew tilts his head, eyeing me with an unreadable expression. "Seen bobcats. A mountain lion once."

"Really?" Gwen perks up at this. "When? Where? How big were they?"

The ranger shifts the chain saw from his left to right hand, as if the weight is getting to him, and Gwen must think the same thing.

"Sorry. Never mind. We should let you go."

Drew reaches into a pocket with his free hand and pulls out a crumpled brochure and hands it to Gwen. "We're giving a talk on the park's wildlife in a few weeks. Come on by."

"Oh." Her voice is light, and her eyes are wide with excitement as she pages through the little pamphlet. "Thank you. I'll do that."

"We'll be there," I add, hoping I'm not working so I can escort Gwen officially.

And then I realize how big this current moment is. Drew is seeing Gwen and me together. Not in any kind of passionate embrace, but still. The two of us are out and about.

Part of me is excited, but another part worries how this'll look in the long run. The truth about Elaine and me still isn't public. Gwen is going to come off like the other woman. Drew doesn't seem the kind to gossip, but he's married to a Winston, and that family is connected all around town. One wrong word, and Gwen will become a villain.

The thought has my stomach clenching in panic.

"Well, it's best we head out. This cat wants to see some views!" I keep my tone jovial as I maneuver around Drew and barely keep from reaching for Gwen's hand to draw her with me. That would only make it more obvious that this isn't an innocent hike between friends, but a romantic excursion into the woods.

Drew nods again and heads off while Gwen folds up the brochure and tucks it into the back pocket of her shorts.

Despite the innocent nature of the encounter, there's a tense cloud lingering over us. I want to say something to dispel the ominous sensation but can't come up with any words. Not even a joke. So, I turn back to the trail and keep going.

The quiet of our trek weighs heavy between us, and I can't help thinking something is wrong. I wonder if Gwen somehow knows what I'm going to tell her. My brain battles between two sides of the issue. Gwen is the one I want to be with; I shouldn't be playacting as another woman's fiancé. But Gwen knows things are over between me and Elaine, and this is just me helping a friend get through a rough time.

This not-yet-a-relationship we have is off-balance, putting more weight on her.

Gwen was exactly what I needed the other night. A comforting presence.

She took to the role intuitively, knowing what would make me feel better without me asking. She didn't try to problem-solve or give me advice about how to cheer up. She just held me and spent time with me and made sure I was okay.

Gwen was my partner.

I want to be that for her.

But how can I when I don't know what she needs? Maybe if I could figure out what's got her so quiet.

Is it the continued secrecy that has her drawing in on herself?

After next week though, I'm going to push Elaine to tell her parents. Before, I backed off the topic, but not anymore. I can only make this breakup so gentle. Eventually, it'll reach a point where it's not a breakup at all. Things need to be officially done.

We hike another quiet mile before breaking through the trees, finding ourselves on a ledge with a view of the Appalachians, a sprawling vista of tree-covered mountains. Going from dense forest to this view has me staggering. A soft hand rests against my arm, steadying me.

"Wow," Gwen breathes out beside me, her eyes wide as she takes in nature's wonder.

"Yeah," I whisper, the word ragged as I stare down at her. "Wow."

"Turn around." She smiles sweetly and gives my side a light poke. "Let Curie see the view."

Better yet, I carefully unstrap my backpack and set it on the ground, so her kitty window faces the sight. I don't know if she's as awed as us mere mortals, but at least she's not napping.

"This was a good idea." Gwen laces her fingers with mine, still gazing outward.

"Listen." *Shit, wait, am I doing this now?* My mouth is moving before I consider if this might not be the best moment to bring up my obligation to Elaine. "I agreed to do something next week. It's not a big deal. Well, it's a big deal to them, but for me, it doesn't mean more than dinner and being there for a friend …" I trail off, realizing I've tangled my free hand in my hair, tugging on the strands, and Gwen is staring up at me with confusion.

"Could you maybe say that again?" she asks. "But this time tell me what you're talking about?"

I huff out a defeated sigh. "I'm having dinner with Elaine and her parents next week. It's not a romantic thing or a relationship thing. They … it's a tough day for their family, and I'm just going to support Elaine."

"Oh." Gwen's focus turns inward, and then understanding flicks in her eyes. The dark moment in Elaine's past isn't exactly a secret. "Yeah, I get it. I'm sure she'll appreciate you being there for her."

Gwen squeezes my hand, reassuring me with her kind acceptance and continued touching.

"This is the last thing I'll be going to," I promise. "No more pretending."

"It's okay, Sebastian. Really."

Gwen stares out over the woods, a smile on her face. The curve has a hint of strain, and I know I'm fucking this up. She's not some sordid secret to be kept. Gwen is sweet and caring and deserves to be cherished without conditions, out in the open for everyone to see.

"We should go on another trip." I want the unbridled joy we shared in Nashville.

This is the way I can support her. Be her travel buddy.

I don't like the way *buddy* sounds. *Partner. Travel partner.*

"That would be fun," she agrees without committing.

My heart rate picks up, and my palms grow sweaty. I *am* messing this up. I know it.

What can I do without also abandoning my promise to help someone I still care about? An idea, a gesture, comes to mind. Maybe *this* could be enough.

"Are you free tonight?"

"You want to go on a trip tonight?" Her smile spreads in a more genuine curve. "I have work tomorrow."

"I know." I kiss her forehead and act like a weirdo by sniffing her sweaty hair because I like the way salt mixes with her floral scent. I want to bury my face in the damp strands. "How does dinner sound? With my family? Kennedy will be there."

Gwen faces me fully, her brows high, as if my invite is some outlandish request. "Me and your family?"

"Yeah. My parents already like you. Y'all will get along great. And my sister's been asking about you ever since we saw Cameron. Those two talk about everything."

"Oh, well, I guess … yes." The flush of exertion started to fade from her face but comes back now with a vengeance. "I'd love to."

Maybe I'm not fucking this up completely.

Chapter Forty-One

GWEN

There is a pinball machine at a bar in Michigan where I officially hold the high score. You're related to a champion. I'll try to remember you when the fame goes to my head.

— POSTCARD FROM RYAN, MICHIGAN

When I climb out of my car at Sebastian's parents' home, I immediately worry that plum lipstick was too bold of a choice.

Well, if anyone makes a comment, I can point out I bought the stick in Kirkwood Drugstore, and then they'll all be happy because I'm a loyal customer.

"Yeah, that's good. I'll do that," I mutter.

"You'll do what?"

Sebastian's deep voice at my back has me yelping. When I turn to find him grinning at me, I'm somehow both more and less nervous.

"Hi!" I squeak. *Damn, I thought I was over this.* "Hello." *Too low again. One day I'll get my shit together.*

Sebastian grins wide as he steps into my space, crowding me back against my car. "You're so fucking adorable."

Then, he's kissing me, warm hand on the nape of my neck, rough beard pricking the edges of my lips, sandalwood scent in my nose and mint on my tongue.

I groan at the pleasure and unfairness and horrible timing.

"Mmm." The pleased noise rumbles from deep in his chest as he gives me one, two, three quick kisses before stepping back, looking way too satisfied with himself.

"Did you smear my lipstick?" I gasp out the question, trying to remember how to breathe.

His hazel eyes drag over my mouth. "It looks great."

"That's not what I asked." I try to scold him with my tone but just sound giddy.

With my hand still in his, I open the passenger door and pull down the visor to check. With a tissue, I'm able to wipe away the few spots his kiss made the color slip outside my carefully constructed lines. Overall, the purple remains, and I like the color even more now that I associate it with the taste of Sebastian. Tossing the tissue in the cupholder, I grab the last-minute gift I bought on the way over.

"Your momma's not allergic to flowers, is she?" I grip the bouquet tightly when I face Sebastian, questioning my decision to bring them for the one thousandth time.

Any other night, I'd pick up a delicious treat from Donner Bakery to bring to a dinner party. A crowd favorite. But going through almost the same exact motions as Elaine had performed yesterday felt weird.

"She loves flowers." He pulls me toward the house. "You don't need to be nervous. They already like you plenty. You're their favorite postal worker."

"People don't usually invite their mail carriers to dinner, no matter how much they like them."

"But you're *everyone's* favorite postal worker. You can't tell me no one has ever invited you for dinner." He lets go of my hand, only to slip an arm around my waist.

"Well, there was one time an Iron Wraith suggested I come into his house and tour his bedroom. And he was holding a burger. Does that count?"

When I glance up at Sebastian, I expect an eye roll and a chuckle. Instead, he stares at me with an uncharacteristically cold expression on his face.

"Who said that to you?" he asks, his voice careful on the question, something lurking behind the words.

Is it anger? Is this an angry Sebastian?

If I ever thought about Sebastian getting angry, I would have guessed the guy would go loud. He's such a lively guy; I would think there'd be a lot of shouting and arm waving.

But even in that made-up scenario in my mind, I don't see him as *truly* mad. More putting on a show for others to laugh at. I guess I can't imagine what a mad Sebastian looks like.

And now, I have one in front of me, and I want to both study him and calm him.

"Don't worry about it. That was, like, over a year ago." That one instance anyway.

I've been hit on more than a few times while working. Hence my bear spray. My male counterparts carry containers of the stuff to ward off aggressive dogs that might try to take a chunk out of their leg.

I carry it for aggressive men. Luckily, I've never had to use it. Knowing I have the bear spray helps ease my fears and allows me to stay confident and undeterred in the face of their flirting. If I cowed, they'd mark me as prey and start pushing my limits.

"I asked *who* said it. Not when." Sebastian holds my eyes with his, as if his handsomeness could hypnotize me into revealing all my secrets.

"No," I say gently. "I'm not going to tell you." And I offer an apologetic smile, hoping that'll lessen the blow of the refusal.

But Sebastian isn't ready to let it go. "I just want to know his name."

"So you can send him a pretty postcard? I don't think I ever thanked you for that, by the way. Thank you!" I rise on my toes and press a quick kiss to his lips, and then I try to tug him the rest of the way to the house. "What do you think your parents made for dinner? I'm sure I'll love whatever it is."

Sebastian has a long arm span, but not enough for me to make it to the front porch while still holding his hand. Since he refuses to budge, I have to stop after only a few steps.

"Just tell me." He uses a coaxing voice. One that says, *I'll make you and your vagina so happy if you just give me what I want.*

Sneaky, swoony bastard.

But I'm made of stronger stuff, and I grew up with an older brother who liked to get into fights.

Or maybe it was people liked to get into fights with him. All I know is, Ryan came home with more than the average amount of fat lips and bloody noses.

Anyway, back to the present moment and the man looking for a fight.

If teasing sweetness won't sway him, then it's time to be blunt.

"Here's the deal. I'm going to have to be selfish on this because telling you the name of the random man who hit on me has absolutely no benefit for me. I mean, maybe you'd have a grand time knocking on his door and punching him in the face or threatening him. But where would that leave me? I'd still have to go to his house every day. And then, instead of being disinterested, he'd be pissed off at me. Telling you his name would put me in more danger than I'm in now."

"You should change routes," Sebastian says, and I want to shake the man as much as I want to kiss him.

"That's not how it works. We're a small town with limited postal workers. I have to drive every route at some point because people need days off. And FYI, the Iron Wraiths don't live in a single frat-boy house. They're all over Green Valley. As long as I'm delivering mail here, I'll be delivering mail to a sketchy biker. And you getting pissed off if one of them hits on me makes my life harder. So, just leave it be."

Sebastian glares at our joined hands, and despite my annoyance at his lapse into Neanderthal-ism, there's also an inappropriate bubble of happiness in my chest at the idea that he wants to defend me.

I don't need it. But I like that he has the urge.

"Fine," he mutters and tugs me close. "I'll leave it alone."

In his arms, pressed against his chest, I hear the pound of Sebastian's heart. The rhythm is rapid, as if he ran a race, and I realize that maybe he wasn't getting possessive for the sake of staking a claim.

Maybe he cares about me and was just scared.

That I can live with, and I stroke my hands down his back to soothe him.

"I promise I take every safety precaution while on my job," I assure him. "Most days, I don't even get out of my car."

Sebastian presses his nose behind my ear. He likes the short hair there, always muttering about how it's the softest and it smells nice. Now, I put in double the effort to remember to scrub behind my ears every shower.

"Are you two ever coming inside?"

The holler from the Kirkwoods' house has me jerking back, but Sebastian's hold keeps me from moving too far from him.

"Yeah, yeah. Calm down." With an arm around my shoulders, Sebastian leads me to where his sister stands, fists on her hips, smirk on her face.

Kennedy is a few years younger than me, so we never really hung out, but I feel like I know a lot about her from chats I've had with Mrs. Kirkwood and then the fun stories Sebastian's told me of his childhood.

"Hello, Gwen." Her eyes track over Sebastian's grip on me, and her expression doesn't change, which means I have no idea if she approves or not.

Kennedy and Elaine could be best friends for all I know, and now, I'm the new girl she doesn't like as much.

Don't worry, I want to tell her. *I know I'm not the forever girl. I'm sure Elaine will be back ultimately.*

And let's not examine how that leaves me bleeding from a gaping wound in my heart.

"Hi, Kennedy," I respond to her greeting. "How's working at the hospital going?"

"I'm amazing at it," she declares. "They're all going to cry when I leave. But that's to be expected." She pulls the front door open and waves us in.

"Stop being so humble." Sebastian reaches out to ruffle his sister's hair as he passes, and she swats him away.

"Ladies gotta brag. No one else will do it for us." She joins us in the front hall and captures me with a laser focus I thought only her brother was capable of. "Let's have it, Gwen."

"Have what?"

"Stop being so intense in Gwen's direction." Sebastian tries to turn us to get me out of her eyeline, but Kennedy is not so easily deterred.

"Give us a brag. Come on. It's good for you." She blocks the hall to the rest of the house, arms crossed, daring me to say something positive about myself.

"I …" *Shoot. What do I do well? I know there are things.*

"Gwen is a talented makeup artist." He gestures at my face, and I'm glad I took a moment to fix my lipstick. "She has close to a hundred videos online, and they all have over a thousand views. Some have over fifty thousand. There. Happy? She's awesome. Now, can we get by?"

"Do I really?" I stare up at Sebastian in shock, earning his curious gaze.

"There're videos of you on the internet you don't know about?" Kennedy's brows dip in an angry V. "That's bullshit. I have a lawyer friend—"

"No, that's not it," I reassure her. "I know about the videos. I post them. I just never look at the view rates."

"Seriously?"

I shrug. "It's just a hobby. Why would I check view count?"

Sebastian's smile spreads slow across his face, and he cups my chin, tracing his thumb over my cheek—a light enough touch that he won't mess up the layer of concealer I applied earlier.

"That's very cool, but it doesn't count because I want *Gwen* to brag about herself." Kennedy recaptures our attention. "There will be no meek mice in this house."

I pretend to glare up at Sebastian. "Great. You took my thing. Now, what am I going to brag about?"

"You also—"

My hand over his mouth cuts him off. "Don't use up any more! Let me think."

The cheeky bastard nips at my hand, then licks it, which has me thinking about the rave review he gave my post-hike blow job. But that's not a brag I'm going to give his family.

"Oh, I know! I just took a self-defense class at Viking MMA, and the teacher said I was the best at one of the moves." I take my hand off Sebastian's mouth. "Can I use you as a fake attacker?" I ask him.

"Go for it."

The second he's finished agreeing, I have his arm twisted and pinned behind his back and aim a firm kick to the backs of his legs, sending him to his knees on the plush rug in the entryway.

"I'm really good at this takedown." I grin at Kennedy from where I have her brother in kneeling submission. "There we go. Self-brag."

The youngest Kirkwood stares at us with wide eyes, and then a grin crashes across her face. "That is fucking amazing. When is this class? I want to go."

"Kennedy?" a voice calls from deeper in the house. "Are they here?"

"Yeah, Momma!" Kennedy shouts back. "We're just chatting!"

Realizing I still have Sebastian in the hold, I release his wrist.

When he doesn't immediately get up, I start to worry. "I'm sorry. Did I hurt you?"

"Well, quit gabbin' and come carve this turkey before your daddy tries," Mrs. Kirkwood says. "You know he'll hack it to pieces."

"Fine, I'm coming." Kennedy strolls down the hall, leaving us on our own.

Only then does Sebastian rise to his feet, his face entirely too red.

"Oh no. I did hurt you." My hands pat over his body as I look for the injury I caused. "I'm sorry. That was a bad idea."

"No." He clears a gravelly note from his throat. "You were fine. I just"—he clears his throat again—"I might have enjoyed myself too much."

That's when I realize he has his hands cupped in front of his jeans.

"Are you hard?" I gasp.

He hushes me with one hand, keeping the other in the protective position. "Just give me a second. And talk about things that aren't sexy. It'll go down."

"Okay, um, not sexy … not sexy …" I glance around the front hall, seeking inspiration. "Lamp." I point at a lamp on a table. Then, I point at the table. "Table."

"Is this you talking about not-sexy things?" Sebastian asks with a strained laugh.

"It's the best I can do on short notice! I'm not some improv star. And you've got to admit, there's nothing sexy about lamps. Unless it's that one from *A Christmas Story*. You know, the leg with the thigh-high fishnet stocking? I've always wondered if the stocking was attached to the leg or if it was a leg lamp accessory that could be taken off. Because, you know, if *I* wore thigh-high fishnets, I'd need to have a garter belt to keep them up. But I guess the lamp leg doesn't move around, so it doesn't need to worry about something sliding down when they shouldn't."

Realizing I've gone on a tangent, I look at Sebastian and find him staring, lips pressed in a line so tight that the skin around his mouth has gone white. And if his hand placement is any indication, he's still dealing with too much wood.

"Sorry. I guess that didn't help."

He slowly shakes his head, then leans in until his forehead rests on mine. "Your punishment is, you have to go into the kitchen without me and hang out with my family on your own for a bit."

"Okay. I can do that. But where are you going to be?"

Sebastian straightens and turns toward a set of stairs. "I'm going to take some me time in the bathroom and think about you wrestling me to the ground in fishnet stockings."

Chapter Forty-Two

SEBASTIAN

It has been raining ever since you left. You took the sun with you.

— LETTER TO MARIA

Tonight's dinner with Elaine and her parents was on a different planet than last week's dinner with Gwen and my family.

Back at my rental, I sit at the kitchen table with a Donner Bakery cupcake in front of me, and I simply stare at the frosting. A perfectly twisted swirl, ready to be destroyed by a single bite.

Mrs. Springfield insisted I take one when I claimed to be too full of dinner for dessert. She made sure I knew the double chocolate creations were Georgie's favorite.

Everything about tonight was Georgie's favorite. Hot dogs, mac and cheese, watermelon with the seeds, applesauce, and double chocolate cupcakes.

Elaine never eats hot dogs, except for this one night a year.

The whole meal was quiet, except for the occasional overly enthusiastic question from Mrs. Springfield about wedding plans. Every one of those clenched like a band around my stomach until I couldn't force down any more of Georgie's favorites.

After dinner, I was able to make my exit, grateful that Elaine hadn't tried to stop me and make me stay for the movie marathon of Georgie's favorite films.

I want to call Gwen, invite her over to spend the night. But that doesn't seem fair. Like I'm using her to clear a bad taste out of my mouth. And like I'm sneaking her in after the main event.

Gwen is the main event.

In a day or two, once the lingering sadness of this anniversary is tucked away for another year, I'll sit Elaine down and tell her things between us are truly done. I won't leave the conversation until she tells me the exact day and time she plans to tell her parents the truth. If she wants help brainstorming a statement for her social media followers, I'm down. If she needs ideas for what to say if the topic comes up during her interview for Channel 5, then I'll improv with her.

But no more lying. What happened with Kennedy's ex won't happen here.

Elaine doesn't need me to be happy, and she'll realize that in the long run.

The decision is enough of a comfort that I'm able to bite into the cupcake.

It should be delicious, but I can't taste anything. Not when all I want is the flavor of Gwen's lips.

Giving up on this day, I stick the rest of the treat in the fridge, then go to get ready for bed. But when I can't fall asleep after an hour, I end up on my couch with the TV on instead. Sometime later, my phone buzzes. In hopes that I'll see Gwen's name, a text asking if she can come over, I snatch it up.

Elaine.

Always Elaine.

This is the thank-you call. One I want to ignore.

If we talk now, I can set up a time for us to get together on my next day off. A time to officially end things, so we can both move on.

That's what convinces me to answer.

"Hey, Elaine."

There's no response. Not a verbal one anyway. But there *is* noise on the other end of the line.

"Elaine?"

Another moment passes, and in that time, I realize what I'm hearing.

Crying.

"Sebastian," she moans. "What did I do?"

I'm already standing from my couch, heading toward the door, one hand keeping my phone against my ear, the other searching for my keys.

"What's wrong, Elaine? Where are you? Did something happen?"

"Hawk's Field." The name stutters out on a hiccuping breath. "I can't … I can't …"

More crying comes over the line as I jog to my car.

"I'm on my way. Are you hurt?" *Did you hurt yourself?*

"No." She drags the word out. "I'm a bad daughter."

In between the notes of misery, I catch a hint of a slur.

Is she drunk?

They didn't even serve alcohol at dinner. Just water and Dr. Pepper. The soda was Georgie's favorite.

"I'll be there in ten minutes. Just stay on the phone with me, okay?"

Her answer is more crying.

If I were in the ambulance, I could have made it in eight minutes, but I have to wait for stoplights and obey speed limits—to an extent. All through the drive, Elaine either whimpers or goes quiet. Sometimes, I hear a sloshing water sound, like she's drinking.

When I ask her if she's still on the line, she says, "I can't," and that's it. But it's enough for now.

"I'm here," I tell her as I pull into Hawk's Field and spot her truck right away.

She used to drive a small four-door, but a year ago, she purchased this huge truck, better meant for a farmer or contractor or a guy overcompensating for something.

I shut off the engine and jump out, hanging up on my way. When I get to the driver's door, I find her slumped over the steering wheel. The truck is unlocked, and I tug the door open.

"Elaine? Hey, talk to me. Are you okay?" I reach for her, worried I'll have to search for a pulse.

She turns her head, meeting my eyes with her puffy ones.

"Momma has a migraine," she says, and I wince.

Mrs. Springfield has chronic migraines. They can pop up at random times, but more often stress will bring one on.

And when they hit, she's down for at least twenty-four hours, pain like nails in her brain, often vomiting. A few times, I went with Elaine to the pharmacy to pick up medication for her momma. But nothing makes them go away forever, and Elaine takes it hard whenever her mom is hit with one.

"I'm sorry. Does she have pain meds? Do you need me to go pick some up for her?" *After I drive you home*, I add silently.

The minute she spoke, I smelled the alcohol on her breath. If I had a match, I could light the fumes; they're so strong.

"I need to be better," Elaine moans, and then she turns and bangs her head on the steering wheel, punishing herself for a mysterious failure.

Watching her fall apart terrifies me.

"Hey now. Don't do that." I slip my hand between her forehead and the wheel. "This isn't your fault. Today was a sad day. If anything set her off, it was just that. Not you."

Carefully, I help Elaine sit up straight, and that's when I see the almost-empty bottle of vodka on the floorboard.

"It's going to be me," she whispers in a hollow voice.

"What is? Elaine, did you drink all of that?" I gesture toward the bottle, but she only stares at her lap. "Elaine?"

Before I can try to coax an answer out of her, headlights spear across the field, followed by a quick flash of red and blue.

The police. *Fuck.*

"Oh my God." The appearance of law enforcement seems to have shocked her out of her distracted state. "Is that the police? For me?" High-pitched fear tinges her words.

"Come on now. It's gonna be fine." Quickly, I unbuckle her seat belt and help her down from the cab of the truck before slamming the door closed. If possible, I'd like to keep anyone from smelling the distillery scent of her front seat.

Her feet are unsteady as I walk Elaine to my car. I'm able to get her in the passenger seat before the cop car parks behind my bumper. Stepping to the side and shielding my eyes, I recognize the figure who climbs out.

Jackson James, sheriff's deputy.

Jackson is a good guy. I've run into him on emergency calls around Green Valley. While we don't hang out outside of work, I'd still say we're friendly.

"They're going to arrest me," Elaine whimpers. "Oh, Momma. I'm sorry."

"Just sit here quietly, okay?" I pat her knee and try not to let my anxiety over this distraught version of my ex throw me off-balance. "I'll talk to him. It's just Jackson."

"Oh God, oh God, oh God." Elaine wraps her arms around her torso, rocking in her seat and quietly crying to herself.

Sensing there's nothing I can say to calm her down, I head toward the cruiser, my hands loose and empty at my sides.

"Hey, Jackson," I greet him when he gets closer.

"Sebastian." He nods and peers around my shoulder. "Everything okay here?"

"Kinda. Elaine's having a bad night." Even as I give him this info, I shield her as best I can with my body, knowing she'd hate anyone to see her in this state.

"Have you all been drinking out here?"

"I haven't. I can do a Breathalyzer if you want. But all I'm looking to do is get her home."

"Sorry, Sebastian, you know I trust you and all, but I'm gonna need to talk to Elaine too."

Hell. Please don't let her get arrested for public drunkenness or something.

Jackson steps around me, and I let him, but I keep at his shoulder. He leans into the driver's side, and I'm surprised by the gentle tone he uses.

"Hey, Elaine. How's it going?"

She lifts a tearstained face from her hands, her normally smooth skin blotchy red and eyes puffy. "My sister's dead."

Jackson thunks his head on the roof of the car, obviously not expecting that.

He stands up, meeting my eyes with wide ones. "What's she talking about? I thought Elaine was an only child."

I shake my head. "She had an older sister." I speak low, not wanting her to hear and start sobbing again. I didn't realize how raw this wound still was for her. Maybe I don't know Elaine as well as I always assumed. "Georgie. She had cancer and died when she was seven. Today's the anniversary."

"Shit. I forgot." Jackson rubs a hand over his mouth, then glances down at the car. "She's been drinking."

"Not till she got out here. And I'm gonna drive her home." When I see him glance toward her truck, I rush on. "We'll come grab it in the morning, or I can call Beau to see if he can tow it now." Although I don't know if the Winston will pick up this late.

"Just go. Take care of her. And get her truck first thing." Jackson glances between me and my car full of weeping woman, shakes his head in a sad move, then heads back to his cruiser.

I sigh in relief, then climb behind the wheel.

"Am I going to jail?" Elaine's question comes out watery, fresh tears leaking down her cheeks.

She's in rough shape, and I'm having trouble remembering the last time she cried in front of me. I think it was a movie where the dog died in the end, and she let out one gasp and a stray tear. That was it. She didn't even cry when I told her I thought we were better off not in a relationship anymore. Elaine is not a crier.

Or the version of Elaine I knew wasn't.

And suddenly, I wonder why I've spent so much time thinking our split would break her. Before tonight, I had no indication she hurt this deeply. Now though, I know. There *is* an acute pain inside her, and I was probably right to be concerned.

"No. Don't worry. I'm taking you to my house, and you can sleep off the booze."

My ex presses her forehead against the window, staring out into the dark night as I drive us back to Green Valley.

When I pull into the driveway of my small rental house, Elaine struggles to unbuckle herself before I even have the car in park. But her drunken fingers slip on the buckle, and I end up having to walk around to her side and unstrap it myself. Then, I steady her as we walk into the house together.

"I don't live here," she murmurs, and I wonder if she forgot what I said on the drive over.

Maybe I should have taken her back to Merryville. But I really didn't want to go all that way with her smelling like alcohol and us needing to grab her truck tomorrow.

I leave her in the bathroom connected to the bedroom and go to fill her up a glass of water and get a bottle of pain meds. Her head will feel like a dump truck come morning.

Giving her space, I linger at the kitchen counter and try to figure out what the hell happened tonight. Elaine is always withdrawn and upset around the anniversary of her sister's death, but she's never done anything like this.

The only change is us.

Guilt roils in my stomach. *Is she like that boy from Kennedy's past? Is this the lead-up to Elaine doing something she can't take back?*

A clatter on the other side of the wall sends me running. I find her slouched on the lip of the tub, staring into space, half of the products previously arranged on my sink now strewn across the floor.

"Elaine? Hey. Look at me."

She blinks at me when I crouch beside her. "I'm so tired," she mumbles.

"Let's get you to bed."

"I don't want to sleep with you."

The declaration has me choking on a laugh.

"Good to know." I run my hands over her face and quickly check her arms and legs to make sure she didn't hurt herself when I wasn't watching her. "How are you feeling? Do you need to throw up?"

Slowly, she shakes her head. "I don't throw up anymore."

That's an odd way to put it.

"Okay. Bed, then water, then pain pills, then sleep."

She lets me lift her to her feet and guide her to the bedroom. The dress she has on is a soft material I figure is fine to sleep in. There are so many lines I've ignored tonight, but I refuse to step over the *undressing my ex-fiancée* one.

I tuck her into my bed and get her to drink a full glass of water and take a painkiller. Then, I stand over her and try to decide what else needs doing.

This is strangely similar to—and yet wholly different from—the night I took care of a drunk Gwen. That was an evening of silliness and hope and longing.

This is sad and scary. There's an ominous note buzzing beneath Elaine's choice to drink alone in Hawk's Field.

"Am I gonna die like Georgie?" Elaine asks me, her eyes blinking and unfocused, the question delivered in such a casual tone that it socks me in the gut.

"No, Elaine. You won't. You're going to go to sleep and wake up in the morning."

"How do you know?"

I settle in a chair next to the bed. "I'll stay and make sure."

Chapter Forty-Three

GWEN

Don't forget to stop by the Winstons' shop and get your oil changed. I mean it.
Those dashboard lights are warning you for a reason.

— POSTCARD FROM RYAN, IDAHO

This is one of the days I absolutely adore delivering mail. The sky is mostly clear with a few fluffy clouds to break up the glare of the sun. It's warm, but not too warm out, so I get a soft breeze through my window every time I accelerate. And in general, people are in good moods. On sunny days, I get an influx of friendly waves. Plus, yesterday, I saw Mrs. Keen and her daughter, Sherry, out on their front porch, waiting to greet me. Sherry promised me a loaf of freshly baked banana bread today. I look forward to having a baked good snack shortly.

Overall, this should be a top-tier day. Which means I can pretend like last night wasn't horrible at all. That I didn't stay up late, researching fun things to do in Atlanta, in hopes that Sebastian might want to visit the city next time we can coordinate time off together, all to distract myself from the fact that he was eating dinner with his ex and her family, who still believe the two of them are getting married.

The weather is so nice that I can almost convince myself that I don't think Sebastian and Elaine are eventually going to get married too.

Instead, I can soak in the gentle warmth and make plans to stop by Sebastian's house this afternoon before he heads out to his evening shift. I wince at the idea of working from seven p.m. to seven a.m. No part of that sounds fun to me, but then again, his entire job is so stressful that I'd break out in hives if I was expected to be the person everyone looked to in an emergency. When I think back, I'm not sure how I didn't totally break down when I found Mrs. Keen all bloody. But I made it through, so did she, and I'm perfectly content with being a hero once in my lifetime.

One of the first stops on my route is the Winston Brothers Auto Shop—and thank goodness. Inevitably, I will get a package for Cletus Winston that makes me nervous.

Admittedly, I've never had a bad experience with his mail per se. But there have been a few occasions where I questioned if I was delivering an item that was never meant to be mailed.

Today, for example. I can't even say the thing came in a box, even though it is technically covered in cardboard. There're too many angles and corners. If someone tried to accost me, Cletus Winston's delivery is the first object I'd grab to defend myself.

There's an element of menace about the not-box. It taunts me.

Gwen, the package says, *don't you want to know what I contain? You might never be the same again ...*

Why does an auto mechanic order items that tempt me to join the dark side?

When I park and reach back to retrieve it, I take a moment to listen for ominous ticking. Assured the not-box won't actively injure me, I cradle it carefully as I approach the garage. As if expecting me, Cletus emerges in a set of grease-stained coveralls, his eyes gleaming above an impressive beard that I've only seen overshadowed by Arthur's.

"Good morning, mail ma'am," he says.

"Morning, Cletus. Got a new oddly shaped parcel for you to sign for."

"Oddly shaped?" His brows dip.

"Well, it certainly isn't one of the standard shapes of priority mail boxes." I lift the delivery higher, showing the extra protrusions.

Cletus tilts his head, as if having trouble identifying the differences. "But if someone were to ask—a jury for example—"

"A jury?"

"Or a judge—"

"A judge?"

"Or a high school principal."

I don't parrot him this time, too lost in this conversation to know where it's going.

"This paragon of postal parcels would surely be considered within the realm of normal," he insists.

I don't know if it's a question, but I offer a nod. "Of course. My mistake. I have no reason to tell anyone your package is oddly shaped."

A delighted grin crinkles his beard, and I realize my wording blunder.

"I appreciate that." Cletus signs my scanner with determined strokes before taking the completely normal, not-at-all strange or menacing package off my hands. "Good day, Miss Gwen." And as the Winston strolls back to his shop, I swear I hear him mutter, "Jenn is gonna love this."

In that moment, I don't care if I accidentally took part in criminal activity by delivering Cletus Winston some black-market baking equipment for his wife or whatever was contained in that not-box.

All I can think about was the pure love in his voice when he said his wife's name. My heart shudders and pounds and *wants*.

Is that how I say Sebastian's name?

I jog back to my Bronco, suddenly eager to continue on my route. It's not long before I approach a familiar street. Well, all of the streets in Green Valley are familiar to me now, but this is familiar in a meaningful way.

This is *his* street. Ahead, I spy Sebastian's rental, the cute house a siren's song to me. I want to walk in that front door and abandon the rest of my workday. Spend every moment I can wrapped up in my sexy paramedic.

Before I don't get the chance to anymore.

A cloud covers the sun, dimming the street in front of me as my joy dims too.

Don't expect too much, and it won't hurt as bad when the good times end.

I breathe in deep and let the air out slow as I come to a stop beside his mailbox.

But why do they have to end? A traitorous thought sneaks through as I reach for the pile of envelopes meant for this address. I fumble the letters and have to restack them in my lap. As I tuck them in their new home and click the little door closed, I do the thing I promised myself I wouldn't.

I let my mind latch on to hope.

Maybe ... maybe this could be something. Maybe he won't want us to end either.

A yellow slip pulls me out of my musings, and muscle memory already has me reaching for a package behind my seat. One that needs to be delivered to his front door.

Even if I can't play hooky from my job, I can still sneak a kiss, right?

The thought has my stomach flamingos line-dancing, each wearing their own set of pink bedazzled cowboy boots.

I'm halfway up the front walk when the door opens. I smile wide, ready to launch myself at Sebastian, but I pause when the sight of the paramedic registers. Dark bags under sleep-deprived eyes, slumped shoulders, wrinkled clothes, hair in disarray, in need of a wash and a comb.

Sebastian stumbles to a stop when he sees me. He lingers half-in, half-out of his house, front door wide open.

"Hey," I greet him, trying to convey with my tone that I see he's tired and I'll just say a quick hi and get out of his greasy—yet still gorgeous—hair.

"Gwen—"

"Sebastian?" a voice—a feminine voice—calls from within the house. "Do you have my keys?"

The birds dancing in my stomach awkwardly peter off as my mind tells me I know exactly who that is.

But I don't. Not for sure. It could be Kennedy. Or Mrs. Kirkwood.

We both stand frozen, and his horrified face solidifies the truth a moment before Elaine steps out of the house behind him. Walking straight through the open door.

I knew it was left open for a reason.

"Never mind. I found them," she says, then spies me. "Oh. Hi, Gwen."

So casual. As if everything in the world makes sense to her and nothing is out of sorts in this situation.

Because nothing is. This is exactly how things were always going to turn out.

"You got a package." I underhand toss the box to Sebastian and turn before I see if he caught the frantic projectile.

"Wait!"

Heavy footsteps pound after me, and the sound makes me want to run. But if I flee, then that means I'm scared of what's happening right now.

And I can't be because I *knew* this was coming.

But when a strong hand encircles my arm, I use another Viking MMA self-defense move without thinking, shoving against his wrist so I slip out of the weak spot between his fingers and thumb.

"Sorry. Hell." Somehow, he looks more wretched than a moment ago. "I didn't mean to grab you. Just … this isn't what it looks like."

Sebastian's voice, heavy and pleading, entices me toward him, but I keep my feet firm on the ground.

Why now? I thought I had longer.

More time to cozy up to him on the couch. More time to wrap my arms around him. More time to hear him call me honey. More time to sink my fingers into his mahogany hair and hold him to whatever part of my body he's kissing in the moment.

More adventures. More memories. More *us*.

But this is the end. And knowing doesn't make me hate it any less.

But knowing will help me survive it.

Even as my heart pounds in a painful way and the self-preservation part of my mind demands I look away from him, I can't help doing my normal scan of Sebastian, searching for that little reassuring note.

But it's not there.

He's not wearing a single piece of pink.

That realization—a small disappointment dropped on top of a massive, heart-crushing weight—breaks my last defense.

I need to get away from here. Now.

"I wasn't—"

"Sebastian?" Elaine lingers in the still-open door, watching us.

She's beautiful, standing there in her cotton dress, long blonde hair falling in waves around her makeup-less face. Her brows rise as she takes the two of us in, the tension vibrating in the air, a radio wave broadcasting what we've been doing. Shame coats my insides because even though they were apart, I knew they'd find their way together again. Now, I'm the blip of a mistake in their relationship story, and that hurts in a new, different way than the rest of it. I didn't prepare for *this*.

"I'm going," I promise her, shuffling toward my getaway vehicle.

"Gwen, just let me explain." Sebastian doesn't grab for me again, but the hand that's not holding the package spreads, palm up, fingers wide, as if asking for something from me.

But I have nothing left to give.

Elaine glances between the two of us. "Sebastian, why are you chasing Gwen?" Her question, simple as it is, rockets through the air and socks me in the chest.

Oof. The air leaves my lungs in one pathetic wheeze.

Why is *he chasing me?*

Somehow, I drag in a single sustaining breath.

"He's not," I announce. Loud. Too loud. *Way* too loud. I stifle the volume and try for a smile and am pretty sure I look creepy as hell. "He. Is. Not." *Because I'm not his finish line. You are.* "He's just saying hi. Because we're friends." My head shakes, my body wanting to deny the words. "Just friends. All I ever wanted to be was Sebastian's friend. And look at that! I am." I flick my gaze between the two of them, unsure of who it hurts more to focus on. "I am your friend. You are my friend. We're all good."

Now, I back away from them, my hands raised, showing I mean no harm.

Sebastian stares at me, some stark emotion on his face that I am incapable of interpreting even if I wanted to try. But I don't because all the flamingos in my stomach are dead with cement on their feet, sinking to the bottom of my gut.

When I get in my car, I keep the wildly inappropriate smile on my face. I shift into drive. I finish delivering mail to the three remaining houses on the street, tensed up as I wait for Sebastian to appear in my window, calling me a liar.

But he doesn't.

When I turn off the road, I start talking to myself. "It's okay. This is okay." The words are stiff and sharp as I force them out of my throat. "This doesn't hurt that bad."

Because how can it? I prepared for this. I knew it was coming. I'd already experienced the worst pain imaginable when I stood next to my grandmother's hospital bed and her chest went down and never rose again.

This can't be anything compared to *that*. I can't hurt too bad when I *knew*.

It's the pain you don't know is coming that truly gets you. So, I haven't been got.

I knew, one day, Elaine would be in that doorway, so it's okay. I'm okay.

Or I would be okay if I could see through this filthy, blurry windshield. With shaking fingers, I spray the cleaning fluid and turn on the wipers. The gesture doesn't help, and I realize the glass isn't the problem.

My eyes are. They're too full of tears to see.

I've made it a few miles from Sebastian's when I pull off onto the dirt shoulder, thankful there're no houses for a stretch. Only trees and fields to witness me breaking down.

"I'm okay. I'm okay. I'm okay." If I say it enough times, it'll be true. It has to be.

The mantra worked all those years ago when I got home from school and hid under my covers and cried over the same boy. For the same reason. Because he chose the same girl.

Who, once again, isn't me.

As tears drip from my cheeks to my hands, I wipe them on my USPS polo shirt. The gesture reminds me of the day I rescued Agnes. The day Sebastian came back into my life.

I should've said screw the mail and driven her to the hospital myself.

At least tears dry clear and my mascara is waterproof. Today, I can continue with my route like everything is fine and dandy. No reason to call Arthur and ask him to take over.

Easy enough to pretend I'm okay when I most definitely am *not*.

Chapter Forty-Four

SEBASTIAN

You were right. I'm leaving him. Life is too short to live with the wrong person.

— LETTER TO MARIA

As I watch Gwen drive away, half of me wants to chase after her while the other half wants to crawl into a hole and forget the world.

"We're friends. Just friends."

The moment the words left her mouth, my whole body rebelled.

Because I realized I don't just *need* her.

I love her.

I am in love with Gwen, but she thinks of me as a friend to fool around with.

And I can't be mad at her. Can't blame her. I've given her nothing but secrets and hiding. All to spare Elaine the discomfort of fully ending our relationship.

In a painful daze, I stride back to my house, not bothering to look at my ex to see if she'll follow along.

"What was that?" Elaine asks, and I realize we're standing in my kitchen.

I didn't even hear the front door close over my heavy, pounding pulse.

"Nothing." Because I guess that's what it was. What we were. Nothing.

"Are you two dating?"

"No." I manage not to groan the word. "We're just friends." I plunge frustrated fingers into my hair, ready to pull it out by the roots. "And even if we were, I can't date anyone. Not when the world still thinks I'm engaged to *you*."

"Don't get mad at me," she snaps. Elaine crosses her arms and glares at the floor while I try to regulate my breathing. "Why? Why did you keep up pretenses with me when you want to be with someone else?"

Why? Why, why, why? Why did I ruin everything?

"Because I didn't think it was fair." The explanation comes on a ragged breath. "Me just ending things. I wanted you to have a choice."

"Seriously, Sebastian? A choice?" Her scoff echoes around the room, buffeting my sensitive nerve endings. "*I* thought you just wanted space. That, eventually, we'd …"

Eventually, we'd get back together. Elaine is a kind, intelligent, beautiful woman, and yet the idea of us resuming our relationship suffocates me. I have to forcefully drag in a breath to keep speaking.

"I'm sorry." I'm sorry for a lot of things.

"A choice," she mutters again. "What would that even change? If we're over, we're over."

"I was scared of hurting you." Sweat trickles from my hairline over my forehead. "What you might do."

Elaine studies my face for a moment before her eyes go wide. "Oh God, like Kennedy's boyfriend?" She paces across the kitchen floor, and a suddenly timid Curie scurries away from the agitated footsteps. "Hell, Sebastian. I'm sad, but I'm not suicidal. That's why you've been letting me drag this out?"

"Is it really that big a leap? After the way I found you last night?"

Her jaw clenches and relaxes. Clenches and relaxes. "I'm not looking to *end* myself," she says. "I just … I don't like feeling out of control. You leaving. My mom hurting. I reacted badly. Last night was a mistake. But I'm fine." Elaine won't look at me, and there's a resentful note to her voice. "Or I'm *going* to be fine. But I don't want some fake, pity fiancé."

Fake. This has all been fake. Elaine didn't need or want the lie. And now, I've ruined something amazing and *real*. For nothing.

I choke, reaching for my collar to loosen its noose-like hold on me. But the fabric isn't what's constricting my neck.

Panic is.

All I can see is the flash of something like agony in Gwen's gaze when she saw Elaine appear in my doorway. What did that mean? What is she thinking?

Fuck.

"I can't …" I pant. "I didn't …" I face the sink, trying to grip the edge of the counter to keep my hands from shaking. But they quiver anyway, the muscles failing to grab hold. "I can't."

I try to do the right thing, but I make it all worse. I'm a screwup. I'm shit.

My heart pulses with rapid, demanding beats, and I realize what's happening too late. No time to hide in my bedroom or get Elaine out of my house.

You can't breathe, my brain shouts. *You're going to die!*

I'm not going to die, I try to tell myself, but the assurance is a whisper against a wailing siren.

"Sebastian?"

Some part of my mind knows Elaine is at my side, trying to ask me a question. But my vision blurs, and my consciousness battles between knowing this won't kill me, yet at the same time knowing it will.

The back-and-forth seems never-ending.

When the panic attack eventually begins to ease, I realize I sank down on my haunches and pressed my forehead against the sink cabinet door. My body continues to shake, covered in a cold sweat, my muscles twitching and tensing as the adrenaline slowly fades. The clock on the wall tells me five minutes have passed, and from the way my joints protest me standing, I must have been rigid the entire time.

"Sebastian?" Elaine's voice is loaded with anxiety. "What just happened? If you don't say anything, I'm going to call 911."

"God, no," I rasp. The last thing I want is for my coworkers to show up in my house, see what a mess I am. Then, they'll tell Chief McClure, and I'll lose my new job.

Who wants a paramedic that has panic attacks?

And that's not even the worst of my sins.

"What just happened?" Elaine repeats her question.

I realize she filled a glass of water and is holding it out for me. I'm not sure I can grip it, and my stomach is a queasy mess. I shake my head, so she sets it down beside me.

"It's nothing." My voice sounds like I smoke two packs a day. "Just, sometimes, I get too worked up."

From the corner of my eye, I catch her pursing her lips, not buying my half-assed explanation.

"How long have you been getting *worked up*?"

Exhausted with every single thing that's happened in the last twenty-four hours, I shuffle to the kitchen table and sink into a chair.

I really thought Green Valley was the answer. That with a low-key environment, less deadly emergencies, I wouldn't have to deal with these episodes anymore.

Guess I was fooling myself about a lot of things.

"Since Merryville."

Her face loses color, and she settles in her own seat. "Is it my fault?"

"No. I swear it's not." Great. One more way I'm making Elaine feel shitty. If someone is handing out prizes for the guy who sucks most at breakups, I'll be looking for my medal in the mail. "This is on me. And it's not a big deal."

Her grimace tells me she doesn't buy it, but something keeps her from pressing. We stare across the kitchen table at each other, feet and miles apart.

"Still, I'm sorry," Elaine whispers eventually.

And that hurts too. Because I never wanted her feeling guilty or wrong. But I guess when two people are together for so long, there's going to be damage during the break.

"You don't have to be sorry. Just … tell your parents. About us." When her lips tighten, I plow on. "I can't lie anymore."

"I know. I don't want you to."

Finally, after months—or maybe years—we're on the same page.

With a groan, I heave myself out of the chair and head toward the front door. "Let's go get your truck."

"What are you going to do?" Elaine asks, following behind me, her keys jingling as she moves.

"About what?"

"Gwen." She whispers the name, but that doesn't gentle the jab to my heart.

I clench my hand around my keys, the sore joints of my knuckles protesting the movement. "I don't know."

Chapter Forty-Five

SEBASTIAN

Don't come back. If I miss you any more, I will lose myself.

— LETTER TO MARIA

After dropping Elaine off at her truck, I wait until Gwen's shift is over to seek her out. And, yes, that means camping out in the Green Valley Library parking lot just across from the post office.

What the hell am I doing?

Oh, nothing, just being a creepy weirdo.

At least I didn't follow her on her route.

Feeling like the worst version of myself, I knock my forehead on my steering wheel a few times. When I look up, I find Sabrina, one of the librarians, paused in the middle of the parking lot, giving me a concerned look through my windshield.

I make my best attempt at a smile and give her a *don't worry; I'm not having too bad of an emotional breakdown* wave.

She pushes dark hair out of her eyes and offers a tight smile in return before giving a friendly gesture toward the library that clearly says, *Whether or not you are, feel free to come inside. Everyone is welcome.*

I nod, my smile slightly more genuine at the kind gesture and unexpected ability to nonverbally communicate with the woman. I wonder if it's a special power librarians have.

Once she walks off, I go back to gazing at the post office in time to spy Gwen pulling into the small parking lot in her familiar Bronco.

Not bothering to drive over, I shove my door open, slam it shut behind me, and jog across the road. Still, I'm not fast enough, and she disappears into the building, carrying a crate full of mail.

Duh, she still has shit to do.

Hesitating on ambushing her at work—any more than I already am—I wait for her to reappear. I misjudged how long her final duties must be when another twenty minutes go by. I spend each one trying not to look like an anxious mess as I hover by her SUV.

Eventually, Gwen pushes through the front door of the post office, but she doesn't see me right away. She has her chin tucked into her chest, eyes on the ground, hands cradling what seems to be a baked good.

"Gwen," I say when I realize we're at risk of colliding.

She jerks her head up, blinking her wide green eyes. "What are you doing here?" Her question lacks all the normal warmth of her greetings.

"I wanted to talk to you. About this morning—"

"It's fine." Gwen holds up her hands—one white-knuckling a tiny loaf of bread —as if surrendering. As if my words are threatening her. "I told you, it's fine."

"It's not fine. I know what it looked like, but I didn't sleep with Elaine. You have to know that."

Isn't it obvious that I'm obsessed with you? I want to ask. How could she even entertain the idea that I'd want to be with someone else?

Unless these past few weeks meant less to her than they did to me.

"It doesn't matter."

For a moment, I stand with my mouth open wide, simply staring at her.

It doesn't matter? Me sleeping with someone else doesn't matter?

"Sorry. I meant to say, I believe you, but even if you did, it's okay." She chews the inside of her cheek as I struggle to comprehend her words. "I mean, not *totally* okay since we were having sex, too, and even with condoms, you should be up front about multiple partners for health reasons. But as for fidelity, we weren't *really* together."

Straight hit to my solar plexus, and I barely keep upright, fighting against wanting to brace my hands on my knees and breathe through the blow.

"Gwen." Her name is a ragged plea. "I'm *not* with Elaine."

"Okay," she agrees. But her tone says she doesn't believe me.

"Seriously." I step forward and try not to let my devastation show when she shuffles back.

"You know I like you as a friend, Sebastian."

And there's a phantom knee to the nuts.

"Sex has muddied all that up." Gwen keeps going. "But I meant what I said. We *are* friends. That's what I want. Just … maybe we take some time. Apart. To recalibrate."

"Recalibrate," I repeat, my lips numb. My whole face grows numb, and my heart pounds hard enough to bruise me internally.

"Yeah. Like, I need you to not show up at the post office unless you're buying stamps." She blinks, green gaze suddenly concerned. "Sorry, are you here to buy stamps?"

Fucking hell. She's so goddamn adorable as she asks me about shipping supplies, as if I can think of anything other than holding her close and kissing her long and hard.

"No, Gwen. I'm not here for stamps. I'm here for you."

"Well …" She anxiously tugs on the short locks of hair just behind her ear. "Only come back if that changes." Her voice is soft, almost chiding.

This sounds so much like *I'm sorry things didn't work out.*

I wish she'd yell at me. Shout, growl, hiss. Give me some sign that while I was falling in love with her and burying my head between her thighs, she thought of me as more than a fuck buddy.

"Gwen." I say her name because I need the single syllable on my lips always. Need something comforting to soothe my pounding pulse and erratic breathing.

My body is on the verge of another panic attack, and I want her to lay my head in her lap and stroke her fingers through my hair and tell me stories about her gran until I'm calm again.

Guilt trickles through me. Is that why I'm here? Looking for a quick fix to my problem? The soothing drug of Gwen's presence to make all the raw panic go away?

"I'm just gonna take some time." She steps around me to her Bronco, not meeting my eyes. "Then, we can be friends, okay?"

Okay. Fuck that word. I used to love it. That was how I checked in with her a moment before I stripped her clothes off and slid inside her.

"Okay?" I'd ask.

"Okay," she'd whisper back.

And now, she's twisting the script.

Okay if I leave you here, brokenhearted? she just asked.

"Okay," I choke out.

Because what else is there to say?

I need you and *I love you* are all tangled up in my mind as I struggle to think straight. I don't want to use Gwen, but I want her. Hell, I want her so bad. But all the reasons are swirling and crashing and melding into each other until I can't speak a single reason if I tried.

"See you around."

Gwen climbs behind the wheel, and I step out of the way, so she can leave the parking lot.

So she can leave me.

Chapter Forty-Six

SEBASTIAN

It's so strange how you were only here for a handful of days, but when I smell freshly brewed coffee, I think of you.

— LETTER TO MARIA

Cameron back in Green Valley is a big deal. At least, to Kennedy and me it is. My sister and I sit on one side of a booth in Daisy's and stare at our brother as he flips through the menu, pretending not to notice our intense attention.

"Hmm." He turns another page. "What's good here?"

"Oh, bullshit, city boy!" Kennedy whisper-yells at our brother, earning a smirk from him.

"How are you here right now?" I ask, baffled.

Kennedy and I got a text in our group conversation, saying: *I'll be at Daisy's in a half hour if you want to grab a bite together.*

"Well"—he sets down his menu—"there's this wonderful invention called a car."

"You're being an ass," Kennedy declares.

"When you have one as juicy as mine, it comes naturally."

"Hi, Cameron." Our waitress appears beside our booth with waters and a smile for my brother. "Haven't seen you around in a while."

No one in Green Valley has. Cameron has never been a fan of small-town life, especially when high school was a long string of bullying. Since leaving for college, he's only ever come back for a couple of days around Christmas. When we want to get together as a family, the Kirkwoods either drive out to Nashville or plan a trip somewhere else.

And yet here he is. Randomly popping up on a Tuesday evening.

Or is it random?

He orders a waffle, scrambled eggs, and bacon—breakfast for dinner, his favorite. Then, he orders a grilled cheese and minestrone soup for Kennedy and a burger and fries for me, proving that no matter how long he's been gone, he still knows us plenty.

"Out with it. Why are you here?" Kennedy holds up her butter knife in a threatening manner.

Cameron gives her an unimpressed stare but relents with a sigh. "Daddy and I are going fishing tomorrow morning. First thing."

The knife drops to the table with a clatter.

"Wait, really?" I ask.

Cameron glances between the two of us, face like stone. Then, he breaks, barking out a laugh.

"God, no. I hate that old boat. You two are so gullible." He sips his orange juice before telling us the truth. "I'm taking him up to Knoxville tomorrow to pick out some birthday gifts for Momma."

"Shit. I completely forgot." Kennedy whips out her phone and starts online shopping.

I already got our mom a new birdhouse, so I'm not worried. I'm also not satisfied.

"Momma has a birthday every year. You never help Dad in person." I'm sure he's done plenty of coaching over the phone.

For a time, Dad and Cameron had a tense relationship. Our father convinced himself his younger son dating boys was a phase. But after too many family gatherings with strained silences, Kennedy made it her mission to educate our father.

And Kennedy does not fail her missions.

After a bombardment of books, podcasts, PowerPoint presentations on the Stonewall riots during family dinner, and plenty of other guerilla warfare LGBTQ+ education tactics, something took root.

The careful circling of each other has faded, and last I visited Dad's office, he had a framed photo of Cameron and Maurice sitting between a shot of Kennedy in her graduation gown and me in my paramedic uniform.

But even that mended bridge never brought Cameron back to Green Valley.

"Why are you really here?"

Cameron sucks on his straw, watching me all the while.

And I know.

Somehow, he found out that Gwen had decimated my heart last week and that I'm barely functioning, and now, he's here to meddle. If Kennedy wasn't blocking me into the booth, I might try to make an escape.

"Elaine called me," he says.

Kennedy's head whips up as I gape.

"What?" I ask the word low and rough.

"Why is Elaine *calling* you?" Kennedy asks. "And why is she calling *you*?" She repeats the question with different emphasis.

I'm not sure I want either answer.

His stare stays on me. "We don't keep in touch, if that's what you're wondering," Cameron says, and a small twist of anxiety eases in my chest. "But she has my number and wanted to tell someone she's worried about you."

Everything tightens back up. *Elaine is worried about me?*

That says a lot, coming from the woman who got drunk alone in a field. Guess watching me have a panic attack is a worrisome thing. I wish she hadn't seen.

"Worried? Why is she worried? What happened?" Kennedy leans over the table, ready to drag the answers out of our brother.

No doubt, this is why Elaine contacted Cameron instead of Kennedy. My brother knows how to quietly listen while my sister immediately goes into defense mode.

He tilts his head to the side, and I almost see his internal decision to keep to the basics.

"You're stressed."

I wait for more, but he doesn't keep going. Okay, maybe we can get through this meal without digging too far into my tender spots. Without me talking about my failures in vivid, unavoidable detail.

"I was more stressed in Merryville, working my old job and dating Elaine."

True. But changing those things hasn't fully eradicated the panic attacks like I hoped.

Cameron tips his head the other way. "Maybe. But I bet Gwen breaking things off hasn't helped."

"What?!" Kennedy yelps, causing multiple diners to glance our way.

"Could you just …" I grind my teeth and bunch up my napkin, not sure what to say other than, *Stop talking about it, but please say her name again because she's all I want to talk about.*

"What's wrong with her?" Kennedy growls, and I spy murder in my sister's eyes.

"Nothing. It's me. What I said … she thought we were a casual thing."

"Why would she think that?"

"Because Elaine. Keeping our breakup a secret until she was ready." I silently berate my past self. "Everyone in town would've thought Gwen was the other woman. I didn't feel right, asking for commitment until that truth came out. Now, it's too late."

"Oh my God, *that's* what you're worried about?" Kennedy groans, dropping her forehead to the table with a loud bang that rattles the silverware. I wonder if I should check her for a concussion when she pops back up and gives me an exasperated swat on the arm. "It's *not* a secret."

The earth must stop its normal rotation because everything around me—life itself—screeches to a sickening halt.

"What?"

I have to wait for my answer as our food shows up, and I'm vibrating with impatience by the time we're alone again.

Kennedy stirs her steaming soup. "I've never been good at keeping long-term secrets, and I won't be shamed for that. Which is why I don't mind telling you, I definitely spilled the beans to multiple people when they kept asking about a wedding date. What was I supposed to say? 'Next summer,' turned into, 'I don't know,' which eventually became, 'There's not going to be a wedding, Flo McClure, so you're going to have to get your cake at the bakery like everyone else!' "

"You promised you wouldn't say anything," I breathe, surprised I still have air in my lungs.

"And you promised it would only be a few weeks. You're *lucky* I lasted three months. Besides, you moved back to Green Valley without her. Got your own place. You two are *never* together. Most everyone knew without me blabbing."

The town knows. Everyone has known for months possibly.

Do the Springfields know?

If they do, they haven't said anything to Elaine.

My sister pokes my arm. "No need to thank me. Now, you don't have to be stressed anymore. You can sweep Gwen off her feet, and everything will be perfect, thanks to me." She takes a victory bite of her grilled cheese.

Cameron takes advantage of her full mouth to grab hold of the conversation again.

"Do you know what I realized when I bought my place in Nashville and fell in love with Maurice?" he asks.

"That you found the perfect life?" I mutter, hating that I sound resentful as I glare down at my fries.

At this point, it doesn't matter if the town knows. I was ready to tell everyone anyway. Gwen is what matters, and she's insisting that we're just friends and that's all she wants.

My brother's eyes bore into my skull until I glance up and can't look away. "I realized that places and people can't fix you."

My gut bottoms out.

How could he know that was my plan? My wild hope?

And how dare he tell me it won't work!

"At one point, I thought Green Valley was my problem." His smile has a self-mocking edge. "That all I had to do was get away and I'd be happy and well adjusted. Poof, no more anxiety! No more anger or stress." He drizzles syrup over his waffle. "Didn't work out that way."

"Great. So, we're all miserable forever, no matter where we are or who we're with." I match his dry tone with my own, unable to be the playful version of myself when I'm in the middle of a hopeless spiral. "Loved this pep talk." I pull my wallet from my back pocket, wanting out of this diner and away from my unhelpful siblings.

"Listen to me, Sebastian. I'm trying to tell you that I *get* it. And I've tried the wrong ways. But"—he waits until I meet his eyes—"I've also found things that help."

A petty part of me wants to continue with my exit.

But what if his help can fix things with Gwen?

"Like what?"

"Drag for one." He leans back in his booth, spreading his arms wide. "It's a release. Something I do entirely for myself. It feeds my joy. Why else would I spend so much time and money on it?"

"Because you crave admiration," Kennedy offers.

Cameron rolls his eyes at her, then refocuses on me. "Why do you think Gwen does those makeup videos but doesn't monetize them? Has all the comments shut off?"

Hearing her name gives me chills. "It's a hobby." And I recall the conversation where I asked her about getting paid to do it. She said she wouldn't want that. It would change it. "She likes it."

"Exactly. Those videos, even though she shares them, are for her. Something she does to make herself happy. And last I checked, you don't have anything like that. You don't do anything for *you*."

I pursued Gwen for me, I'm about to argue.

But I think about that moment outside of the post office with her. When I felt the panic rising and I wanted her to soothe me. To make all the bad feelings go away.

Even if she could, that's a lot to put on a person.

Cameron braces his elbows on the table, leaning toward me. "You don't talk about it, but we know you've seen horrible things on your job. And just because you're in Green Valley now, it doesn't erase all that shit. You need to find something to help your mind cope."

To stop the panic attacks, he doesn't say, but I read it in his eyes.

Elaine must have gone into a lot of detail on their call.

"I don't think drag is for me."

The joke falls flat.

Both of my siblings are staring at me now, and I think this might be the most honest conversation we've ever had.

"You work with more darkness than most people," Cameron says. "You need more than a hobby to cleanse your brain."

"Then, what are you talking about?"

"Therapy." He snaps his fingers in front of my face when I begin to frown. "Stop that. Therapy can be wonderful if you do it right. I go."

"You do?" It's hard to think of my confident, self-assured brother spilling his guts to a stranger.

"Less so now *because* it was so helpful. But there were times in my life when I went weekly. Started in college, and I haven't stopped."

"I didn't know that," I mutter to my plate, feeling like I've missed some key information about my brother.

"Yeah, well, sometimes, I have trouble admitting it. The stigma and all that. I bet you're listing off people in your head right now who would judge you for going."

It's freaky how well he knows me. In my mind, I was imagining the reaction at the station. They're a good group, and I don't know for sure if they'd give me a hard time about it.

But would they trust me at their backs anymore if they knew about therapy? If they knew about the panic attacks?

"Sebastian." Cameron's stern voice brings me out of my worries. "If I didn't go —if I'd never gone—I wouldn't be with Maurice. I wouldn't have been able to love him the way he deserved if I couldn't figure out how to take care of myself."

The confession sits heavy between us all.

"Shit," Kennedy mutters, and I have to agree.

And once again, I read the silent message underneath his words.

How can you make things work with Gwen if you don't take care of yourself?

Chapter Forty-Seven

GWEN

Sometimes, I think being stuck in traffic is what hell will be. Or maybe purgatory.

— POSTCARD FROM RYAN, MASSACHUSETTS

Watching the glitter beard video was a mistake. I knew it the moment Sebastian turned toward the camera and smiled.

I'd held out for a full week after the Elaine encounter. But today …

It was too much.

I've been trying my hardest not to shy away from basic interactions with Sebastian. He lives in Green Valley now, and I told him I wanted to be friends. And I figure friends wave at each other.

They do not gape though. But that's exactly what I've been doing each and every time I've seen him.

Can anyone blame me though?

Monday, the fire department got a few packages that needed to be carried into the office, which happened to take me past a workout station set up with machines and weights. And there was Sebastian, hanging from a bar, slowly pulling himself up.

Over and over again.

When he let go, our eyes met.

I plopped the packages on the closest table, said, "Howdy, buddy," saluted him, and then made my escape.

Overall, I gave myself a seven out of ten for the reaction, proud of my ability to form any coherent words at all.

Tuesday, I was happy to see there were no packages for the department, only mail for the outside mailbox. But Sebastian was on duty again, and I know this because he was outside, washing the ambulance, his white shirt soaking wet and sticking to every inch of his chest. When I was able to breathe again, I realized he was waving at me. I waved back and tried not to peel out.

Wednesday, he wasn't at the department. He was at his house, mowing the lawn, grass adhering to his bare, sweaty chest.

Thursday, he was back at work, washing the fire truck. I guess the vehicles are too large to scrub them all in one day. A fact that only means I suffer for longer.

Friday was my day off, and I refused to leave my house, for fear I'd see him out and about, looking too good, his magnificent hair in disarray around his face, begging for my fingers to comb through the strands. His hazel eyes telling me to give in and pretend happy endings were possible.

Today, I was back out on my route, trying to remember what his work schedule was and if I could get through the day safely. My whole body was tense as I approached the fire department. And then I saw it. The third bay was open, another emergency vehicle pulled out into the front drive.

And there, yet again, was a wet and soapy Sebastian.

Something in me broke. I didn't look at him when I waved. Just flicked a hand, shoved the mail in their box, and drove away with my stare resolutely out the windshield.

And when I got home, I watched the video.

Mistake.

The sight of us smiling and joking together brought back too many painfully good memories. Halfway through, I shut it off and tried to convince myself I was fine.

But I am *not* fine.

To take my mind off the abysmal state of my social life, I try to at least make myself look pretty on camera. Another mistake.

"And this, my lovely viewers, is the look you get when you let a three-year-old handle your makeup!" The false cheery smile melts from my face as I take in the mess I've made of myself on the little video box on my computer screen.

There is no child to blame. I'm the one who made this monstrosity.

I'm not even sure what my end product was supposed to be. I just picked up some brushes and went to town.

This video will go with me to my grave.

I drop my brush, pink powder exploding from the bristles in a damning cloud, and I bury my face in my hands.

What is wrong with me? We reached the end I had known was coming. Why can't my heart and libido accept that?

Raising my chin, I stare at the small green dot that tells me the camera is still recording. I remember the first time I did this. Made a video of me doing my makeup. Some books on grief said journaling could help, but I didn't want to write things down. Instead, I decided to do a video journal. Talk to myself while I did my makeup.

But in the beginning, I ended up talking to Gran.

The little green dot became her. I pretended she was sitting on the other side of the screen, smiling quietly, listening as I told her about my day. When that got boring, I'd talk about the makeup, the new techniques I was trying and why I liked certain colors and what I thought I might do in the future.

At some point, all my talking centered on the makeup, and that was when I decided to start posting the videos. In case there was someone in the world like me. Lonely and looking for someone to listen to.

I haven't felt this lonely in a while. And my heart hurts with missing people.

Sebastian.

My grandmother.

"Hey, Gran," I say to the little green light. "It's been a while."

And I tell her all of it.

How I decided to stop avoiding adventure and stop avoiding the boy I liked. How I thought he'd liked me, too, all those years ago. How I'm sure now that there's something between us.

But I don't think that something is enough. Not for him anyway.

Not when Elaine lingers as a possibility. Ignoring her existence was the perfect way to get my heart broken.

But wasn't it already cracked?

Because right now, there might as well be a fissure running jagged down the middle, leaking fluid and affection, scalding my insides with missed chances.

Was there ever a time for us?

Even when we were together, I never felt we were truly on our own. A shadow lurked just over his shoulder. Or maybe over mine.

Was it in the shape of Elaine? I always imagined so, but maybe I was wrong.

Because right now, that destructive shadow looks an awful lot like me.

In sad clown makeup.

"So, that's where I am, Gran." I swallow back tears. "I miss you. So much. I wish you were here."

The green light quietly stares back at me, existing but never answering. I click to stop recording, and the light dims, which makes me want to cry all the more. But I turn to my mirror instead, facing the mess I've made of myself.

"This is going to take so many wipes," I mutter, poking at purple dots I think I meant to be freckles.

If I let myself ponder how much makeup I wasted in this endeavor, I might finally start sobbing, which would make this a truly horrendous look.

From downstairs, I hear the sound of the front door opening, and I wonder which of my parents got home. Either way, they tend to leave me to my own devices when I'm in my bedroom. They're thoughtful like that, and they seem content to have me live here as long as I'd like. I had to strong-arm them into letting me pay part of the utilities bill.

Thoughts of Sebastian's small rental come to my mind. When I move out, I'd like to find a place like that. I don't need a lot of space.

My mind goes on a twisting tangent I can't wrestle away from. Of me showing up on his doorstep, a few cardboard boxes in my trunk. And I pretend he'd give me that medicinal smile that would cure this cardiac rupture—or whatever paramedics call a broken heart.

I rub my chest, wishing the pain didn't feel so real. Shouldn't emotions stay in my brain? Isn't that what we learned in school? That all the thoughts and feelings are electrical pulses in our noggins?

So, why does my whole body hurt?

My heart … God, my heart. It's just supposed to pump blood. Not hold this terrible longing. Maybe I'd understand all of this if I'd gotten a chance to dissect a frog in Biology.

But if I'd gotten that chance, my whole life would be different.

My bedroom door flings open, causing me to yelp and almost tumble from my chair.

But then the world rights itself when I stare into a familiar bearded face and hear a rumbling laugh I've missed.

"What the hell did you do to your face?"

Chapter Forty-Eight

SEBASTIAN

Sometimes, I still hear your laugh.

— LETTER TO MARIA

After a satisfying thunk of my ax, two halves of the tree stump tumble in opposite directions.

Gotta save the good ones for later, I remind myself, one ear turned toward the road. Listening for the familiar rumble of a Bronco engine.

I want to make sure a certain postwoman gets a good view of me, out in my yard, chopping wood.

I'll admit, this isn't my best plan. But how else can I re-seduce the woman I love, who claims we're just friends? If she's telling the truth—that friendship is all she wants—then seeing me shirtless, in one of my tighter-fitting pairs of jeans, won't matter one lick to her.

Just like her delivering mail to the fire station when I happened to be out front, washing the ambulance—my white T-shirt getting real wet—didn't make her beautiful eyes go wide or her tempting mouth drop into an adorable O.

And it's not my fault the fire truck needed washing the next day I was on duty.

And that I've needed to mow the grass and chop some wood on my days off. Gotta get ready for the winter.

Therapy. Cameron's recommendation rattles around in the back of my head. I haven't dismissed the notion completely, but I don't see how talking to someone about my panic attacks is going to get Gwen to admit we're more than just friends.

The sun beats down on my back, sweat forming streams on my skin and sticking my hair to the back of my neck.

Maybe she'll remember how I got her all sweaty when I pushed her against my kitchen counter …

The sounds of tires and the rumble of an engine have me diving forward to grab a hefty log. As the vehicle approaches, I let loose a mighty swing, cracking the wood in half with one blow.

What d'ya think of that, honey?

I should keep going, pretend like I don't know she's here. But I can't pass up the little interaction she's still willing to give. My daily wave. Whether I'm washing the emergency equipment or splitting logs or doing some other task I hope turns her on, I always pause long enough to wave. And she waves back.

I need that wave.

All I want is to see her. A quick glimpse of her arm stuck out the window, taking a hand off that steering wheel that's on the wrong side. Maybe catch sight of the sun on her hair. From this distance, I won't be able to see the makeup she's done for the day unless she went drag-queen bold.

I kind of hope she did, just so I can catalog more details about her before she drives off.

But when I turn to eye the car, my shoulders sag, and I dismiss it. Not her Bronco. Not Gwen. Just someone driving by.

Only why are they stopping at my mailbox?

The arm that reaches out is not the slim, lightly tanned one I was hoping for. Instead, it's a beefy arm with darker skin and a lot more hair. Then, I spy the prominent black beard of another postal worker who should *not* be delivering my mail.

I'm halfway across my yard before I realize what I'm doing. The guy has plenty of time to drive off, but we lock eyes, and he stays parked. Waiting for me to approach.

"Hey, Arthur," I say when I get within hearing distance, hoping my voice doesn't come out as desperate as my pounding heart is.

Arthur's only response is a single brow raise. Damn, that move is badass. I've only ever been able to raise both, which leaves me looking surprised rather than coolly disdainful.

"Isn't this Gwen's route?" I ask. "I thought I'd see her working today."

With intimidating precision, he lets his single brow drop back into a linear position with his other, and he gives me another long pause that has me remembering I'm a sweaty mess, trying to look like a mountain man wet dream for Gwen. And I'm clutching an ax.

Not the best way to hold a casual conversation.

"I was"—I clear my throat and toss a thumb over my shoulder—"just chopping some wood."

"I gathered that." He does not sound impressed. But so what? He's not the one I'm trying to get hot and bothered.

The heat of the day, mixed with an anxious twinge in my chest, keeps me sweating, and I peel my baseball cap off, the material gone dark pink with perspiration. I use the shirt tucked in my back pocket to mop up my face.

If Gwen isn't coming, I don't want to keep standing out here. But I need answers.

"Does this work?" Arthur tilts his chin toward me, then glances at the overly large wood pile.

I've been out here a while. I didn't want to miss the mail delivery.

And now, I've been found out.

Briefly, I consider pretending I don't know what he's talking about. But Arthur is Gwen's friend, and the guy can smell my bullshit. If I ever want him even close to my side, I need to stick with honesty.

"Well, I'm standing here, talking to you instead of the woman I wanna be talking to. So, you tell me."

Arthur's beard might twitch at that, but it's hard to tell. There's so much hair, and whatever expression might have started is gone the next moment.

"You don't know," he finally says. Not a question.

My lungs squeeze, refusing to allow me to fill them the entire way.

"Know what?" I eke the question out.

"Gwen's gone." Then, the man shifts his car into drive and pulls away, leaving me in frozen panic.

Gwen is gone? Like *gone*, gone?

It can't be. I just saw her yesterday, right before Grizz came out and told me that if I washed the trucks any more, the paint would peel off.

Where would she even go?

But then I think about her travel plans. All the trips she's apparently spent years mapping out. The far-flung friends her Gran had.

She could have gone anywhere. For any length of time. For *forever*.

"No," I mutter to myself, dropping the ax and plunging my hands into my hair, fisting my fingers. "She wouldn't have just *left*."

But I don't know that. And I'm not on the top of her list of people to tell her traveling plans to.

I need to find someone who is.

Arthur, obviously, is out of the question. The guy seems to like the idea of torturing me with this information—fuck him very much.

I need to find someone nicer.

After stripping off my sweat-drenched clothes and splashing some water on my face—too impatient to take a full shower even though I sorely need one—I get dressed and head out. I drive across town, hoping that because it's summer, the person I'm looking for will be home.

I park in front of a small house with white siding and blue shutters. The last time I was here was high school, when Gwen and I had a group project. She had invited me over, and I ate peanut butter and jelly sandwiches her mom had made and tried not to stare too obviously at my partner as she wrote our project information on a bright orange poster board.

When I knock, I cross my fingers in my pockets, hoping for the best.

After the count of five, the door opens to show an average-height woman with wavy brown hair, starting to show a touch of gray at the roots. Her smile is so familiar that I stop breathing for a second, then start back up again because I'm frantic for information.

"Hello, Mrs. Elsmere. Good to see you, ma'am. Hope you're doing well."

The woman with similar cheekbones and nose to her daughter gazes curiously at me. "Sebastian Kirkwood. How are you?"

"I'm …" *Miserable because your daughter is missing from my life*. "I'm getting by. Sorry to disturb you, ma'am. Only I'm wondering if Gwen is home."

This has her brows dipping further. "You're looking for Gwen?"

"Yes. Uh, we've reconnected recently. We're friends."

We were more, but she insists friends is all we are, so that's what I'll stick to. For now.

"Oh. I'm sorry. I didn't know."

That has me flushing with shame. Of course Gwen didn't tell her mom about us spending time together. I'd asked her to keep it all a secret.

"I think your daughter is amazing," I say, overwhelmed with the urge to speak the truth to anyone and everyone who's around to hear it.

She gets a quizzical smile on her mouth and leans a shoulder against the door, not inviting me in, but not shooing me away. "I think so too. And she's taken her amazingness out of town. Gone off on an adventure."

"Alone?" I choke out.

Of course alone. Because she doesn't need me. Not like I need her.

Mrs. Elsmere slowly shakes her head. And that's all she gives me. I wonder if she's been taking lessons from Arthur.

"Well, thank you for letting me know, ma'am. Any idea when she'll be back?"

Mrs. Elsmere narrows her eyes at me—an expression the middle school teacher honed to a point on misbehaving students. "She didn't say."

The bottom of my stomach seems to be missing, and no doubt, Gwen's momma can see the anxious sweat on my palms when I give her a wave. "All right then. I'll just … keep an eye out for her. Have a good day, ma'am."

Mrs. Elsmere smiles, but not with her eyes. "Of course, dear. Oh, and congratulations on your upcoming marriage."

Ah. Yes. I guess Kennedy's blabbering didn't make it *all* the way around Green Valley. Don't I look like the slimiest asshole?

"Thank you for the well wishes, but Elaine and I aren't together anymore. Haven't been for a few months now." My brain wants to keep going, add more to the statement.

And I love your daughter.

But I keep my lips closed because I want Gwen to be the first person to hear those words from me. I pray that wherever Gwen is, she decides to come home. Preferably on her own.

Chapter Forty-Nine

GWEN

I miss you all. Think I'll have to stop home soon.

— POSTCARD FROM RYAN, GEORGIA

T wo days in a truck cab with my brother, and I'm trying to convince myself I'm not bored.

And I'm failing.

"So, I've told you all the Green Valley gossip you missed over the past years."

"Thanks for that," Ryan grumbles, not sounding thankful at all.

"Okay, now, it's your turn."

"My turn to what?"

"To entertain me with stories. Tell me all the drama and adventures of living life on the road."

He glances my way, thick brows dipped, before returning his attention to the highway running through Oklahoma.

This is the farthest I've ever been from home, and part of that is exciting. Ryan said we'll make it to Texas by the end of the day. But I'm also slightly underwhelmed. The highway is like any other, and the landscape is just an endless stretch of flatness.

Not really the explore-the-world plans I had in my mind.

But I'm here with my brother, who I barely ever see, and he promised to stop laughing about the makeup mess he found me in. Although he sometimes lets out a stray chuckle, and I can see the memory playing behind his eyes.

"Didn't you read my cards?" he asks.

"Of course I did! Every one of them. I still have them too."

"Well, there ya go."

"There I go what?"

"I send you all the interesting stuff. When it happens, I find a postcard, write it down, and send it to you."

"Those are *all* your stories? You don't have any more?"

Ryan gives me a disgruntled side-eye, then taps his phone to life, where it's mounted on the dashboard. "No. Put on some music. Or a podcast."

"You've got to be kidding me. We barely ever see each other, and you're saying we've already run out of things to talk about?"

"Wanna talk about why you're so sad?"

My mouth hangs open. I'm struck quiet by his question. After a moment, I snap my jaw shut and swallow down my discomfort.

"It's not a big deal. And you could make me happy by chatting with me."

Ryan shifts in his seat, and I wonder if his butt ever goes numb, like mine sometimes does on longer days of driving. When that happens, I usually pull off to the side of the road and do some jumping jacks. Good to keep the blood pumping. Also earns me strange looks from random people driving by.

"Nah. I think it is a big deal."

I scoff. "It's not." I won't let it be.

Ryan pinches his lips and taps a thumb on the steering wheel. "If it was, would you tell me?"

"Sure." The word sounds like a lie when I say it, and I stare out the truck window, hoping he doesn't notice.

"Who else would you tell?"

I sigh dramatically. This was not the kind of chatting I had in mind. "I don't know. But I don't need to know because it's *not a big deal*."

Because if I admit it is, then that would mean something like my heart is broken. Which is impossible because I prepared for things to end. I knew the happiness was temporary, so I'm *fine*.

Not wanting him to pick at me anymore, I give in, reach for his phone, and bring up a classic country station to listen to.

The first song that starts playing is "9 to 5" by Dolly Parton, and I gasp as the memory of the drag show hits me. Such a colorful memory of joy and freedom and meeting Sebastian's eyes throughout the night and knowing we were sharing the thrill of the experience.

I skip the song, ignoring Ryan's protest.

A few more miles pass under the tires before my brother pauses the music.

"I never apologized," he says, taking me by surprise.

"For what?"

"For Gran."

The topic shocks me so much that I flinch. Talking about her doesn't hurt as much as it used to, but people don't bring her up much. And when they do, it's not to apologize.

"Why would you need to? It's not like you gave her cancer." I stare at the side of Ryan's face, trying to read his mind. But I guess that's a psychic connection reserved for twins because I've got no idea what's rattling around in his noggin.

"I meant, when things got bad. Momma and Gran and Dad decided how much to tell you. I didn't like the idea of lying, so I left. Got this job and avoided the hard stuff. But I should've told you the truth. So, I'm sorry."

And I'm back to gaping at him.

I know now that when my grandmother got really sick, my family tried to keep the worst of it from me, but I didn't realize that was why Ryan had left. I thought he was just the restless sort.

"Well …" My throat is all full of gravel. I cough to clear it. "I don't hold anything against you."

"You don't?" He sounds surprised. "You should."

"So … you *don't* want me to forgive you?"

Big brothers don't make sense.

"I'm not saying that. But it wasn't right. You deserved to know the truth, no matter how hard it was. Gran was your best friend, and then she was gone. And you hadn't known it was coming, and I've thought about that so much in the years since. It tears me up, thinking about it."

With only a side view of his face, I can still see the devastation.

"It was rough, but I got through it. And I don't blame you for anything. Why are you even bringing this up now?"

"Probably because I found you sobbing in your room, looking like a birthday clown who just got fired, and it's been days, and you still refuse to tell me what's wrong." He taps his thumbs in an agitated rhythm. "I figure you don't trust me anymore. And I deserve that. But I wish you did."

The truck cab vibrates with the rumble of the engine and the weight of my shocked silence.

Not trust Ryan? I want to scoff at the notion. Tell him he's being ridiculous. Claim he's breathed in too much exhaust over the years and it's messing with his brain.

But when I open my mouth, no words come out.

Is he right?

Though it was the worst time in my life, I take a moment to remember the days, weeks after Gran passed. I felt like I was a piece of wood someone had taken an ax to. Split me right down the middle and tossed my other half in a nearby fire. She was gone, and I would never be whole again.

Everyone I loved had assured me there was nothing to worry about before the end.

They were wrong.

My hand clenches and releases on my thigh. I'm a whole piece of wood again, though battered from the loss. But how much of me would remain if an ax split me again?

That's what I'm afraid of. Losing myself when I lose someone else. If I don't love someone as much as I loved Gran, then it can't hurt as much when they go.

Sebastian's face comes to my mind—hurt, bewildered eyes holding mine. I told him he was my friend and that was all I ever wanted. The first part was true, but the second was a lie to keep him from eventually cutting me in two.

"I'm not with Elaine." Sebastian's voice plays through my head.

I didn't believe him. Not really. Yes, I acknowledged that they hadn't slept together because I can't fathom Sebastian intentionally lying to me.

But when he told me they were over, I refused to trust him. Refused to trust that the feelings he might have for me would stick around.

Just like I've stopped trusting Ryan to be here for me if I need him.

Dang it. My brother's right.

Hate when that happens.

"I was crying about a guy. Because I like him"—*more than like*—"and he likes me." The confession is an olive branch.

Ryan grunts. "So, what's the problem?"

"Me, I guess." My fingers pick at the worn seat cover.

My brother sits quietly for a stretch, then pulls a package of gum out of the center console and offers me a piece. The minty flavor and companionable chewing are oddly soothing.

"You having trouble believing a good thing'll last?"

"Something like that." *Exactly like that.*

"Because …" he starts the sentence and lets it linger in the air for me to finish.

"Because," I huff, "I planned a life of good things with Gran. Because I thought she'd get better and she didn't."

He slants a gaze my way, as if to say, *See? Told ya so.*

"Yeah. Hush your knowing looks. Maybe you're right." Maybe I have trouble with trust.

"Now, will you take my apology?"

"Fine. Apology accepted."

"Good. So, who's this guy? I know him?"

When I admitted the truth, I knew we'd get here. Still, I try not to cringe or sound too suspicious. "You've met a time or two."

"Hmm." Ryan pops on his gum as he thinks. "Is it one of those guys you work with? Arthur or Lance?"

"No. We're just friends. He doesn't work at the post office."

"Well, come on now. Give me a name. I'm not one of those Neanderthal brothers who'll threaten him with a shotgun just for giving you heart eyes."

"You sure?"

"Course I'm sure."

"You promise?"

"Want me to swear a blood oath or somethin'? Just tell me who this fella is. I won't say a bad word against him."

He should learn not to make promises he can't keep.

"What if it's Sebastian?"

"Sebastian …" He chews the name over before recognition flashes in his eyes. "Sebastian Kirkwood? Are you screwing with me? No way. No way in hell." He slams a fist on the steering wheel. "That man is dead to our family."

"Come on, Ryan. You cannot still be holding that grudge."

"You bet your ass I can. That grudge will die with me."

"It was just a piece of cake!"

"It was *pie*. And it was the *last* piece. That fucker knew I was going for it, but I dropped my fork. One second, I was bending over to pick it up. The next second, I was standing, and he was strolling away with my piece of pie."

"Okay, so everything you just said about believing a good thing, I should toss that out the window because when Sebastian was seven, he accidentally took the dessert you'd wanted at the Jam Session?"

"Ha! You're in love with him, aren't you? You'd have to be to take his side over mine. He's already corrupting you."

"You spend too much time alone in this truck."

"That way, I never have to deal with the pie thieves of the world."

"Do you think, for me, you could give him a second chance?"

With aggressive movements, Ryan shoves a second piece of gum in his mouth and starts chomping violently. A full minute passes before he answers. "Fine." He chews for a moment more. "So, what are you gonna do about the dirty, rotten pie thief?"

Chapter Fifty

SEBASTIAN

I wish I had known sooner. I'm afraid I'll never see you again.

— LETTER TO MARIA

"I t's nice to meet you, Sebastian." The dark-haired woman leads me into her office and waves for me to sit. "Now, why don't we start with what has you coming in today?"

I try not to fidget on the couch cushion as I meet Dr. Linares's eyes. There's no reason I should find her office uncomfortable. She's decorated the place with muted colors; a few plants sit by the window, and abstract art hangs on the wall. The temperature is warm, but not stifling. No odd smells or distracting noises.

Just the tapping of my fingers against my jean-clad legs.

But I can't stop the nerves creeping through me, knowing this next hour is all going to focus on me. My brain. My emotions.

"My brother suggested it. This. Therapy. He goes. To therapy, I mean."

Hell, now, she's going to start taking notes. *Patient can't form proper sentences.*

Dr. Linares smiles, the expression gentle as it creases the brown skin around her cobalt eyes. She doesn't write anything.

"That's not uncommon. To find therapy more approachable when we know family and friends are also going."

She makes a good point. It would have been one thing if Cameron had just told me to go. But the suggestion felt less … judgmental, I guess, when he said he's been in therapy for years.

"So, your brother recommended you come. Do you know why?"

I open my mouth to make a joke. To tease and banter and make this woman laugh, so she doesn't try digging deeper.

But that's not going to fix anything. I swallow, then try again.

"I have panic attacks sometimes. They … I don't know. I can still work." That last bit comes out more defensively than I meant. "Sorry, ma'am. I only mean to say, I've found ways to deal with them." Hide from everyone nearby until the episode passes. "But I want to stop having them."

"That makes sense. We can certainly work on that. Why don't you help me get a better idea of your daily life?"

She has a voice as calming as her room, and while I don't find it easy to fill up the conversation with facts about myself, I try to outline how I've been living these past few months.

"You made a lot of life changes at once." Dr. Linares does make a note then. "How'd you come to those decisions?"

"My mom. Uh, wait." I wave my hands, then clasp them in my lap to keep from flailing. "That didn't sound … sorry."

"You don't have to apologize. Tell me however you need to."

"Okay." I breathe in deep and try to ignore the sweat gathering in my pits. This is worse than a workout at the station on a ninety-degree day. "I was talking to my mom on the phone, and I felt one—an attack—coming on, so I hung up fast. She must have picked up on something because she called back soon after and asked if anything was wrong."

"What did you tell her?"

"I—everything, I guess." I remember that day. I was too tired to keep all my worries to myself, so they flowed out of me, unchecked. "Well, not everything. I didn't tell her about the panic attacks. But I admitted my job was fucking—sorry, ma'am. I mean, *messing* with my head. How I was picking up extra shifts because I didn't want to go home, but every shift, I felt like someone was going to die and it'd be my fault. Because I—" I cut myself off, not ready to talk about that yet. Maybe not ever. "And, yeah … then that somehow had me telling her I thought the wedding was a mistake and I didn't know what to do and how I felt so … trapped."

If she noticed my slip, she doesn't mention it. "And then what happened?"

"She thanked me." I still can't believe it. I'd braced for a lecture on responsibility, but she seemed grateful for what I'd said. "She told me that whatever I decided, going forward, she would support me. And that I could always come home. After that, I couldn't stop thinking about her saying I got to decide how to move forward. Like I had a choice. A few days later, she texted me about the job opening in the Green Valley Fire Department. And I don't know if it was a sign, but it had me realizing I could pick a different direction. And maybe escape these panic attacks."

"What happened with the panic attacks? Once you moved?"

"I thought they went away." Weeks without one, and I finally started relaxing. "Thought that working in a low-key place was doing the trick."

"But they came back?"

"Yeah, I … well, bad shit—sorry, ma'am—bad stuff happens everywhere. And I'm still a paramedic."

She sketches another note. "And the attacks happen at work?"

"Uh, no actually. I mean, I think they happen after bad days at work. But I'm usually at home or maybe in my car."

She nods and gazes at me with an understanding tilt to her head. "Though it might be unpleasant, what I would like you to do next is explain what was happening—what you were saying, doing, thinking—right before your last attack."

My guts turn watery at the thought, but I give a stiff nod and think back to that moment. It was on the drive home after talking to Gwen's mom. I pulled over on the side of the road, once again battling that dueling perspective of knowing I wasn't dying, but my brain shouting at me that I was, as I gasped for breath and my heart beat too hard and my vision blurred. Luckily, no one came along to ask me if I was all right.

"So, you were looking for this woman, Gwen, and couldn't find her. Can I ask what your relationship is with her?"

Wouldn't I love to have an answer to that?

"It's complicated. We were together. Now, I guess we're friends, but it still feels romantic for me."

The doctor nods and makes a note, and I don't know what she's writing down, but I hate the idea of her thinking anything bad about Gwen.

"And did you work that day?"

The shift of focus has me blinking and redirecting my brain.

"Uh, no, ma'am. Not at the station anyway. I'd been chopping wood all morning."

She nods. "And the attack before that. What was happening in the moments before?"

A grimace twists my mouth. "I was fighting with my ex. About how we were pretending to be together so she didn't have to tell people right away about our split."

At least I know that argument won't come up again. Elaine texted a few days ago to tell me she finally broke the news to her parents. I tried calling her, but she didn't pick up. Instead, she texted that she needed time. There's still guilt lingering in my gut whenever I think about what Elaine must be going through, but I know I have to trust her to deal with this in her own way.

We're not a unit anymore. Even though that's what I wanted, I still care.

"And were you working before that argument?"

"No. I was off that night, but I was up for most of it anyway because she'd … overindulged. I had to pick her up and keep an eye on her."

"And the call with your mom. What were you discussing before the attack came on?"

I rub the back of my neck as I try to recall the words. "The wedding, I think. My ex and I were engaged before I broke it off. Mom was asking about plans and offering to help."

"And did you work that day?"

"Yes, ma'am. Just finished a twelve-hour shift. Had a lot of calls that night."

The therapist nods, as if I just confirmed something for her. "Well, there does seem to be a pattern."

"What do you mean?"

She glances at her notes, then back to me. "This is only a theory at this point, but it seems as though your panic attacks come on when you are both exhausted and faced with relationship stress."

I blink at her for what feels like a good five minutes.

"Huh?"

Dr. Linares offers me another of her gentle smiles. "That's likely oversimplifying the problem. I'm sure there are many nuances. But you said yourself, the attacks don't tend to happen while on your job. That doesn't mean that the mental stress of your career doesn't contribute, but it also doesn't seem to be the trigger. Situations related to your romantic partners do."

"So, what? Stop dating, and I'll stop having panic attacks?" Not going to happen.

If Gwen gives me another chance, I'll find a way to deal.

But the doctor is already shaking her head. "No, I would never suggest that. What we want to do is identify the causes, make *reasonable* lifestyle changes, and develop exercises to help you cope when you feel an attack coming on."

That sounds doable. But it can't be that easy. And she doesn't know about *the* event.

"Someone died," I blurt, then immediately wish I could take the words back.

I don't know this woman. Telling her about what happened—that should be weeks, months, years down the line. If ever.

But I also can't handle the thought of this therapist trying to give me hope without knowing all the darkness. She thinks it's relationships? It can't be. It has to be *that* night. My mistake. My screwup.

"What do you mean, Sebastian? Who died?" Her eyes are all concern, no judgment.

That'll change soon. Might as well get the truth out. See the disgust on her face now.

"When I lived in Merryville, I took on too many shifts. I knew I was working too much, but I couldn't sleep, and being around Elaine—my ex—and acting like we were some perfect couple was … I was a coward. I ran to work. And one night … fuck. Sorry, ma'am." But I can feel the tears in the back of my throat as I remember.

And over the next half hour, she coaxes the story out of me. How there was a call to a house where a woman was having a bad reaction to some drugs. We got her in the bus, got her Narcan, left for the hospital, and thought everything was taken care of.

But there was someone else in the house. Someone we'd left behind, and by the time we got the call to go back for him, it was too late. He was gone.

"The attacks started after that night," I confess.

Dr. Linares nods, but her expression doesn't condemn me. "And you think you're at fault?"

"Yes." The word is ragged.

"Did you have a partner?"

"I … yeah."

"Is it their fault too?"

Thinking back, I realize I never blamed Craig, the EMT working with me that night.

"I should have checked the other rooms," I say in response.

She doesn't agree or disagree. "It's clear this weighs heavy on you, and I wouldn't doubt the event is connected to your feelings of panic. Like I said, these things aren't clear-cut. Our brains make connections and have reactions we don't expect."

A silent nod is all I can manage.

She leans forward in her chair, holding my eyes. *Seeing* me. "Dealing with your attacks won't be a quick fix, Sebastian. It'll take work and dedication. But I think therapy can help. If you'd like, we can set up weekly appointments."

Despite the raw sensation in my chest, I also feel … not better exactly. But productive maybe? As if I've stepped forward instead of staying stagnant in my miserable memory.

And I want to keep going.

"Okay."

Chapter Fifty-One

GWEN

Been stuck driving back and forth through deserts these past few days. Back and forth. But I'm heading to the coast finally. Need some water in my eyeline.

— POSTCARD FROM RYAN, TEXAS

Ryan asked me what I was going to do about Sebastian.

Well, turns out, I'm going to trust him.

So, I demanded my brother drop me off at the closest town with a bus station, so I could get home and try to fix the mess I'd made. Or maybe the one *we'd* made. Neither one of us had gone about this the right way.

Because even though I want to trust Sebastian, I can't keep doing this secret relationship.

If he needs more time to end things with Elaine, then he can have it. And I'll have to trust that there's a time for us in the future.

Luckily, Arthur is kind enough to pick me up from the Greyhound station in Merryville. I'm gonna give my friend a huge birthday present this year.

"So, you're in love with Sebastian Kirkwood," he says by way of greeting when I slide into his passenger seat.

"What?" I yelp. "Why—who—I would never ..."

Fuck a duck, how'd he find out?

He gives me a heavy dose of side-eye. "Seat belt."

With nervous fingers, I strap myself in and try to think of a misdirection. I can't be telling Sebastian I love him the same time I admit I somehow blabbed his secret.

"Calm down," Arthur grumbles. "Everyone knows."

I groan, letting my head drop back to the seat. "God, everyone? For how long? Was I that obvious?" Someone must have seen me drooling over the paramedic while he was washing the fire truck. "The whole town must think I'm some kind of hussy. Or just pathetic, panting after a taken man."

"I meant, everyone knows about their split." Arthur's no-nonsense voice cuts off my anxious rambling. "For a month now, I'd say. That Kennedy Kirkwood cannot keep a secret." Arthur merges into traffic leading out of Merryville, pointing his car toward home. "Doubt anyone knows about you two though."

Everyone knows? "I'm lost."

"It's not a brainteaser. People know Sebastian and Elaine are over cause Kennedy let it slip. I've seen you two talkin'. Now, you're rushing back from your trip 'cause you need to *tell someone something important*, you said. So, I figured it out."

He did.

Everybody knows.

A few days ago, that wouldn't have mattered much to me. I still would've convinced myself that there was no future for Sebastian and me. Wouldn't have realized how I'd withheld my trust, believing he'd always go back to Elaine.

Good things can happen to me and not end in disaster, I remind myself.

If all the Green Valley gossips know about the breakup, there's nothing stopping me from getting loud about what I want.

And I want Sebastian Kirkwood.

"Good job." I smile over at my friend. "You guessed it. I'm in love with Sebastian."

Arthur gives a curt nod, like he just crossed off an item on his to-do list.

Check—my friend is in love with the handsome paramedic.

The car goes quiet for a stretch, and I try to figure out what I'm going to say to Sebastian when I show up. Blurting *I love you* won't be enough. I shoved him away, and he needs to know why.

"What does it feel like?" Arthur asks abruptly.

"What?"

"Love. Loving Sebastian."

"Oh." My mouth hangs open as I try to put into words something I know but don't have a clear way to explain. "I guess … it's this pressure. Or a pull inside me." My fingers fiddle with the front of my shirt, where my heart threatens to escape my chest. "I'm getting tugged toward him. I want to be around him. Hear his voice. I want to talk to him. About anything. I just want more of his thoughts. And there's the physical stuff, too, but that's just part of it. I want *him*." I grimace. "Sorry. I don't know a better way to put it."

"Hmm," is Arthur's response.

"You've never been in love?"

He shakes his head slowly. "I love people. But never like you're saying."

"Well, I'm sure you'll find it. If you want it, I mean. You don't have to fall in love. But you could find someone easily, I'm sure." My nerves about the upcoming interaction have me babbling a bit. "You're kind and funny and good-looking. Sebastian asked once if you and I were dating. I think he was jealous of you. But I told him we've only ever been friends."

Arthur grunts. "Well, we did kiss."

That's one way to shut down my brain. "What?" I stare at his face, searching for a smile or some other indicator that he's joking. "No, we didn't."

"Yeah, we did." His thick brows dip as he glances over at me before refocusing on the tree-lined road. "Halloween. Two years ago."

"Halloween …" I mutter to myself, then gasp in horror, recalling the shitshow I was that night at the Jam Session. What I can remember of it anyway. "Cletus Winston gave me moonshine! I forgot my own name that night. You're saying we kissed?"

"You kissed me."

My mind is a black hole when it comes to that night. "Then, what happened?"

"You said, 'Wow. That was god-awful. No, thank you.' Then, you fell asleep in that seat." He gestures to the one my butt now occupies.

"Oh hell, Arthur. I'm sorry."

He shrugs. "Wasn't meant to be. I'm okay with that."

The way he says *meant to be*, as if the words carry extra weight, I could believe Arthur is a secret romantic.

"Thank you for still being my friend even though I said our kiss was awful."

His beard twitches. "You're welcome."

As we pass the town sign, all my words dry up. I chew on the inside of my cheek and twist my fingers together, trying not to play out all the bad scenarios in my head.

Remember, I think hard to myself, *there are good outcomes too. The only way to get them is to try.*

"Your house or his?" Arthur asks when we pause at a Stop sign.

"His. And I need you to drive away right after you drop me off, so I don't chicken out."

My friend huffs out a laugh but doesn't argue.

Other than a large pile of chopped wood in the side yard, Sebastian's house looks the same. Not that I expected it to change in the few days I was away, but everything seems different now, and I half-expect the world around me to reflect the shift.

Through the front window, I spy Curie lounging on the back of the couch. The sight has me smiling. Has me hopeful.

"I officially owe you a whole week of coverage and a box of Daisy's dough-nuts," I tell Arthur as I climb out of his car.

"I accept those terms." He gives me one of his rare smiles. "Good luck."

And like I asked, he drives away. Leaving me stranded.

I hike my backpack high on my shoulders and march to the front door, hoping determined steps will imbue me with confidence. Halfway to my destination, I realize there's a car in the driveway. A green one. The shade reminds me of the skin of a frog.

And it's not Sebastian's car.

My stomach flamingos, which reanimated at some point during my life reevaluation, tremble in discomfort at the thought of finding Sebastian here with someone else. Elaine or maybe another woman he started dating after I insisted we were just friends.

I'm tempted, so very tempted, to turn around and hike back to town. Pretend I never showed up here and avoid the heartbreak of his rejection.

My feet stop moving, adhered to the walkway, waiting for my direction.

"Elaine asked me to the Sadie Hawkins dance." Sebastian's voice comes to me across a decade.

I mumbled a response, like *cool* or *fun*, when what I should have said was …

That sucks because I wanted to ask you. In case it's not obvious, I have a huge crush on you, Sebastian Kirkwood.

Teenage Gwen never had the courage to say those words.

Adult Gwen will have to make up for it.

I force my feet forward, straight up to the door, and knock. From inside the house, I hear footsteps. Anticipation and dread pump in my veins.

The door swings open, and I jerk back at the fierce scowl that greets me.

"Where the fuck have you been?"

Chapter Fifty-Two

SEBASTIAN

What does home look like for you? Could it look like here?

— LETTER TO MARIA

As I pull into the driveway of my house, I recognize a car already parked there. The sight has me sighing, but I decide avoidance isn't the best tactic.

When I walk in the front door, I can see straight down the hallway to the kitchen. There's a rolling chair not where I left it.

"Hello?" I toss my bag to the corner and watch as the chair swivels around, revealing my sister.

Kennedy is here to check on me. Again.

Ever since our sibling chat at Daisy's, she's been on high alert. I think the breakup—if I can even call it that since Gwen and I were never officially together—triggered an alarm in her brain. The memory of her ex-boyfriend no doubt playing on repeat. And with Cameron suggesting therapy, she's probably imagined every possible worst-case scenario, which means she's constantly showing up at my house *just because*.

I don't know if telling Kennedy about the panic attacks will ease her mind or give her rabid, protective impulse more focus. At least everything she does comes from a place of love, and I try not to let myself get frustrated at her urge to babysit me.

"Hello, Sebastian." My sister looks like a villain from a cheesy movie, sitting in the chair with Curie in her lap, stroking the cat's fur as she contemplates me.

I spread my arms wide and do a slow turn, showing every part of me is still in working order. My heart is what's malfunctioning, but I can keep that under the surface.

"What's with the creepy greeting?" I move around her, heading to the fridge for a snack.

She swivels to follow my path, petting my cat all the while. Purring fills the room.

"A little guard duty until you got home. I stopped by to check on you, and an unsavory character showed up."

When I straighten from the fridge, cup of yogurt in hand, I notice what the large office chair is blocking. A smaller kitchen chair shoved under the doorknob of my bedroom.

"Do you …" *She wouldn't.* "Do you have someone locked in my bedroom?"

"Yes." She strokes Curie another time. "And she's not coming out until she promises not to hurt you again."

When the reality of her words soaks through my work-tired brain, I drop my yogurt. The top ruptures, and white goop splatters across the floor, enticing Curie to jump out of Kennedy's lap. But I don't care that my cat is lapping my food off the floor.

All I care about is who's behind that door.

"Are you—is she—is *Gwen* in there?"

"Hi!" an achingly familiar voice calls out from behind the thin door. "And I'm not going to hurt him," the disembodied voice adds. "I'm just going to talk to him."

"There're a lot of ways to hurt someone!" Kennedy shouts back.

"I know."

There's a mournful note that has me stumbling, then striding forward.

Kennedy launches out of the desk chair, sending the thing spinning, and plasters her body starfish-style in front of my bedroom. "You can't just let her out!"

"You can't lock people in a room because they make you mad, Kennedy! This is kidnapping!"

"It's a ground-floor bedroom with a window," my sister retorts with a tone born for irritation. "She *wants* to be locked in that room. Because she knows what she did was messed up."

If there's retaliation from the woman in question, I'm too busy removing obstacles to hear it. First, I bend to scoop my sister in a fireman's hold.

Used to this tactic, she doesn't fight, instead going boneless. I've never understood the physics behind how a body somehow becomes heavier when relaxed as opposed to stiff. Something about throwing off balance. Either way, I'm trained to haul bodies around—and larger ones than Kennedy's. I walk her to the opposite side of the kitchen, plop her on a section of free counter space, and rush back to the bedroom door before she can try getting in my way again.

Removing the chair takes no time at all, and my breath comes in short, excited pants at the thought that I'm about to see Gwen.

Just one more barrier—

The doorknob doesn't turn.

I rattle it, grip harder, and try to force it in both directions. Shove forward, pull back.

Nothing budges.

"Gwen, the door is locked on your side." I press a flat palm against the surface, as if I could feel her through the wood.

"Yes. True." There's a pause that has me considering breaking the whole thing down to get to her. But she stops me with her next words. "See, the thing is, I kind of like the door where it is. Just for now. I think it'll help."

"Told you she wanted to be in there," Kennedy mutters, pouting as she leans against the kitchen counter.

I hush her with a growl, then lean my forehead on the barrier.

"Okay. We'll keep it closed for now." And yet I can't loosen my grip on the knob. I stand there, braced for the moment I can push the door open and see her again. "You said you wanted to talk?"

"I do." Pause. "I've been thinking a lot." Pause.

Every moment without words is torture. Without her face, her hands, her body in my eyeline, I have no clues as to what's coming next. There's just waiting.

"What have you been thinking about?" I prompt.

"You. Us. Why I can't date you."

My whole body sags.

"I told you, no hurting!" Kennedy shouts.

"Sorry! Sorry! I meant, why I *think* I can't date you."

Not a whole lot better, but adding that single word makes the statement less definitive.

"Talk it out with me, Gwen. Tell me why you think that."

There's a light thud on the other side of the door, and I can imagine her resting her forehead against the cheap material, just like me, only a few inches lower.

Open the door. Let me hold you.

I keep the words to myself.

"I've wanted to be with you since I was sixteen years old," she says.

Now, I'm the one pausing, absorbing the claim. *Since she was sixteen? Since Biology class?*

I had a crush back then too. And I thought she might. Was almost sure of it. Then, things shifted between us.

The jokes stopped. No more teasing or playful notes or silly faces or eye rolls shared when Mr. Parish said something ridiculous.

I never could figure out why. One time, she mentioned something about needing to get her grade up, and I figured maybe our playfulness was distracting her. It was distracting me, but in the best way.

Still, I didn't push her.

And we faded apart from each other until Mrs. Keen's accident forced us back together.

"I was going to ask you to the Sadie Hawkins dance," she says.

Now, that's an event I remember vividly. Because it was my first date with Elaine.

Could that have been why things between us changed? Would everything have been different if Gwen had asked me?

I imagine it. Me picking up Gwen in my dad's old Toyota truck, helping her tuck her skirt up away from the door and trying not to let on how sweaty my hands were.

Elaine smiled quietly at me the whole ride to the dance. I was a riot of excitement and nerves, wondering if I was doing my first official date right.

Gwen would have teased me. She would have joked and blushed and talked in her squeaky, high voice if I said something that surprised her.

That night with Elaine was good.

But that night with Gwen would have been *right*.

"Why didn't you?" I'm hoping she doesn't hear any accusation in my voice.

I don't blame her, but now, there's this whole life of what-if playing in the back of my mind. A life with Gwen. One where we passed more risqué notes in class and made out under the bleachers and shared a picture-perfect kiss in our graduation robes. A life where I met her gran and held Gwen when she found out about the diagnosis. Years where we cared for each other, supported each other, and made each other laugh. And maybe in that life, I still would have taken too much on at work and seen bad things and had panic attacks.

But I would have had Gwen combing her fingers through my hair and coaxing me to take time off to visit family and have little adventures.

Or maybe that's not how it would have gone with us. But we'll never know.

"Frogs," she croaks.

"Huh?"

"The day I was going to ask you was the same day we were going to dissect frogs in Biology. Mr. Parish saw me in the hall before class and told me to help him carry the containers into the lab. But I was wearing these new shoes—my whole outfit was new because I wanted to look pretty when I asked you—and they had heels, and I never wore heels because I was already so tall. Anyway, I tripped and fell. The container landed on top of me, the lid popped off, and I was drenched in formaldehyde-soaked frogs."

There is no universe where I imagined *that* being what had kept us apart.

"To this day, it's the grossest thing that has ever happened to me. I ran to the restroom and threw up. When I came out, Mr. Parish told me I could go home and we wouldn't ever have to talk about it, which sounded right as rain to me. If anyone had found out, I would've been dead-frog girl for the rest of my life."

Dead frogs. It's so hilarious and so tragic, and now, I'm pissed off at amphibians and my old high school teacher.

"But the next day—" I start.

"The next day, I came to class like nothing had happened. I asked you what I missed, and you listed off a bunch of things, *including* that Elaine asked you to the dance. And you said yes. And for sixteen-year-old me, that was a tragedy. All that time, I'd thought we were flirting. That you liked me."

If the situation were reversed, no doubt, I would've felt the same. But I said yes to Elaine because I was eager to have a girl be romantically interested in me. Gwen was funny and sweet to everyone. I figured I had a crush on a girl who only thought of me as a friend.

"I *did* like you. Of course I did. It's impossible not to."

There's a dry chuckle from the other side of the door. "Thank you. But I'm trying to—I don't know. Explain some misfiring in my mind."

"Okay, keep going."

"After I got over being weepy"—*shit, I made her cry?*—"I told myself I misread everything. And that it wouldn't have hurt so much if I'd never thought you liked me that way in the first place. That the best thing to do was to get over my crush. To move on."

Hell, is that what she's trying to do now? Repeat the past? Get over me?

"I get it, Gwen. That sucked. I sucked. But I'm here now, wanting to be with you." I flex my fist against the door, grinding my knuckles into the surface. "Is Elaine still a problem?"

"Kind of."

My stomach dips. "I swear we didn't sleep together. I was helping her ..." I want to go into more detail, but as much as I've claimed I don't owe Elaine, that doesn't mean I'm going to spread her dirty laundry around for anyone to see.

"I know. I believe you," Gwen says.

"If you do, why is Elaine a problem?"

Pause.

"She's a problem because there's this voice in my head that keeps telling me, at some point, you'll go back to her."

Damn it. I know how hard those mental voices can be to ignore.

"But I'm telling you—*swearing to you*—that's not what I want. We're over. For good."

Pause. Pause, pause, pauuuusssse.

My breath shudders from my body, and I wonder if I should run outside to see if Gwen is in the middle of climbing out of my bedroom window.

Then, I hear the rumble of her clearing her throat. "Up until a few days before my gran died, I thought she was recovering."

There's a soft intake of breath from behind me, and I realize Kennedy is still lurking in my kitchen. I glare at her over my shoulder, but she's staring at her shoes, unable to see my censure.

"I'm sorry, Gwen. That must have been hard." I'm not sure what this has to do with us, but if Gwen is ready to be vulnerable with me, I'll take that as a good sign. "Holding on to that hope for so long."

"That's the thing." Her voice gets a desperate edge to it. "It wasn't hope. It was knowledge. I *knew* she was going to get better. Because up until that last bit, everyone had told me she was. Every single person I loved—except for my brother, who just didn't say anything—had lied to me."

That revelation floors me. Kennedy lets out a hiss behind me. My sister does not abide lying about important things.

"I know it sounds naive," Gwen continues, obviously misinterpreting our silence. "I mean, I was with her in the hospital every day. I saw her wasting away. But she told me it was temporary. That the treatments were making it look worse than it was. And if you ever spoke to my gran, you'd get it. When she told you something, you just believed her. It was impossible not to. So, I did. I believed her when she said the doctors were shocked by her recovery. That it was a matter of time before she got out of the hospital and then we'd travel the world together." The last word comes on a choked hiccup, and the sound batters my chest, breaking ribs like CPR. "And then she died. I had so little time to come to terms with it. I think it broke something in me—to be lied to like that. And I know she was trying to make it easier on me. But now, whenever someone tells me something good is going to last, all I think is that they're lying to make me happy." She clears her throat. "Or they're flirting, but they don't mean anything by it."

Fuck. Fuck a duck.

My high school screwup has melded with the emotional scarring left by her family's loving lies. No wonder Gwen hesitates to believe heartfelt declarations.

"What can I say? What can I do?"

Curie lies at the bottom of the door, swiping a paw through the crack, demanding to be let in. I can sympathize.

But Gwen is the one who has to remove this last barrier between us.

Chapter Fifty-Three

GWEN

Mountain roads in the Rockies are beautiful, but they're also fucking scary. Still, sometimes, you gotta drive them.

— POSTCARD FROM RYAN, COLORADO

W*hy am I still hesitating?*

I came to Sebastian's house with a purpose. To confess the brokenness in my soul and try to see if he could still care for me. But here I stand, frozen a foot from the door, clutching a pillow to my chest that smells of his sandalwood shampoo. This single pillow has a pink pillowcase, and the sight comforted me so much that I latched on to the plush object like a lifeline.

He's right there. Go get him!

But I can't move.

Because the fear still lingers. The nasty voice that whispers, *This is temporary. Don't get attached.*

I thought it would go away. I shone a light on it, figured out where the voice had grown from. I *understand* myself now.

So, why won't the worries go away? Why am I not better now?

Why can't I be the confident, *no doubt in her mind* woman that Sebastian deserves?

I shouldn't open the door if I don't deserve him.

"Gwen," he calls out, "if you think this—relationship, huge feelings—doesn't scare me, too, you're wrong."

"I know you're trying to make me feel better—"

"I'm serious, Gwen. I have …"

When he pauses, I lean closer to make sure I won't miss a word said in his deep voice.

"I have panic attacks. Like full-body, freak-out, *my brain's telling me I'm about to die* panic attacks. And a lot of times, relationship stuff triggers them. At least, that's what my therapist thinks."

There's a high-pitched exclamation that must be from Kennedy.

Sebastian huffs out a half-growl, half-laugh. "I cannot deal with sisterly concern at the moment, okay?"

"Oh God! Are you—right now?" Guilt has my fingers shaking as I reach for the door handle.

"No." Sebastian's steady voice stops me. "It's okay. I'm good. I mean, I wish I could see your face. But I'm not having one. I just …" He trails off again, and I wonder if my hesitation puts him on edge the way his does with me. "I want you to know that I get what it's like to be scared of the future. Scared of how things will turn out." There's a shuffling noise, and I imagine him moving his body closer to the door. Closer to me, as if we could melt through the wood and meet. "And I promise, if you'll let me, I'll hold you when that fear comes on. Because I love you, Gwen."

The house goes still, quiet, every mote of dust pausing to hear his words.

"And maybe, when I need it, you could hold me too."

A silent question plays under that last request.

Could you love me too?

My heart shatters and reforms with Sebastian's words acting as the glue, binding the ragged edges together.

In that beautiful, painful moment, I realize exactly what I've done.

I'm the one with a closed door. Figuratively and literally.

If I was being honest with myself, I knew when Sebastian showed up outside of the post office that day that he was there for me and me alone. But I wasn't ready for him.

So, I shut the door on us.

And now, I'm the only one who can open it.

I have to accept that this fear lives in me, but it doesn't have to make my decisions for me. Moreover, I *refuse* to let my fear force me to think my loved ones are liars. People make mistakes, but that doesn't make them unworthy of trust.

I love Sebastian Kirkwood.

I need to trust him too.

Tossing the pillow to the side, I lunge forward and fumble with the lock. The moment it clicks, I wrench the door open and have to brace the full body of a man stumbling into me. But a second later, Sebastian catches his balance and scoops me into his arms. I expect him to seek out my mouth for a kiss, but he only does what he promised.

Sebastian holds me.

Arms a vise around my waist, face buried in my neck, he breathes me in.

"I love you too," I whisper, wrapping my arms around his neck, resting my cheek against the side of his head, reveling in the soft press of silky hair against my skin. *God, I missed this.*

When I blink my eyes open, I meet Kennedy's stare from across the kitchen.

Thank you, I mouth to her.

She smirks, though her gaze holds a hint of concern when it lands on her brother's back. Still, she gives me a tight nod and strolls out of the kitchen. Leaving us alone, except for the cat twining around our ankles.

"Could you say that again?" His question is gruff, the heat of his breath against my neck sending goose bumps racing over my body.

"I love you, Sebastian. And I believe you."

He loosens his hold then, enough so we can finally look at each other. Last time was only a matter of days ago, but it feels like ages.

"Hey, honey," he says with that medicinal smile spreading over his face. "I missed you."

"I missed you too." I swoop in for a quick kiss. Then linger for a long one.

When we break apart, we're both breathing hard.

"Where'd you disappear to?" he asks.

I grin. "My brother took me on a long-haul adventure. Gotta admit, I preferred Nashville with you. But don't tell him that."

Sebastian's brows lift. "You're telling me a trip with Ryan Elsmere somehow convinced you to give us a chance?"

"What's so unbelievable about that?"

"Well …" Sebastian dips his chin, looking guilty. "Because the man's hated me since I stole a piece of blueberry pie from him at the Jam Session a while back."

"You remember that?" Chuckles steal my breath, and my face hurts from smiling so big.

"He knows how to hold a grudge." The laughter in Sebastian's eyes tells me he's not too concerned.

I comb my fingers through his thick hair and enjoy his grumble of pleasure in response. "If he tries to start something at the next family gathering, I'll ask Kennedy to lock him in a room till he calms down."

Sebastian grimaces. "I'm gonna have a talk with her about that."

"No need," I assure him. "I'm glad she did."

"Oh, really?"

The teasing tone, so familiar, heats my body until I want to strip off every piece of clothing I'm wearing.

"Yep. In fact"—I let go of his neck with one arm and reach for the door handle— "I was thinking we might lock things up again."

With that, I tug him into the room, managing not to trip over Curie in the process, and close the door on the world.

Ready for some alone time with the man I love.

Epilogue

SEBASTIAN

Heaven is an empty road and a good song on the radio.

— POSTCARD FROM RYAN, TENNESSEE

I fell in love with you. Thank you. It was glorious.

— LETTER TO MARIA

A Little Over a Year Later

"Well, if it isn't my knight in shining armor." Mrs. Keen waves in greeting as she crosses the post office parking lot toward me.

I push off from where I was leaning on the side of my car.

"Afternoon, ma'am. And your true knight is still inside, finishing up her shift." I grin in anticipation of Gwen getting her sweet behind out here, so we can start our next adventure.

"Let's be fair and say it was a joint effort." Her strong, wrinkled fingers grip my forearm like a small hug. "You two make quite the pair. I'm glad our Gwen has you."

Heat and happiness fill my chest until I'm worried I might melt on the pavement. Almost a daily occurrence now that I get to constantly remind myself a particular mailwoman is in love with me.

"I'm the lucky one." I pat her hand. "You here for mail or makeup tips today?"

Agnes chortles. "Just need a few of these."

She waves a book of stamps in the air, and I spy the design.

Frogs.

Fuck a frog.

But I set aside my prejudice, smile wide, and wish the woman luck with all her letters as she walks off to her car.

Over a year later, and Mrs. Keen is all healed from her fall, but Gwen still checks in with her almost daily on her route, just in case.

A plaintive meow from my backseat has me seeking out Curie. I lean in through the open back window to get a better look at where she's strapped in. She's not happy about being contained within her cat carrier. My feline friend would prefer to have free rein in the car.

"Sorry, sweet girl. Safety first."

Her response is to gaze at me through the mesh fabric prison, blinking her set of huge green eyes that say, *I'm innocent. Why do you choose to torture me?*

"I'm not *that* easy of a pushover," I grumble at her.

"Oh, really?" The honeyed voice sounds from over my shoulder and has me grinning wide.

When I straighten, I find a gorgeous postal worker checking me out. Meanwhile, her grumpy coworker stands at her side, rolling his eyes, no doubt at me conversing with Curie. Well, Arthur can deal with it because my woman loves herself a devoted cat dad.

"Now, what's that supposed to mean?" I try frowning at Gwen, but I can never quite manage it. "I'm an immovable force. The intimidating disciplinarian."

Arthur snorts, and Gwen scoffs.

"Last night, you were sharing your ice cream with her. From the same spoon." She strolls up to me, and with one finger in the center of my chest, Gwen gives me a delicate shove that has me teetering back on my heels. "Pushover."

She's so cute when she teases me. I can't stop myself from leaning forward and kissing her sassy mouth.

"PDA," Arthur mumbles. "Gross."

Once Gwen and I went public with our relationship, all aspects of our lives started weaving together, including friends. Arthur might pretend to be annoyed by the air I breathe, but he always has a seat for me in his backyard and even brought out a spare guitar for me to fiddle with when I mentioned I took lessons when I was younger. In turn, I invited him to join a poker night at the station. I'm still waiting for him to take me up on the offer, but ever since I made it, I've noticed he's friendlier with me. At least, as friendly as a stoic, quiet type gets.

All this to say, I'm more amused than offended by the postman's commentary.

I break off the kiss, only to place another on Gwen's forehead, then meet his eyes with a shit-eating grin. "Brace yourself—the cutesy nicknames and baby talk are coming next."

Gwen giggles and wraps her arm around my waist. "Gonna take more than that to drive him off. Our dear friend Arthur has a special house guest he's avoiding."

The man glares at Gwen and shoves his hands in his pockets. "I'm not avoiding her."

"Oh, okay." Gwen shrugs and keeps smiling her innocent smile. "My mistake. Tell Robin I say hi."

With another scowl, the man stalks off across the parking lot, as if to prove he wasn't lingering.

"Isn't Robin his cousin's girlfriend?"

She answers me with a kiss. "It's a wild story that I suspect is only beginning. But we've got plenty of time on the road for me to tell it." Gwen pats my chest before jogging around to the passenger side of the car, sliding into her seat and turning to say hello to Curie.

When I settle in, I don't immediately start the engine, content to watch Gwen sweet-talk my cat. Our cat now since she moved in two months ago. Only took me ten months of begging and countertop orgasms.

But Gwen had insisted on taking our time, not rushing forward just to prove our fears wrong. Not every moment has been perfect. I still get the occasional panic attack, although therapy has helped me find healthy ways to deal with them. And Gwen had admitted part of holding off on living together was worry over our longevity.

So, we work together. Building trust and love every day.

And we've adventured. Atlanta, Savannah, New Orleans, Chicago. More to come.

This time though, we're headed back to Nashville. Cameron is going to help me ask a special question.

"I got a new postcard from Ryan today," Gwen tells me when I finally turn the key and get us moving. She shimmies her delicious butt and maneuvers a colorful card out of her back pocket. "Looks like he's in California." She holds up the image, showing a seal lying on a beach towel under a rainbow umbrella.

"What's it say?"

"It says, *I stopped to eat a sandwich on the beach, and a seagull stole the last bite when I wasn't looking. Reminded me of your boyfriend.*" Gwen grimaces. "Sorry. I'm sure he'll get over it someday."

But I just grin and plan on buying the guy another pie when he stops in Green Valley for a visit. There's no malice in his jabs anymore. They feel brotherly now.

"Speaking of food, I packed snacks." I dip my chin toward a plastic bag at her feet. "All extremely unhealthy, as required. The theme is *pop*."

"Let me guess …" She drags the snacks into her lap. "Pop-Tarts. Of course. Popcorn. Pop Rocks. Amazing. Oh! Ring Pops. I haven't had one of these in forever." Gwen tears open the packaging and tries the candy on each finger until she finds the right fit.

Left hand. Ring finger.

My mind goes to a little box in my duffel bag. A more durable piece of jewelry.

This time, I remember every moment in the shop. My nose to the glass as I tried to figure out which ring said *Gwen* to me. Kennedy came and held up her phone, so Cameron could video conference in. We all agreed the round pink diamond, set in a simple gold band, was the perfect choice.

"Want a lick?"

Gwen extends her hand, offering the cherry-red sweet directly in front of my mouth. I keep my eyes on the road as I tongue her fake jewelry and listen to her soft laughter.

"Okay, that's enough!"

She tugs her hand back, and I let the candy go with a pop. Then, with a saucy grin, Gwen immediately sticks the lollipop in her mouth, and hell, if that doesn't make me fall in love with her a little bit more.

"Honey," I purr better than Curie could. I take one hand off the steering wheel, reaching over to wrap my grip around her thigh, fingertips brushing the inner seam of her jeans. "When it comes to you, I'll never get enough."

Acknowledgments

A small but mighty group of people helped me make this book a reality. Thank you, Kate, for answering my random medical questions. Thanks to my insightful beta readers Stephanie, Sylwia, Amy, Katy, and Kimberly. Your feedback made this story so much richer. Jovana Shirley, my amazing editor, once again I say my words would be a mess without you!

Then there is the lovely SPRU team. Thank you to my fellow SPRU authors who were so welcoming and let me borrow a few of your characters. Thank you, Fiona and Brooke, for guiding me through this process. And most of all, thank you Penny for kindly opening your world to me and letting me take up residence in the Green Valley Post Office. This is a dream come true, and I hope I did your world justice.

About the Author

Lauren Connolly is an award-winning author of contemporary and paranormal romance stories. She's lived among mountains, next to lakes, and in imaginary worlds. Lauren can never seem to stay in one place for too long, but trust that wherever she's residing there is a dog who thinks he's a troll, twin cats hiding in the couch, and bookshelves bursting with stories written by the authors she loves.

Find Lauren Connolly online:
TikTok: https://www.tiktok.com/@laurenconnollyromance
Instagram: https://www.instagram.com/laurenconnollyromance/
Twitter: https://twitter.com/laurenaliciaCon
Facebook: https://www.facebook.com/LaurenConnollyRomance/
Pinterest: https://www.pinterest.com/LaurenConnollyRomance/

Find Smartypants Romance online:
Website: www.smartypantsromance.com
Facebook: www.facebook.com/smartypantsromance/
Goodreads: www.goodreads.com/smartypantsromance
Twitter: @smartypantsrom
Instagram: @smartypantsromance
Newsletter: https://smartypantsromance.com/newsletter/

Also by Lauren Connolly

https://www.laurenconnollyromance.com/book-list

Also by Smartypants Romance

Green Valley Chronicles

The Love at First Sight Series

Baking Me Crazy by Karla Sorensen (#1)

Batter of Wits by Karla Sorensen (#2)

Steal My Magnolia by Karla Sorensen (#3)

Worth the Wait by Karla Sorensen (#4)

Fighting For Love Series

Stud Muffin by Jiffy Kate (#1)

Beef Cake by Jiffy Kate (#2)

Eye Candy by Jiffy Kate (#3)

Knock Out by Jiffy Kate (#4)

The Donner Bakery Series

No Whisk, No Reward by Ellie Kay (#1)

Dough You Love Me? By Stacy Travis (#2)

Tough Cookie by Talia Hunter (#3)

The Green Valley Library Series

Love in Due Time by L.B. Dunbar (#1)

Crime and Periodicals by Nora Everly (#2)

Prose Before Bros by Cathy Yardley (#3)

Shelf Awareness by Katie Ashley (#4)

Carpentry and Cocktails by Nora Everly (#5)

Love in Deed by L.B. Dunbar (#6)

Dewey Belong Together by Ann Whynot (#7)

Hotshot and Hospitality by Nora Everly (#8)

Love in a Pickle by L.B. Dunbar (#9)

Checking You Out by Ann Whynot (#10)

Architecture and Artistry by Nora Everly (#11)

Scorned Women's Society Series

My Bare Lady by Piper Sheldon (#1)

The Treble with Men by Piper Sheldon (#2)

The One That I Want by Piper Sheldon (#3)

Hopelessly Devoted by Piper Sheldon (#3.5)

It Takes a Woman by Piper Sheldon (#4)

Park Ranger Series

Happy Trail by Daisy Prescott (#1)

Stranger Ranger by Daisy Prescott (#2)

The Leffersbee Series

Been There Done That by Hope Ellis (#1)

Before and After You by Hope Ellis (#2)

The Higher Learning Series

Upsy Daisy by Chelsie Edwards (#1)

Green Valley Heroes Series

Forrest for the Trees by Kilby Blades (#1)

Parks and Provocation by Juliette Cross (#2)

Letter Late Than Never by Lauren Connolly (#3)

Story of Us Collection

My Story of Us: Zach by Chris Brinkley (#1)

My Story of Us: Thomas by Chris Brinkley (#2)

Seduction in the City

Cipher Security Series

Code of Conduct by April White (#1)

Code of Honor by April White (#2)

Code of Matrimony by April White (#2.5)

Code of Ethics by April White (#3)

Cipher Office Series

Weight Expectations by M.E. Carter (#1)

Sticking to the Script by Stella Weaver (#2)

Cutie and the Beast by M.E. Carter (#3)

Weights of Wrath by M.E. Carter (#4)

Common Threads Series

Mad About Ewe by Susannah Nix (#1)

Give Love a Chai by Nanxi Wen (#2)

Key Change by Heidi Hutchinson (#3)

Not Since Ewe by Susannah Nix (#4)

Lost Track by Heidi Hutchinson (#5)

Educated Romance

Work For It Series

Street Smart by Aly Stiles (#1)

Heart Smart by Emma Lee Jayne (#2)

Book Smart by Amanda Pennington (#3)

Smart Mouth by Emma Lee Jayne (#4)

Play Smart by Aly Stiles (#5)

Look Smart by Aly Stiles (#6)

Smart Move by Amanda Pennington (#7)

Lessons Learned Series

Under Pressure by Allie Winters (#1)

Not Fooling Anyone by Allie Winters (#2)

Can't Fight It by Allie Winters (#3)

The Vinyl Frontier by Lola West (#4)

Out of this World

London Ladies Embroidery Series

Neanderthal Seeks Duchess by Laney Hatcher (#1)

Well Acquainted by Laney Hatcher (#2)

Made in United States
North Haven, CT
14 August 2023

40284892R10207